DANCING WITH THE VENGEANCE DEMON

FOILS AND FURY BOOK TWO

LAURETTA HIGNETT

CHAPTER 1

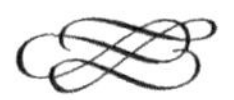

The woman sitting in my salon chair raised one eyebrow a tiny fraction of an inch; it was stymied by way too much Botox. "Well, I'm *sure* you can handle it, Sandy," she said haughtily, enunciating her vowels dramatically, sounding like a mighty queen bestowing a great favor on me. "I have *every* faith in you. You come *highly* recommended."

I wasn't fooled. We'd been talking for twenty minutes already, and I'd gotten nowhere with her.

Mrs. Tull had been half an hour late for her appointment, and never apologized. Her posh accent roamed around several different European countries – despite the fact that she came from Missouri – and she'd already interrupted our consultation twice to loudly chat to her friends on her phone. She might as well be wearing a whole dress made out of red flags instead of head-to-toe Prada.

"Mrs. Tull," I said, trying to keep the frustration out of my voice. "Do you think you could pick the color you were after on the swatch, here?" I held up a cardboard strip with tuffs of different-colored hair on it.

She curled her lip slightly. "Well, *none* of those, Sandy, darling. I said I want it bright blonde, but with no yellow at all."

"So like this?" I pointed out the natural level-nine sample on my cardboard strip.

"No. That's not light enough."

"This one?" A pretty natural level ten.

"Too much yellow."

I stuck my finger on the level ten ash sample. "And this one?" I already knew the answer.

"No. I don't want my hair gray. That's why I'm here in the first place," she twittered.

"This one?" I pointed to a clean, clear light-blonde shade.

"No. That's too dull."

I pressed my lips together. She'd already rejected every single color sample I could find, insisting that I should just color her hair *exactly* as she described.

Trouble was, what she was describing didn't exist.

We got this all the time. Managing client expectations was such a bitch, and it was the reason why I didn't start coloring anyone's hair until they'd pointed to the exact color shade they wanted. Relying on verbal descriptions was always a one-way ticket to Disasterville, population zero, because all the residents of Disasterville were zombies, and their houses were all on fire.

The thing is, everyone described color differently. It was quite common for someone to say something like, "I want a nice auburn tone, but with no red in it." Except, auburn *is* red. It's literally the base undertone for auburn. Auburn with no red in it just wouldn't be auburn.

"I don't know what the problem is, Sandy," Mrs. Tull said, her voice slightly frosty, using my name for the fiftieth time. Using someone's name in conversation once or twice is polite – it shows that you respect them enough to remember it. Using it constantly, like Mrs. Tull did, was a little condescending. She pouted. "Why can't you just color it the way I'm describing?"

I resisted the urge to sigh. "I just want to make sure we're on exactly the same page, Mrs. Tull. I don't want to do something you don't like."

"Well, you can't *possibly* do any worse than the last girl that did my hair," she said with a bitter laugh. "It took me *years* to grow out that disaster! Years!"

She'd already told me what happened. According to her, she'd asked for a bright-blonde with no yellow or no ash. The stylist had gotten it badly wrong, and had damaged her hair trying to fix it.

Upon slightly more questioning, it seemed that the stylist had delivered the requested bright blonde shade, but Mrs. Tull had bullied her into re-bleaching it because she decided it wasn't quite blonde enough. Then, the stylist was forced into toning it with a golden tone to make it brighter, then, when it was *too* gold, Mrs. Tull bullied her into bleaching *that* out, and putting an ashier tone in. Then – you guessed it – she demanded the stylist bleach out the ashy tone because it was too dull.

Mrs. Tull, it turned out, had never been happy with anything a stylist did for her. Now she was sitting in my chair, and I had that sinking feeling in my chest, the one where you realize your day is about to take a nightmare turn.

Ruffling her dress, metaphorical red flags flapping like a hurricane blowing through them, Mrs. Tull declared that every single hairdresser she'd ever had was a silly girl, obviously inexperienced, uncomprehending, an idiot that could not understand basic instructions. "I'm *sure* you're not like that," she said to me in her fake plummy accent. "I'm *sure* you and Chloe can deliver *exactly* what I describe."

Chloe was crying in the back room, desperately flicking

through all our hair magazines, trying to find the exact cut Mrs. Tull asked for. Again, it didn't exist. You can't have soft face-framing, but no short bits, and textured layering, but with thick, blunt ends.

I suppressed a sigh. The demon inside of me chuckled, enjoying my discomfort. Mavka had been annoyed with me lately. Apparently, I was a killjoy.

You are, she murmured softly to me. *This city is thick and ripe with evil manflesh, I ache to consume it. You* are *a killjoy.*

And you're a joykill, I shushed her, trying to focus.

Ha. Ten more minutes with Mrs. Tull and you'll be begging me to eat her. She sniffed dismissively. *Too bad she's not my type. Not enough Y chromosomes.*

I clenched my teeth, and immediately tried to relax my jaw. I was usually good with difficult clients, but my patience was wearing thin. Mrs. Tull was the most difficult one I'd had so far here in my new salon.

My two best friends – Chloe, the gorgeous, soft-hearted, slightly ditzy blonde, and Prue, the razor-sharp raven-haired beauty – opened this upscale boutique salon five years ago, and were soon fully booked. Now that I'd come along, there was room in the appointment book for some new clients, and inevitably, a few hard cases ended up in our chairs.

I don't mind dealing with picky clients, or wriggly ones, or the ones with high standards. I didn't mind the ones who had no idea what they were after. But these clients like Mrs. Tull – the ones who wanted something that existed only in their imaginations – were the *worst.*

I tried again. "If you could just point to the color that is closest to what you were after?"

"It's none of those," she said dismissively, waving her hand over every single blonde shade known to mankind. "You don't have it here. But I can tell you that it's a light, bright blonde. With no yellow–"

"And no ash, yeah, I got it." I took a tiny breath in, trying not to make it too deep. "Do you have a photo of the color at all?"

"No." She gave a haughty chuckle. "Why would I? You're the stylist, Sandy. Can't you figure it out?"

I grabbed the tablet and brought up a screen full of blondes. "Any one of those?"

She ran her eyes over them. "No. Not bright enough… too ashy… too dark… too purple… Look, Sandy," she said, a shade angrily. Her grand, know-it-all persona was starting to erode. "I don't know why this is so difficult for you. I've told you what I want. I've told Chloe exactly what type of cut I want."

"Mrs. Tull." With enormous effort, I kept my tone even. "Do you happen to have a photo of yourself at a point in your life when you had this color?"

She frowned at me. "No. No one has managed to get it exactly right, yet."

"So no hairdresser has been able to do the *exact* shade you're describing?" I was hoping she'd get what I was gently trying to imply. The color you want does not exist. It does not even exist in your mind. It's a bunch of words, not an actual shade.

Unfortunately, my subtlety wasn't going to penetrate the rhino-hide of her ego. She let out an exasperated huff. "I don't understand why this is so hard, Sandy," she snapped. "You're supposed to be a professional. Why can't you *do* what I'm *asking?*"

Just then, Prue appeared behind me, holding a Prada trench slung over her arm. "Okay," she sang out loudly. "That's enough." She dumped the coat onto Mrs. Tull's lap. "You're done here. Off you go."

Mrs. Tull bristled. "Excuse me?"

"Are you deaf? I said, you're done." Prue eyeballed the

older woman steadily.

"I most certainly am not. We haven't even started yet."

"You're not going to start. We're refusing service." Prue pointed towards the door. "Get out."

Mrs. Tull mouthed in outrage for a full minute. "How *dare* you," she finally spluttered. "I have not even finished this consultation yet."

"The consultation is over. You don't know what you want, and no matter what Sandy and Chloe do for you today, you'll hate it, you'll complain, and you won't pay your bill. So I'm cutting you off to save ourselves all the drama." She snapped her fingers and pointed towards the door. "Go on," she said cheerfully. "Off you fuck, on your merry little way."

Mrs. Tull looked like she was going to explode. She turned to me, her eyes bulging. "Why can't you just do what I'm asking?"

I opened my mouth to gently explain, but Prue cut me off. "What you're asking for doesn't exist. That's why you can't find an exact color sample or picture, and that's why Chloe can't find an example of the haircut you were after, either. You're throwing out adjectives that contradict each other, and you're too dumb to see it. You want a bright ash. A golden neutral. Feathery blunt ends," she snorted. "It's all in your over-botoxed little head."

Mrs. Tull spluttered. "My…my over… little…"

"The 'tox must have seeped into your head, it's affecting your brain. Jog on, sweetheart."

Mrs. Tull's cheeks turned puce. "How *dare* you?" She exploded.

"You should be thanking me," Prue said. "I'm saving you a whole afternoon of drama." She paused and pointed at her. "Don't bother trying to rebook your appointment, you're banned. Get out, don't come back."

After a long moment of outraged spluttering, Mrs. Tull

scooped her coat up, clutched her hideously-expensive designer bag to her chest and stomped out the door.

Then, she stomped back in, stuck her hand into the bowl of candy on the podium, took a huge scoop, shoved it into her designer purse and stomped back out again.

"Bitch." Prue snatched up a crocodile clip and hurled it at her. Mrs. Tull closed the door just in time, and it smacked against the glass window.

Wow.

I turned, very deliberately, to look at Prue.

She stared blithely back at me, and shrugged. "What?"

"That was a little… forthright. Even for *you*." I peered at her. "Are you okay?"

Prue pursed her lips. "I'm fine."

"Is she gone?" Chloe poked her head out of the back room, and let out an enormous sigh. "Thank God. That woman might as well have been carrying pom poms made out of red flags. She could have done a cartwheel and a split on the floor, and screamed *I'm big big trouble! B-I-G! T-R-O-U-B-L-E!"* Chloe walked over to my station and wrapped her arms around Prue, kissing her on the temple. "Thanks, Prue. My knight in shining Prada."

"Get off." She stayed still and let Chloe cuddle her, though.

"You're not okay, though, are you?" I peered at Prue closer. "Don't get me wrong, babe, I love how assertive you are, but that was a little extreme, even for you."

Prue let out a reluctant groan. "Jesus, don't make me talk about my feelings, Sandy." She said *feelings* in the same way that one might say *anal warts.*

"You can share, you know." I made a circle with my arms. "This is a safe space."

"Fuck you," she muttered, picking at her cuticles. "Urgh,

fine. I'm a bit on-edge, I suppose. We're having some family drama."

Prue had a big family; three older sisters, a handful of nieces and nephews, several aunts and uncles, and a ton of cousins, so there was plenty of opportunity for family drama. She'd been a surprise baby herself; her mother popped her siblings out when she was in her early twenties, but Prue came along when she was almost forty years old.

There was some drama there, too. Prue's dad had died before she was born. In fact, it was touch-and-go whether or not he died before she was even *conceived*. Prue never talked about that, though.

I didn't blame her. I guessed she had enough childhood trauma, considering she'd drowned in the bath as a toddler, and her mother, insane with grief, had subsequently dived head-first into the darkest blood magic to bind Prue's spirit back to her body. It worked – but her body was already dead. Prue's mom was left with an animated baby corpse, a rotting toddler whose skin flaked and peeled off with every diaper change, and who lost chunks of flesh while playing hide and seek. She'd been left with just a skeleton, which, inexplicably, grew to adult size.

I'd known Prue for six years, and I had no idea of any of her history. Prue, as far as I was concerned, was completely normal. I found out almost three months ago, when my whole world changed for good.

When I thought about my life, it was insane how easily and firmly it divided into Before Mavka and After Mavka.

Before Mavka, I was living in Emerald Valley, married to my no-good lazy husband Terry, living paycheck-to-paycheck, crying over bills, juggling my beautiful boy Dexter while working fifty-plus hours a week at a salon for my slave-driver boss Jenny, and puking my guts up every ten minutes with morning sickness. Apart from Dexter, my life was absolute misery, but I'd never had a chance to stop and take stock of how much of a nightmare my life had become.

After the demon possessed me, everything changed. I *saw* everything.

Not just magical things, like fairies and fae dogs. After Mavka, I saw the ordinary things as they really were, too.

My husband wasn't a charming, shambolic, absentminded fun-loving sweetheart. He was a lazy manipulative asshole who spent a good amount of energy taking away all my options so I couldn't escape from him.

I mean, I kinda knew before. I knew it, deep inside, but I never confronted that knowledge until I was lying on the floor of my kitchen in the arms of a strange woman, with my parish priest standing over me flicking me with holy water.

I'd been possessed by a pontianak – a vampire-ish demon that eats the internal organs of evil men; the vengeful spirit of a woman who will never give birth. Perhaps she was drawn to me because I was pregnant, overworked, overburdened, over-extended, and on the verge of collapse. Or, perhaps she'd been drawn to Terry, playing video games and eating cereal all day while I slaved away at a salon for pennies and comforted my toddler when he woke five times a night.

Whatever the reason, Mavka took hold of me, and did her best to eat Terry's spleen. He was saved in the nick of time by my beloved priest, and a mysterious badass girl called Imogen, who apparently wrangled supernatural creatures for a living.

Imogen hauled the demon out of me and trapped her in a banana, and me and Terry tried again. Or, I tried. Terry did not. Within a week, we were back to normal, and the stress and pressure broke me for good. My Cinderella-like situation caused me to miscarry our baby. In the hospital, I lost my mind for a moment, and ate the haunted banana.

Nothing happened. I thought the banana was a dud, no

demon inside at all. That is, until I ran into a human trafficker in a gas station.

Mavka took over my body, and *ate* him.

She wasn't what I thought she was. A pontianak, yes, but she was more than that; an archetype, a goddess of sorts. The spirit of feminine rage. The scream of a million wronged women.

She ate evil men.

And now, because I'd eaten the damn haunted banana, she was inside of me. Sharing my body. We were a two-for-one deal: Buy one cheerful, vegetarian blonde hairdresser, and get a furious vengeful man-eating monster absolutely free.

Now, back to Prue. Because I'd been thoroughly exposed to the supernatural, when Prue showed up in Emerald Valley to rescue me, I saw her for what she really was: A skeleton. Until that moment, I'd only ever seen a projection; an image of what she thought she might look like if she had flesh and skin and hair. She was gorgeous, of course, with thick black hair, alabaster skin, high cheekbones and almond-shaped eyes.

Looking at her now, pursing her lips and narrowing her eyes as if she'd been sucking on a lemon, I was reminded how shocked I was when I first saw her as she really was. An animated skeleton, a terrifying monster, standing in my front yard yelling at my husband that she was taking me away forever.

It says something about my mental state at the time that I was willing to go with a terrifying bone-creature rather than stay with my husband.

Prue saw me watching her, and wrinkled her nose at me. "What are you looking at, loser?"

"I'm looking at my gorgeous best friend," I told her, patting her gently on the arm. "Now, what family drama? What's going on?"

She pursed her lips. "Stuff."

"Do you feel like elaborating on that?"

She groaned melodramatically. "*Fine*. My mom has been pushing me to learn the craft. We've been butting heads over it."

"Has she?" I glanced over quickly to see where Chloe was before I said anything else, but she was at her station, happily finishing up her last client. Our beautiful friend had no idea about any of the supernatural. She'd been exposed to a few things, but she had never Seen. Chloe was as innocent as a lamb. And, sometimes, as dumb as a sack of rocks. I doubt she'd notice anything out of the ordinary even if a dragon waved his willy in her face.

I leaned in closer and lowered my voice. "I thought your mom had sworn off magic?"

"She did. I think she's feeling… impotent, at the moment. She's itchy for power but she knows it's too dangerous for her, because of how tempting the power is. So she's pushing me to learn the ropes instead. She's under some sort of weird impression that I'm destined to be a great witch."

I cocked my head, peering at her closely. "Why is she itchy for power?"

Prue squirmed. "My niece has gone off the rails a little, and it's making my mom edgy. She's sneaking out to parties, coming home wasted, that sort of thing."

"Which niece?"

"Ginger."

I remembered Ginger. Before I'd accidentally gotten pregnant and Terry had strong-armed me back to Emerald Valley, I'd hung out with Prue's family quite a lot. Ginger Nakai, the oldest daughter of Prue's sister Isabelle, was a firecracker – as feisty as Prue, and strong-willed, with bright-green hair and a pierced septum. She was also a straight-A student, a representative on the student council, and she had founded her own charity, so her mom found it really hard to reign her in.

I frowned. "I can't imagine Ginger going too far off the rails."

"She's just going through a rebellious phase, that's all," Prue said airily. I wasn't convinced by her casual tone. "Isabelle doesn't understand, of course. That bitch can't say boo to a goose."

Prue's sisters were completely unlike her – calm, well-mannered, responsible women who had cookie-cutter houses in the suburbs and corporate jobs. They even ironed their socks. They'd rebelled in their own way by turning their backs on their magical heritage. Instead of cauldrons and candles, they had coupons and car-dealerships. Instead of rituals and runes, they had R.V's and rodeos. They married mild-mannered balding white men, and went yachting in their holidays. One of her sisters even went to a Catholic church, just to twist the knife in their mother's back.

All of Prue's nieces and nephews were straight-laced, studious, polite and mostly quite shy. She had a nephew who played the French horn, and another the cello. One of her nieces even represented the state in Mathletes. Ginger, to Prue's great relief, was almost exactly like her.

"Ginger is your favorite niece, isn't she?"

Prue gave me a scornful look. "Of course! She's a bad bitch, I love her. She paintbombed the Lexicore building after those racist tweets, and she led the pro-choice march in the fall, too. She even founded an on-campus support program for rural kids who struggle to cope in the city."

"But now she's getting wasted at parties?"

"Like I said, she's just going through a rebellious stage. I'm just happy she's not wearing button-downs, playing a lute, and converting to Methodism," Prue snorted.

"So why is your mom so worried?"

Prue shifted uncomfortably. "Ginger has always been... honest. Like me. Blazingly forthright. But something's going on with her, and she's not telling anyone what it is."

"Not even you?"

"Not even me," she sighed.

"... So your mom wants you to learn magic so you can help her?"

"Kinda," Prue muttered. "She's been bugging me to learn the craft for ages. She thought when I moved in with Aunt Marche, I'd definitely take the opportunity to learn from her. I didn't, though." Another thing I'd been completely in the dark about until Mavka set up shop inside my body: My great-aunt Marcheline – my grandmother's sister – was the most powerful high priestess on the West Coast.

"Why..." I swallowed, hesitating, in case this was a touchy subject for Prue. "Why didn't you learn, though?"

"I don't know. It might be because it's so touchy-feely airy-fairy. I can't imagine myself in a circle holding hands with a bunch of bushy-haired women chanting prayers."

"Prue, you've run naked in the woods on a full moon before, shouting the lyrics to Taylor Swift songs. *That's* a distinctly witchy thing to do."

"I was high as a kite. That doesn't count." Her expression grew thunderous. "Maybe I just don't want to do what my mom did. I don't want to be like her. She struggled with the power; she still does. She's still tempted. Every day is a hard day."

That was the problem with magic. Your results depended on the ingredients you used. Crystals, herbs, candles – they all carried a little energy that could be transmuted into manifesting whatever you desire.

The problem is, some witches want more. You can only go so far with flames and herbs. Soon, they'll discover how much power is in warm, freshly sacrificed blood. It's potent and explosive, but it's dark and corrupting. Prue's mom, from what I understood, was an exception to the inevitable downward spiral that comes once a witch starts to dabble in blood magic. She came back from the dark path. She came back to look after her hyperactive, giggling, mischievous corpse baby.

I shook my head. "I can't imagine what it was like," I said, thinking of Zombie Prue as a toddler. "Having that sort of power."

"She's like a recovering drug addict. Always hyperaware of every situation."

"Poor woman. And poor *you*," I rubbed her shoulder again. "It must have been so hard for you." I assumed Prue's childhood trauma caused a few of her more interesting personality traits.

"Nah. I didn't know any different," she said dismissively. "All I knew was that I wasn't allowed out of the house for two whole years. Mom hid me for as long as she could, trying to figure out a way to fix me. I had no idea I was a stinky rotting corpse until Aunt Marche got her mitts on me, you know. Once Marche stabilized what was left of my body – which by then, was just a skeleton– and put the permanent projection in place, I was five and finally ready to start school. My mom was devastated, totally broken, and she begged Aunt Marche to bind her, so she did. Mom can't do any magic at all now."

"So why is she on edge all the time?"

"Dark magic *could* break the binding," Prue explained. "Aunt Marche is a magical heavyweight, but there's only so much you can do with runes and crystals. Mom knows that she could break the binding at any time with blood magic. That's why she's so aware of her addiction."

"Oh. Why bother with the binding, then?"

"Temptation," Prue explained. "Even performing the most

benign spells would be like an heroin addict taking a sip of beer on a hot day. One thing might lead to another, and all of a sudden she's thrusting a dagger into the heart of a homeless man so she can get the money for a new kitchen renovation."

"Yeesh. Is... is that what she did? To bind your spirit, I mean? Did she sacrifice a homeless man?"

"I don't know what she did," Prue said darkly. "She never told me. We don't talk about it."

"But now she's pressuring you to learn the craft? Why would she think that's a good idea, considering it's so dangerous for her?"

Prue looked away, not meeting my eyes. "I have no idea."

She was lying. She knew why; she just didn't want to share it with me right now. "Maybe because we're all so worried about Ginger. She's being... really weird. She's gone boy-crazy." Her nose wrinkled. "It's gross."

"Boy crazy? How so?"

"She's going to a lot of frat parties," she said, shuddering. "And she's not going to, I don't know, protest or burn them down or whatever. I think she has a crush on a boy." Prue sighed. "I don't know. Like I said, she's always been forthright and serious, but now, she's sneaking around and lying to me. To *me*, Sandy! She knows she can share anything with me."

"Well..." I said tentatively. "Whatever it is... maybe she doesn't think she *can* share it with you."

She looked at me sharply. "What do you mean?"

"Prue, I love you. But I stopped telling you stuff about Terry because I knew you'd get mad."

She cracked her knuckles. "And murder him."

"No, I just thought you would give me a hard time about how he'd been treating me. I know it doesn't make sense, but for me, there was no way out of my marriage. As far as I was concerned, I was stuck for good. Every time I told you about something bad that he'd done, you got *so* mad."

"Of course I did! That man is a douchecanoe of the highest order. I was never mad at you, Sandy. You know that."

"Yes, but that's not the point. You'd get mad and insist I leave him. You'd make a fuss. And I know this is irrational, Prue, but to *me*, you were rubbing my failure in my face. I had a husband who treated me like shit, and you calling him out only made me feel worse because I didn't feel like I could do anything about it."

Prue looked at me, aghast. "Babe. I never– I never wanted–"

I waved my hands. "No, I understand now. Now that I'm out. But I stopped telling you all the shitty things he'd done, because it only made me feel worse." I gave her a tentative smile. "Maybe Ginger is exactly the same. Maybe she's fallen in love with someone she knows you definitely won't approve of, some asshole of a dude, and she's lost control of herself and the situation."

Prue's face froze. Literally shut down, as she processed what I was saying. After a long moment, she sucked her bottom lip. "I suppose that does make sense," she sighed. "And you're right, I'll be pissed about it if she's gone and fallen in love with some chino-shorts-and-polo-shirt-wearing, campus-conservative-club-attending, beige-colored soy-boy."

I rolled my eyes. "See? Why would she confide in you if you're going to threaten to kill her boyfriend? Anyway, we don't know if that's it. It could be something else. She might be coming out as gay, or something like that."

"No. I *wish* it was something like that." Prue sighed despondently. "It's not, though. Like me, she has always been pissed about the fact that we're sexually attracted to men."

"Just keep the lines of communication open. She could just be on drugs," I said.

"Oh, I *hope* it's drugs. Not boys."

Chloe appeared behind Prue and draped her arm around her neck. "Are we talking about boys?"

"Just how much that we hate that we love them."

"Oh, you're singing my song," Chloe said. "I've sworn off men for a while. Bloody liars and cheats, the lot of them."

The last guy Chloe dated had secretly stolen her phone and transferred all her photos – including the nudes she took of herself – to his own phone, and spent several long weeks taunting her with the idea he was going to send them to her entire contact list. With the help of Mavka, who can hear evil intentions, we'd scared him so much he wet his pants in Scarlett's wine bar.

I grimaced when I thought of it. I'd broken his wrist. I thought it was Mavka, but no, it had been me, and I remembered far too clearly the man who sat on the barstool watching me with a smile on his face.

Reading my mind, Chloe nudged me. "Still haven't heard from him?"

I shook my head. "Nuh-uh."

"Bastard," Prue hissed. "It's been months."

I didn't want to think of him right now. I clapped my hands. "Let's clean up," I said, resisting the urge to break into the 'clean-up' song I used when I was at home with Dexter – it activated him as effectively as if he was some sort of Russian sleeper agent. "Since you've chucked out our last client, we're done for the day."

Chloe whooped.

"Silver linings," Prue grinned back at me.

CHAPTER 2

I should have been happy when I left the salon – I was on my way to pick up Dexter early. I adored my kid. The inevitable mom guilt I felt for leaving him collided with the blazing overwhelming love I felt for him, and I was practically jogging towards Love Bugs Daycare in Foggy Bottom.

But I was not happy.

Neither was Mavka. She was hungry.

What about that one? She metaphorically jabbed me in the ribs as we strode down the busy sidewalk. *He has charmed some terribly old people into letting him store their money in a pyramid. He seems to believe they are not going to get it back, and he is positively giddy about it.*

"A pyramid scheme, Mav," I murmured under my breath. "He's just a fraudster. On the Scale of Evil, he rates just below Terry. You can't eat him."

She cursed in an ancient, unknown tongue. After a moment, she perked up again, and pointed. *That one? He screams at women every day, he demands they work harder and harder, he pushes them to the very brink of collapse. His thoughts are thick with glee right now, coming up with new insults to fling at them.* She growled; a low, dangerous noise. *He made a woman vomit this morning, he is very proud of that.*

I glanced over at the taut young man in bike shorts and sighed. "That's the Circuit Cycle instructor, Mav."

He is evil?

"Yes, of course he's evil, he's a personal trainer. But women literally pay him to yell and scream at them, though, so you can't eat him."

Oh.

We walked in silence, and I tried to shake off my mood. I was going to pick up my kid and have a fun afternoon with him.

It's normal to be sad after a funeral, Mavka suddenly piped up.

"I'm not sad because of that." Not *just* because of that, anyway. My beloved parish priest – Father Benson – died a week ago, and I'd just gotten back from his funeral. I was blindsided by how upset I was when I heard the news, even though the priest was as old as the hills and couldn't walk two steps or say two words without wheezing like a defunct steam train.

I'd known Father Benson my whole life. He'd been a rock for me through a whole bunch of childhood trauma – my dad dying, my mom remarrying a bully, my brother running away. And, of course, he'd been there for me when Mavka first took hold of my body.

Father Benson had a heart of gold. He was a little unorthodox for a Catholic priest; he welcomed anyone and anything into the church, including, as it turned out, supernatural creatures. Apparently he went to Zumba classes with a vampire, had coffee with a witch, and counted an immortal half-breed as one of his best friends.

I'd snuck down to Emerald Valley to go to the funeral. I

kept to the edges of the crowd, though, dressed all in black, hoping no one would notice me. I paid my respects to Father Benson and said goodbye. Yes, I was sad that he was gone, but I was happy he'd had such a full, loving life. So that wasn't the reason I was feeling blue.

Maybe it was my mom. I hadn't talked to my mom since I left. I was still avoiding her.

My mom hadn't believed I would ever leave Terry. As a born-again, fundamentalist Evangelical Christian, she thought she'd done a good enough job bullying me into accepting my fate as a submissive housewife.

Now, she called me every single day, demanding I speak with her. I let every single call go to voicemail. I wasn't ready for her, yet. I had been strong enough to leave Terry, but I wasn't strong enough yet to withstand the constant barrage of her telling me I was going to go to Hell.

I tested my feelings gingerly, like you'd poke a sore tooth with your tongue. Yes, I was mad with my mom, but it wasn't her causing the deep, restless despondency that lingered inside me.

I found it relatively easy to avoid her at the funeral, despite my son's best efforts. Dexter was infuriatingly indifferent to the fact that we were trying to keep a low profile. At one point, he'd wandered out of the church gardens with a fat tortoiseshell cat in his arms, and declared that the cat's name was Gor'gamuth, and it wanted to come home with him.

I had gently directed Dexter to put the cat down. Then, I cajoled him, then tried to bribe him, and finally, I outright threatened him, but he refused to let go of the cat, and screamed loudly when I tried to take it out of his arms. In an effort to get him to give the cat up, I hustled him into the local vet's surgery, but curiously, it seemed the cat had somehow managed to chew out its own microchip.

Even more curiously, Mavka had been giggling like a schoolgirl since we laid eyes on the cat.

"He's mine," Dexter announced for the hundredth time. "Mine!"

Let him take Gor'gamuth, Mavka had murmured to me. *A life filled with boredom is a life unlived.*

Feeling like I was being held to ransom – I was trying to keep a low profile, dammit – I finally acquiesced. Since we'd gotten home, Dexter and the cat had been best friends. The damned thing was weird. I swear those yellow eyes glowed.

It wasn't the cat that was bugging me now, though.

It was probably Terry. I'd dropped in on him after the funeral, trying to get him to sign some divorce and custody papers. He hadn't contacted me at all since I'd walked out, and from what I could gather, he wasn't interested in visitation with Dexter.

That bothered me. My poor kid.

To my surprise, Terry didn't answer the door when I knocked. A girl did. I was even more surprised when I realized I knew her. It was Kate Samuels, one of the young women from my mom and stepdad's church, a quiet, shy girl, timid as a mouse. I didn't know her very well – her mom was best friends with my mom, but she was five years younger than me, so we'd never hung out.

A flare of fear sparked in her eyes when she saw me on the doorstep. I quickly put two and two together: Terry had a new girlfriend.

Shoving down the anger I felt – Kate was *so* young – I hastily reassured her that I was only there to get Terry to sign some papers. She hustled away, and Terry appeared on the doorstep. He signed the initial separation papers, but, with a vicious gleam in his eyes, said he'd think about the custody arrangements.

Asshole. He'd managed to snag himself a new slave, and

she was perfect; obedient, hardworking, just like I had been, so he was happy to let me go. But he was going to make me sweat about the custody. The fear had been niggling at me ever since.

You should have let me eat him.

"Yeah," I sighed. "It wouldn't be right, though."

Of course it would have. The man is a slaver; a blight on humanity. He lies and manipulates vulnerable women to get what he wants.

"The spectrum, Mav," I reminded her. "Remember? The Scale of Evil? Yes, he manipulated me, but I did reluctantly consent to most of the bad stuff he did. And he wasn't violent."

It's only a matter of time, she declared. *To kill the snake, you must cut off its head.*

"He's not a snake, he's a human man."

And they are all evil.

I rolled my eyes. Men.

Good grief, there was that feeling again. The aching, gnawing emptiness. I rubbed my chest, suddenly realizing what had triggered it.

Detective Conrad Sinclair hadn't called me.

It had been over two months since I saw him last, in Scarlett's wine bar. He'd been grinning at me because I broke Chloe's blackmailer's wrist. Sinclair had given me a contract and asked for my help in tracking down and destroying the Blood Kings, an insidious group of rogue supernaturals that had banded together and infiltrated every level of government. Headed up by a mysterious, powerful figure called Lord Seth, the Blood Kings had one goal: Take over the world.

It was chilling stuff. According to Sinclair, every decade or so some rogue supernatural will decide that their species deserves to be on the top of the totem pole. Because of the delicate balance between vampires, shifters and witches, they were taken down by either their own people, or their rivals.

This time was different. The Blood Kings were supes working together; shifters, vampires and blood witches, a merry band of misogynists. Under the leadership of Lord Seth, they'd bound together with a common enemy in mind. Women.

Detective Sinclair had sought my help to read the mind of Linus Brady, a blood witch and scion of the Blood Kings. What I learned was terrifying. The Blood Kings despised women, thinking them as property, servants, little more than cattle. Their plans were simple: Take away every woman's right that they'd fought the past two hundred years to obtain, and keep them as slaves. No owning property, no jobs, no votes, no divorce, no birth control, no bodily autonomy, no passports, no legal right to refuse sex with their husbands... Of course, the political arm of the Blood Kings, which Linus Brady was a part of, promoted their values as a way of 'returning to the good old days.'

Armed with a little information Mavka got from reading his thoughts, Sinclair took down a lair of the Blood Kings, but he never found Linus Brady.

And he never would. Because Mavka ate him.

I should probably be happy that Sinclair never called me again. He'd asked for my help, thinking I was just a psychic. If he ever found out that I shared my body with a bloodthirsty, man-hating vengeance demon, he would probably feel honor-bound to kill me. It was his duty as the Enforcer, the city's designated supe cop.

I still wanted to see him, though.

Sinclair was a wild storm, a force of nature, powerful and deadly, phenomenally, brutally gorgeous. Every single supe in D.C. was either terrified of him, or secretly in love with him. Or both.

I just wished he would call me. I sighed, turning down the side-street that would take me to Love Bugs Daycare.

Not here. Take the next crossroads over, Mavka urged me.

"Why?"

There is a shortcut.

"But it's…not." I frowned. "Love Bugs is that way."

She bristled inside me. *Are you calling me a liar, child? You think I would deceive you?*

"Oh." I remembered that Mavka couldn't lie. Maybe there was a shortcut down the next turn. I awkwardly crossed the street in front of me and continued in the direction I'd been going in. The next left was a small street, practically an alley-way, but I scuttled down it, dodging trash cans and makeshift cardboard cubby houses.

It really didn't seem like this was a shortcut. I'd have to turn left again, and walk a block back the way I'd come to get to Dexter's daycare. Mavka couldn't lie, but she might just be plain wrong. I kept going, though, and the buildings condensed around me, hugging the tiny street, turning the afternoon sun into a watery dim light.

A muffled scream hit my ears, and I stopped in my tracks. Listening hard, I heard sounds of a struggle, a heavy body thrashing against a dumpster.

Edging forward, I peeked around the corner, a tiny lane between two buildings. A large, heavyset man held a terrified woman against the dumpster, her business shirt and jacket bunched in his fist at her chest. In the other hand he held a knife, the glinting sharp tip pointed at her face. "Wallet and phone," he grunted. "Now."

The woman rummaged desperately around in her bag. Decidedly middle-aged and respectable-looking, I guessed she was an office worker, an admin manager, or even a librarian. But now, she was being mugged in the most horri-fying way possible. She was scared out of her mind.

Oh! Mavka stage-whispered inside of me. *Hekate spare me, there is a vile act taking place here! A violent man, behaving violently! Towards a woman!*

I grimaced. "Bitch, are you serious? You just lied to me!"

I did not.

"You said this was a shortcut!"

No, I specifically said THERE IS a shortcut. And look, spare a glance for that poor woman he has trapped. See that cut on her wrist? Would you say it was a long cut?" She let her words echo around our shared brain for a few seconds. *Or... would you say it was a... short cut?*

She'd tricked me. I suppose I couldn't blame her. She heard a man doing something terrible. What was she supposed to do, ignore it?

I was still annoyed, though. "For fuck's sake," I muttered. "I just wanted to get my kid and go home."

And I'm starving.

"Urgh, fine. Here we go, I suppose."

I stomped into the lane, making no effort to keep quiet. The mugger, wholly preoccupied with pocketing the woman's things, didn't even turn, so I kicked over a trash can.

He didn't turn. To my horror, he plunged his hand inside her shirt and ripped the buttons, exposing her bra. With a revolting chuckle, he grabbed her breast and squeezed.

"Oi!' I shouted. "Asshole!"

His head whipped towards me; face soft and flabby-red, his little piggy eyes peered at me. He was a big guy, towering over the terrified woman. I stared back at him, my face blank, but I was quivering with rage. "Why don't you pick on someone your own size?"

Unoriginal, Mavka drawled. *And thoroughly without teeth. That sounds like something a perky idiot would say. You sound like a Jack Russell yapping at a Doberman.*

The man looked behind me, down the alleyway, checking to see if I had backup. When nobody appeared, he let out a low chuckle. "You'll do for dessert," he said, letting out a dirty guffaw. It sounded like he was slurring his words. "This bitch is dried up. I gotta admit, I like 'em young." He waggled his tongue at me. "You're even a little old for my taste, but I'm not going to turn down some clams when they're put on a plate in front of me, am I?"

Shoving the woman against the dumpster one more time, she let out a wail of terror. He let her go and turned to face me. He was so big, and the laneway so narrow, his shoulders almost brushed either side of the buildings surrounding us.

I felt Mavka twitch inside me. I let her power fill my body, her dark magic seeping into my limbs, letting her take control of my body but keeping my head.

She was surprised. *Will you remain in the vehicle, child? Do you wish to witness?*

"No," I muttered. "I just want to make sure she's okay."

Thinking I was speaking directly to him, the mugger chuckled. "That bitch is far from okay. You ain't either." He stepped close and thrust his arm out, aiming for my throat.

Letting Mavka use my body, I blocked him, and struck out with my own fist, catching his neck in my hand. I turned him sideways and threw him onto his knees, pressing his body into the brick wall. Mavka's strength was insane, otherworldly, in fact; one quick squeeze turned the mugger's face purple. She eased off slightly, and he choked for air. Quickly, cringing, I rummaged around his dirty, stained pants and got the woman's phone and wallet out of the pocket.

I jerked my head towards the sobbing woman, desperately trying to hold her shirt together. "Go," I said to her, throwing her the wallet and phone. "Here's your stuff. Report the mugging." I turned to her, and let Mavka's ruby red sheen roll over my own eyes. "You never saw me. Okay?"

She nodded frantically. Ducking around us, she ran off down the alleyway.

The mugger's eyes were wide open, staring into my face. Mavka started to purr as I checked out of consciousness, disappearing into the place of dreams, and left her to it.

CHAPTER 3

I made spaghetti for dinner. Dexter played happily in his highchair, conducting an epic battle between his dinosaurs and his spork. While I salted the water and gently placed the pasta in the saucepan without breaking it, I thought about my grandmother.

Grandma Moira had emigrated to America with her twin sister – my great-aunt Marcheline – when she was only sixteen years old. Born in northern Italy, the twins had lived in a village in the shadow of a mountain.

The people they called their parents weren't the ones who actually conceived them, and it wasn't a secret. They'd always known they were adopted, but it wasn't talked about.

Despite frequent beatings, the twins grew up rebellious and headstrong. One day the girls broke into their adoptive father's writing desk and found their adoption certificates, and discovered that their birth mother had died in an insane asylum in the town nearby only days after giving birth.

She'd been admitted to the asylum as the Italian equivalent of a Jane Doe. Nobody knew who she was, and she didn't have a name. When she was brought to the asylum, heavily pregnant and gibbering incoherently, the only thing in her possession was a notebook filled with nonsensical scrawl. The words were all in English.

Entranced, the twins were convinced that their mother was an English princess, the heir to a vast fortune, locked up against her will in a remote country asylum just like The Man in the Iron Mask. The girls pored over the notebook, trying to decipher where their birth mother may have come from, finding clues in the various place names that lay printed in a jumble on the pages. After a while, they realized the place names were mostly American, so they decided to run away and try their luck in tracking down their birth mother's family. They ended up in Emerald Valley, where my Grandma Moira met my grandpa. Gilbert was also Italian, a recent immigrant much, much older than her. They married, and had my mom.

I didn't know if they found out anything about their mother. I must have asked about it once or twice growing up, but I never got an answer. I knew my grandma had a twin, of course, but she never talked about her except to spit in disgust when her name was mentioned.

Great-Aunt Marcheline didn't stay in Emerald Valley, instead, she headed to the nation's capital and built her fortune there. I assumed that the twins had some sort of falling out, and became estranged.

Grandma Moira was a tense, devout, uptight woman, so my mom's stories of the rebellious little girl who ran away from Italy didn't make much sense to me. I assumed that Marcheline led her astray, and that was probably true. Moira was deeply religious, a devoted Catholic, and best friends with Father Sampson, the parish priest – Father Benson's predecessor. She raised my mom as a strict, God-fearing woman.

The only time she relaxed was when she was cooking.

I adored that time with her. She was like a different person. She taught me how to roll gnocchi with a fork and how to gently spoon filling into ravioli and pinch it closed. She taught me about balance of flavor, and how powerful simplicity could be when it came to cooking.

She died when I was ten years old. She was often cold and mean, and very quick to hit me with a wooden spoon for any imagined infraction or blasphemy, but I missed the tender side of my grandmother that came out when she was cooking. The grandma that gently instructed me on how to shape pasta, the one that loved lemon and olive oil, the one that always smelled like garlic.

We all had different sides to us, I guess. We were all capable of change; look at me. Three months ago I'd been a doormat, overworked to the point of exhaustion from picking up after a husband who treated me like a slave. Now, I was a happy single mom, working my dream job, living in an apartment I adored, with a bloodthirsty demon inside me, happily singing ancient songs to herself and picking gristle out of her teeth...

Mavka sighed with satisfaction. *That man was delicious.*

"I'm mad with you," I told her. "You tricked me."

Child, we saved a woman's life today. You cannot possibly be mad about that.

"Yes, but you killed someone, so it cancels out the life you saved."

It was a man. So it does not count.

"It does," I said firmly.

He was a monster.

"People are capable of redemption, Mav. And we don't know his history. He was drunk, and he looked a little homeless."

She shrugged. *I'm not seeing your point.*

"Trauma can cause people to do terrible things," I said.

"You know that as well as anyone. What if that guy was homeless, on the streets, and someone did something awful to him and he just snapped, and was robbing that woman for... I don't know... Insulin? Because he was diabetic?"

You should be grateful, then, child.

"Why?"

He's not homeless anymore, is he?

I groaned. "That's because you *ate* him." I stirred my pasta sauce violently. "You're being deliberately obtuse, you know."

Because you are being ridiculous. I heard his thoughts. His head was a veritable cesspool. He'd done much worse than mug a woman for common currency, you know.

I sighed, and slid the pasta into the pan and gave it a stir to combine it.

Dinner was almost done. All it needed was a squirt of fresh lemon, and approximately twenty pounds of parmesan cheese on top. My grandmother would strangle me with her apron strings if she saw me doing that in her kitchen. She was dead, though, and this was my kitchen.

You seem... less vivacious than usual. I could see Mavka in my mind's eye, tilting her head and regarding me carefully. *Almost morose. Is your dull mood anything to do with the Enforcer?*

I snorted. Trust Mavka to go to the source of my gloomy mood. "I guess it is, yes."

Why on earth would you be sullen about a man?

"He said he'd call," I sighed. "And he hasn't."

Would you like me to eat him?

"No! Mav!"

She tittered. *I could, you know. Technically, he's done some terrible, awful, downright evil things.*

My spoon paused mid-stir. "Has he?"

Of course! He is a man, after all.

I continued stirring. "Is this one of those times when you

are going to trick me? I was under the impression that Sinclair didn't bother you very much."

The evil stench that resides in the blood of evil men is only a memory within him, she said cryptically. *Again, technically, I can still eat him.* She made a face.

I frowned. "Does that mean he used to be bad, but now, he's very very good?"

Your comprehension skills are astounding. I watched her in my mind's eye, inspecting her long black claw-like nails. *Once upon a time, your Detective Conrad Sinclair would have been absolutely delicious. Now...* She sighed sadly. *I think he and I have more in common than I'm comfortable with.* She shuddered slightly. *He is a man, after all.*

"Ew. Boy cooties." I giggled. Twirling the pasta with a fork like my grandma taught me, I placed it in a perfect coil on a plate and deposited it in front of Dexter with a flourish. He gave a hoot of delight, shoved both fists into the spaghetti and jammed them in his mouth. Wiggly wet strands hung down his chin, and he slurped them up happily. "Bisketti!"

"Glad you like it, buddy," I ruffled his hair.

Terry never let me make spaghetti for dinner. Dexter usually ended up throwing a handful or two around the room, and Terry hated how much of a mess it made. He'd demand that I clean it up while Dexter was eating it, so I would end up trying to serve dinner to Terry and wipe up tomato sauce spatter as it appeared, and I wouldn't get to eat my own dinner.

Terry would never help, of course, because it was my fault – I'd made the spaghetti in the first place. And after dinner I'd clean up everything, because if I gently cajoled Terry into doing it, he'd leave red ring-stains on the counter and pasta in the pans which inevitably turned to concrete and became impossible to get off.

It was astonishing how the memories kept coming back

and assaulting me; memories that I'd distorted in my head, filtered, photoshopped and altered until they were more palatable so I could go on with my life and not confront how abusive my husband was. It was like watching an old movie you used to like, a light-hearted family comedy, when suddenly you realize it's actually a horror movie. I'd convinced myself that Terry was just a bit haphazard, absent-minded, charmingly child-like.

And now, I remembered quite clearly Terry sulkily rinsing the pans under cold water, dumping them on the sideboard and saying to me, "There, done."

"Honey," I said gently. "You need to use hot water, and give them a scrub."

He'd thrown his arms in the air and shouted so loud that I flinched. "It's never good enough for you, is it? You just want everything to be perfect. Nothing I ever do will be good enough! Can't you see how *exhausted* I am? I'm out at work all day, my job is so physical, I'm tired, Sandy!" He'd slammed his hands down on the counter, and I cringed. "I suppose you want me to fold the laundry now? Tidy up the lounge? Play with Dexter?" He rubbed his face. "God, I'm so tired! I'm sick of not being good enough! I suppose you're going to leave me now, too, are you?"

His mom had walked out on him and his dad when he was thirteen, and it had cut him deep. He confessed to me on our first date he had abandonment issues, and I was in awe of how brave and honest he was for telling me.

I told him I'd never leave him. I'd never hurt him like his mom did.

"It's okay, it's okay," I had said, moving towards the sink. "I'll do it."

And I did. The dishes, the laundry, the cooking, the cleaning. I did it all, while Terry played Xbox in the living room.

Thinking back on it now, I could slap myself for how well

he'd manipulated me. His mom didn't abandon him – she'd had a total mental breakdown and had to be hospitalized. Within a week of her treatment, she filed for divorce and never came home.

Now, I could see it quite clearly. I'd heard all the town gossip – how his mom had been a hard worker, a loving, supportive wife, shy, quiet, devout, clumsy, devoted to her family... Underneath it all was a hushed implication of domestic abuse.

I just never really took it in. It was horrifying how similar our stories were. Terry's dad was a big man, like Terry, and he'd even said to me on our wedding day that he'd kill me if I ever left Terry.

I decided he was joking, and I'd merrily laughed.

We should return to Emerald Valley and eat him.

"Stay out of my thoughts, Mavka."

A strange, low-pitched meow yanked me out of my memories. Dexter's cat wandered into the kitchen, waving his tail in a jerky, eerie way. Dexter pointed. "Gor'gamuth!"

The tortoiseshell cat looked up at him, padded his paws on the ground for a second, then leapt up onto Dexter's chair. Before I could move him, he'd nestled in next to my son. Dex carefully placed a spaghetti noodle in front of the cat, and he delicately nibbled it into his mouth.

"That thing gives me the creeps," I sighed. "Why couldn't you start with a hamster, or a goldfish, or something?"

"Gor'gamuth." Dexter hugged him.

"And that's a crazy name." When Dex had named him, I assumed it was a random bunch of sounds, and that he'd forget it and change it several times. He'd stuck with it, strangely enough.

It's his actual name, you know. Mavka eyed the cat with interest. *He must have divulged it to your son, which is interesting. Knowing a beast's name gives you power over him, and he will do your bidding. He must have found a kindred spirit in your son.*

"You've obviously never met a cat before," I mumbled to her. "No one ever has power over a cat."

Obviously. She sniggered.

I frowned at her. "Is there something you're not telling me? I get the feeling you're laughing at a joke that only you understand."

There are many things I am not telling you, she drawled. *Just because we inhabit the same body does not mean I am beholden to you, child. I am a goddess, remember. Many things you will not understand. Besides, it is in your best interest. You will worry, when there is no cause for concern.*

I gritted my teeth. "I will worry about what, exactly?"

Suddenly, I heard a scream, floating down from upstairs, and the sound of a door slamming. I frowned, and glanced up.

You know you cannot see through the ceiling, don't you?

"Don't be a smartass. That was coming from Prue's apartment," I muttered. "I wonder what's going on?"

Perhaps we should go and check on her?

Mavka was very fond of Prue. Kindred spirits. I blew out a breath, and scooped Dexter out of his highchair. "Come on, bud. Let's go see Prue."

Prue lived on the second floor of the building, which was entirely owned by Aunt Marche. There were two apartments on the bottom two floors, and one grand suite at the top which Marche occupied by herself. Damon – her surfer-dude acolyte – lived in the apartment opposite me, which was handy, since Damon often babysat for me. Prue lived right upstairs from me, and the apartment opposite her was kept for short-term stays – visiting witch friends of Marche, refugees, students, that sort of thing.

I climbed the stairs, feeling the burn in my calf muscles.

Dex was getting heavy. Prue's door was open, so I knocked quietly. "Everything okay up here?"

As usual, I got a tiny glimpse of Prue's true form before her illusion snapped into place. A terrifying skeleton stood in her living room, with empty black eyes and snappy teeth. It put its bony hands on its hips. Then, suddenly, it was Prue, pursing her lips and glaring at me. "Does everything *sound* okay? No." She ran her hands through her hair in a gesture of exasperation and flung her hand towards the bathroom door. "Ginger is here. She's upset. She won't tell me why."

"Oh."

"She's locked herself in the bathroom and she won't come out."

"Oh," I said again. Dexter wriggled in my arms, so I set him down. Prue eyed him suspiciously for a moment, waiting to see what objects he was planning to destroy inside her apartment. Her decor was decidedly minimalist – Scandinavian, she said, with beige-on-beige furnishings and clean, bare surfaces – but Dexter could wreck anything if he put his mind to it.

He toddled back towards the door, and called out. "Gor'gamuth!"

The damned cat walked straight in.

I glanced up at Prue apologetically. "You're not allergic, are you?"

"I don't have nasal canals, dumbass."

"Right. Okay." Dexter stomped over to the kitchen and set up camp in the pantry with Gor'gamuth, moving little boxes and storage containers around. It looked innocent enough, so I returned my attention to Prue. "So Ginger hasn't told you what's going on?"

Prue groaned. "No. She showed up here, all upset and stuff, and I tried talking to her. I asked her if it was a boy, like you thought, and she went apeshit and screamed and now she's locked herself in the bathroom."

"Right. Okay... Do you..." I cast around for ideas. "Do you want me to pick the lock?"

Prue squinted at me. "Can you do that? Do you know how?"

"Yeah." I'd taught myself how to pick a lock. It was a necessity. "I've got a basic kit on my keyring – just a couple of picks and a tension wrench. I can run downstairs and grab it if you want."

"Why do you..." She shook her head, bewildered. "You know what, never mind. Don't worry. She can hear us pretty clearly anyway. She'll probably barricade the door."

"I've already done that!" Ginger wailed from inside the bathroom. "You can all fuck off! You can't help me!"

"Bitch, why did you even come here if you don't want help?" Prue yelled back.

"I *want* help. I want it! But nobody can help me!" Her wails dissolved into sobs.

I glanced over at Dexter, pottering away in the pantry. As I watched, he pinched something between two fingers and went to put it in his mouth. Quick as a snake, Gor'gamuth slapped Dexter's hands with his paw, and Dex dropped it.

I squinted at the floor, trying to see what it was. It was a tiny fridge magnet.

Maybe the cat was a good companion after all.

"Dex," I called. "Come over here, buddy. Leave Auntie Prue's pantry alone."

"Don't call me Auntie," Prue shuddered. "Aunties are old and dried up."

I suppressed a grin. "Isn't that your niece locked in the bathroom? What does she call you?"

"She calls me Bad Bitch Bones, of course."

"Of *course*," I murmured sarcastically. I scooped up Dexter and moved closer to the bathroom door. "Ginger?" I tapped the door gently. "Do you remember me?"

There was a pause. "Sunshine Farts?"

I pressed my lips together. "I forgot about that nickname." Back when I'd lived in D.C, before Terry got me pregnant and strong-armed me back to Emerald Valley, I'd been an innocent, relentlessly perky, ridiculously optimistic young woman. Fifteen-year-old Ginger, curling her lip, said I was so stupidly cheerful I must fart sunshine.

"Yeah, that's me," I said. "Do you know what happened to me?"

There was a moment of silence. "Yeah," she said hesitantly.

"I'm guessing Prue filled you in. I've had a rough few years, Ginger. Apart from having Dexter, who is the best thing ever, I've been through a really hard time."

I waited, but she didn't say anything.

"Like you, I didn't want to tell anyone what I was going through," I went on. "There were a lot of reasons why, but the main reason was that I didn't think anyone could help me."

The door cracked open, and Ginger poked her head out. She looked the same, even though she was nineteen now, wearing a black tank top and a long black sequin skirt that I wouldn't put together in a million years, but looked fantastic on her. She still had the same bright-green hair and septum piercing that had given her mother a heart attack four years ago. "Nobody can help me, anyway," she muttered. "It's too late."

Prue visibly stiffened and inhaled sharply, about to explode.

"I'm not *pregnant,*" Ginger snapped. "I'm not a fucking idiot." She glanced at me. "No offense."

I threw my eyes to the heavens. "Teenagers know how to cut you right to the core, don't they?" I exhaled heavily. "No offense taken, Ginger. Listen… I don't want to sound trite or dismissive, but if you tell us what's going on, we're not going to judge you, okay? We won't be mad, no matter what you've done. Right, Prue?"

Prue crossed her arms over her chest, glaring furiously.

I nudged her. "*Right*, Prue?"

She pursed her lips. "Yes, fine. Right. Whatever."

Ginger hesitated. There was a long, long moment of silence. Suddenly, her eyes filled with tears. "I… I…" Her chin wobbled.

I walked forwards and took her hand. "Sit down, honey. Here." I dumped Dexter on her lap, and he immediately started playing with the sequins on her skirt. "Hold this." I figured the distraction might help her get the words out. It worked in the salon – as soon as I started playing with people's hair, they spilled their darkest secrets to me. "Now, start from the beginning."

"I– I– I started seeing this guy," she said tentatively. Prue opened her mouth and I silently shushed her. "His name's Jeremy – Jem, we call him. He's best friends with my friend Lexi's brother. He's a junior, studying architecture. He's in a frat."

"Ew." Prue couldn't help herself.

"He's cool, though," Ginger said defensively. "His dad made him join the fraternity. His dad's a total asshole, but Jem's great, he's just putting up with his dad so he'll pay for his tuition. One of the conditions is that he had to join and live in the frat house. Lexi's brother is in the frat as well," she added. "They go to these wild parties, not in the frat house, but someone hires out these warehouses and basements and they put on proper rave parties on the regular. Me and Lexi and Cameron have been really getting into electronicore…"

"Is that some kind of drug?" Prue glared at her.

"No, moron. It's dance music. Like metal, with trance and dubstep."

I nodded thoughtfully, trying to make it seem like I understood what she was saying. "Yes, of course. Ginger, go on."

"So we'd go to these parties with these boys. Jem – that's my man – was always really lovely. Lexi's brother Olly is a bit of an arrogant prick, and his friends are bastards, but we never let it bother us. We were only at the parties for the music, anyway."

She paused, and took a deep breath. We waited patiently. "A couple of weeks ago, a girl from my geoscience class was found in her dorm room, unconscious. They couldn't wake her up," Ginger explained, finally meeting my eyes. "There was nothing wrong with her as far as they could tell, but she was in a coma. She'd been at the party the night before," Ginger's voice dropped to a whisper. "I remember seeing her on the dance floor."

"Okay," I nodded. "Was it drugs? Did she take something at the rave?"

"Her tox screen was clear." Her eyes hardened. "And we would never take drugs bought from a stranger at a rave. Only an idiot would do that."

Prue nodded forcefully. "Good."

"I buy my drugs from my neighbor Carol," Ginger added. "She's almost finished her chemistry degree and she doses herself first, so I know they're always good."

"Gah," Prue threw up her hands and stormed away.

So it wasn't drugs. "What happened to your friend from your geoscience class?"

"She's still in a coma. They've transferred her to a ward at the university hospital."

This was ringing a bell inside me. I'd heard about this

from somewhere else. "She's not the only one, is she?" I asked Ginger.

She shook her head. "Two other girls from my classes were found in exactly the same state, a week later. Comatose, with no explanation why. One of them had been at a rave; I'd seen her. I'm not sure about the other one." She chewed on her bottom lip for a while. "I started to get scared, and told Jem I didn't want to go to the raves anymore. He laughed and said I was being silly. He thinks it's just a coincidence that the coma girls were all at the rave, and he thought it might be some kind of virus going around."

"He called you silly?" Prue cracked her knuckles. "That fucker."

"He's cool, Bones." Ginger waved her hand. "He's a great guy." Her expression fell into a glare. "Olly is an idiot, though. He mocked me and Lexi and Cameron and called us all chickenshit for being worried about the girls in the comas."

I nodded, waiting for her to go on. She gently smoothed Dex's hair down, gathering herself. "Lexi and Olly are twins, and they've always had quite a volatile relationship. She never said as much to me, but she always seemed… a little scared of him, I guess. I know he has anger issues. Jem says he's a good dude, but he's had a bit of trauma in his life so he can be a little mean sometimes. I don't like him, but he's my best friend's brother, and my boyfriend's best friend."

Prue was making a very obvious wrap-it-up motion, just out of Ginger's line of sight. I scowled at her. "Go on," I said to Ginger.

She took a deep breath. "Just this past weekend, there was another rave. I didn't want to go, but Olly talked us all into it, so we all went. I left early, with Jem. I wasn't feeling it. Lexi stayed with her brother, and Cameron went home with some random girl." Ginger's hands, gently patting Dexter's back, started to tremble. She bit her lip and looked up at me, eyes filling with tears. "Lexi's mom called me a few days ago. She's in hospital. In a coma."

"Oh, honey."

She started to cry. "I just *know* it's something to do with Olly. I know he's done something… And I can't talk to Jem about it, because he'll think I'm insane." She took a shuddering breath. "I've looked into it – there's five girls in comas at Georgetown University Hospital. Five! They're keeping it out of the press because they don't want to cause a panic. But I know it's something to do with the raves, and I know Olly has something to do with it!"

I glanced over at Prue, who had raised her eyebrows.

Ginger let out a sob. "My best friend is in a coma, and her twin brother is still going to those damn raves! Jem doesn't see anything wrong with his behavior," she added bitterly. "He says Olly is upset, and needs the distraction. He's planning on going to the next party with him this Saturday, and he wants me to come along." She wiped her cheeks. "I like him, Sandy. I like him a lot. I don't want to break up with him because I suspect his best friend is some sort of magical serial killer. I'm really worried that I might be next." She took a shuddering breath in. "Stuck in a coma, like poor Lexi, with no idea how to get her out."

I nodded thoughtfully. "I understand."

"No you don't."

"No, seriously. I get that your situation is a little… unique." I frowned. "But I can see what a massive problem it is."

Ginger stared at me for a moment. "Yeah," she finally said in a little voice. "It totally is." She took a deep breath. Her posture straightened up. "So what do I do about it?"

Sometimes, all you needed to do was listen. I gave her a tentative smile. "Will you let us help?"

She curled her lip. "What can *you* do to help?"

"We can come to the rave with you. Check it out. See if we can figure out what's going on with these girls."

She held back a snort. "You're too old."

"We're both twenty-six, you little shit," Prue snapped. "It's a university party. There are people older than us there."

"You're my auntie," Ginger said scornfully. "You're too old."

"Don't call me that!"

I cleared my throat. "Ginger, I've been told I look a lot younger than–"

"You've got a baby." She dismissed me with a click of her fingers. "That means you're, like, *old* old."

"You only think that because you know us, Ginger," I said patiently. "If you didn't know us, and we dressed appropriately, I think we'd blend in at a college rave quite easily."

She stared at me stonily for a moment, then bit her lip again. "What if it happens to you?" Her voice had dropped to a whisper. She looked up at Prue. "What if you wake up, here, in a coma?" She pointed towards Prue's bedroom.

"You can't *wake up* in a *coma*, you idiot," Prue screeched. "Besides, whatever's happening to those girls, it won't happen to me. I don't have a stomach, so I can't be drugged. I don't have a circulatory system, so I don't catch viruses."

"You don't have a sense of rhythm either, so you'll stick out like a sore thumb at a rave."

"Fuck you."

Ginger pressed her lips together, obviously thinking. Her gaze swung towards me. "What about you, though? It could be so dangerous…"

A loud, clear voice called from the front doorway. "Oh, she can *definitely* help."

We all turned to see Aunt Marche standing in the doorway.

Ginger scrambled to her feet, and bowed her head deeply. "High Priestess. I'm sorry, I didn't realize you were here."

"None of that, child." Marche waved her away.

"I don't want to bother you–"

"You're not bothering me, honey."

Ginger's attitude shift took me by surprise. I glanced over at Prue, who rolled her eyes in an odd, self-deprecating gesture.

Ah, I got it. Until three months ago, I had no idea that my great-aunt was the most powerful witch on the eastern seaboard; to me, she was just a nutty old lady. Ginger, for all her sassiness, was the granddaughter of a witch who had almost been lost to darkness, and the niece of a woman who could have been stuck as a horrifying monster forever. But Aunt Marche had saved Prue's mom, bound her, and fixed Prue the best she could. Ginger loved her family, despite roasting them every chance she got, so she was grateful to the witch who had duct-taped her family back together.

Aunt Marche stepped into the room and took Ginger's hands in hers. "Prue and Sandy can help you, Ginger," she told her, staring deep into her eyes. "Especially Sandy. She's amazing at reading people, she'll have the bad guys wrapped up in a bag in no time at all." Over Ginger's shoulder, she winked at me.

"Thank you," Ginger exhaled gratefully. "I've just been so scared..."

"It will be okay, darlin'." Marche gave her a hug. "I know everything is going to work out–" Her eyes swung towards the kitchen, and she froze; her eyes bugged out. "Holy fuckballs!"

I jolted. "What? Aunt Marche... what's wrong?" I looked into the kitchen. Prue's pantry doors were still open; Dexter had made a bit of a mess moving cans and boxes around.

Gor'gamuth was still sitting there on the kitchen floor, blinking his bright-yellow eyes lazily.

Marche was staring at him. "What– what is *he* doing here?"

"Oh." I walked to the kitchen and scooped the cat up. He wriggled in my arms, reaching for Dexter like a baby, so I plopped him down on my kid's lap. Dexter was obviously getting strong – that cat weighed a ton, but Dex held him as easily as a Barbie doll. "That's Dexter's new cat. The stray I told you about."

Marche looked from the cat, to me, then back at the cat. "A stray?"

"Yeah." I chuckled awkwardly. "Dexter found him in the woods behind the cemetery at Father Benson's funeral and refused to let go of him. His name is Gor'gamuth."

There was a long, long pause, then finally, my great aunt let out a hoot of laughter. "Is that right?" She studied the cat with interest for a moment, then turned her gaze on me, giving me every impression that she was trying to meet Mavka's eyes, inside me. "Gor'gamuth, you say?"

Nestled in my son's arms, the cat narrowed his eyes.

I shrugged. "Yeah, it's a weird name. Dexter came up with it."

"I doubt that very much," Marche chuckled. "Very well, very well…" She walked over and scooped up Dexter and gave him a tight hug. "I'm so happy, little man. So happy."

I creased my forehead. "Why are you so happy?"

"My great-grandnephew has a lovely new pet, that's all. I'm allowed to celebrate the little things, you know, Sandy. It's good for the soul. Celebrate the first cup of tea in the morning, celebrate getting out of a parking ticket, that sort of thing. It makes your life richer, and you'll feel more blessed."

She was deliberately withholding something from me.

I mentally poked Mavka, who shrugged. *I've got no idea. Your High Priestess is female; I cannot read her.*

Prue uncrossed her arms. "Aunt Marche, did you watch the smoke for signs? Have you read the leaves? Will we be able to help Ginger and her friends?"

Apparently it was time for witch-talk.

"All signs say yes," Marche told her, moving into magic 8 ball mode and frowning deeply, suddenly deadly serious. "Lives will be lost, though, I warn you, this path is fraught with danger, and you must take care. The girls who seem to sleep too deeply are not asleep." Her eyes filled with sadness. "You must help them."

"We will," Prue said, clenching her fists.

"Another warning," Aunt Marche said, holding up her finger. "These evil deeds are the tip of the iceberg. A monster awakens and is feeding, growing bloated and fat like a great leech of chaos. This is the beginning," she said, her blue eyes glowing. "The start of war."

Mavka purred. *This is going to be fun.*

CHAPTER 4

According to Ginger, the next rave was due to be held on Saturday, which gave us some time to hunt for clues. Those parties seemed to be the linking factor between all the girls, although Ginger was not certain that all of them had been there. There might be other clues, other similarities they all shared, other reasons why they'd fallen asleep and couldn't be woken up. We couldn't discount anything.

We decided to head to the University Hospital and try to sneak in to see them. Hopefully we could talk to their relatives, pretend to be concerned friends of all the girls, and find out as much as we possibly could.

Aunt Marche had also given us a contact. A man named Dr. Herd – one of the doctors at the hospital – was an old friend of hers, and perfectly placed to help us with trying to figure out what was wrong with the girls. In fact, she said, he was probably already working on trying to diagnose them. She said she'd call ahead, so he knew to expect us.

We locked up the salon and headed off in Chloe's little Mazda. Chloe wanted to come with us, and to my surprise, Prue not only agreed, but also filled her in on what we were doing. It wasn't until we'd hit the road that I realized she'd left out every single reference to magic or unexplained phenomenon.

Prue had a whole lifetime of this, I realized. I'd been friends with her for almost seven years, and not once had I raised my eyebrows at any of her antics. Now that I could See, there was no chance she'd ever leave Chloe out because she wasn't aware of the supernatural. Prue was fiercely loyal, and wouldn't shut Chloe out for any reason.

It helped that Chloe was blissfully naive. Prue told her that Ginger's friends were in a coma and we didn't know why; that we suspected drugs or hypnotism or something, all stemming from illegal rave parties they'd attended, and Chloe just nodded happily and came along for the ride.

Chloe was innocent, and would remain so, until she saw something that couldn't be ignored. Like me, possessed by a vengeance demon, or my own brother, who had no idea about the supernatural until he was attacked and almost killed by a vampire.

It was unthinkable that something traumatic might happen to Chloe. Prue and I had a job to do, though, and Chloe wanted to help.

I couldn't decide how I felt about it. I didn't want her to be left out; her feelings would be hurt. But if she came with us, she'd be in danger.

And if she *wasn't* with us, she might be in even more danger. At least if she stayed by my side, Mavka could sound the alert for any dangerous men around. It wasn't like I had a choice in the matter anyway. Chloe wanted to come, and Prue was happy to have her.

We drove to Georgetown and found a parking lot a million miles away from the hospital. After a brisk walk, we entered the beautiful red-brick building and approached the reception. We'd decided to pretend to be Lexi's friends, coming to visit her. Ginger had already been in a couple of times, and told us that since Lexi had been cleared of any infectious diseases, the doctors were encouraging friends and family to come in and speak with her, to try and get her to wake from her coma. The receptionist signed us in and gave us wristbands, and directed us up to the ward. We found Lexi's room easily.

The door was open. A woman was inside; I could hear her voice clearly, reading out loud. I paused for a second at the door and listened. It was an Enid Blyton book. The woman sat right next to the bed, where a young woman lay, deathly still, fast asleep.

Chloe knocked softly and walked in. "I love that book," she said. "The Magic Faraway Tree. It's one of my all-time favorites."

The woman looked up, her expression haggard, worry etched into every line on her face. She gave us a tentative smile. "It was Lexi's favorite when she was a child, too. She would laugh so much at the old-fashioned names – Dick and Fanny. Every time I read one of those out loud, she'd dissolve into giggles and I'd have to wait until she calmed down before I could keep reading."

She stroked Lexi's hair with trembling fingers. "I was hoping she'd wake up and laugh." Her lips quivered for a moment. Taking a deep breath to steady herself, she looked up at us again. "I haven't met you girls yet; are you friends from her classes?"

Prue nodded. "Yeah. From biochem. We hung out at parties sometimes, too."

"I'm Lexi's mom, Christine."

We murmured greetings. Christine pointed at Prue. "You look a little familiar. Are you related to Lexi's friend Ginger?"

"My cousin," Prue murmured. Close enough, anyway.

Christine nodded. "She's been here to visit a couple of

times already. Keeps shoving headphones on Lexi's head with the most appalling screechy thumpy music, hoping to wake her up."

"Electronicore," I said, nodding.

"That's it. Awful stuff. Although, if it can wake her up..." She stared at her daughter again, and I took a second to look over Lexi, to see if I noticed anything strange.

She is not in there, Mavka whispered to me. She sounded shocked.

What do you mean? I hated speaking to Mavka internally; it wasn't direct enough, and sometimes she misunderstood me. But she understood me perfectly now.

The girl, she whispered. *She is not in her body.*

She was still alive though, clearly. I pushed my attention towards the monitors, which showed her vital signs and body functions, behaving, as far as I could tell, quite normally. In any case there were no frantic beeps or red lights flashing. Where is she, then?

I do not know. Mavka was unsettled, which worried me. She was never unsettled. *This is rather unprecedented. Normally, when a spirit leaves the body, the body dies. It is the way of this realm, of our universe.*

So her spirit isn't in there?

Mavka didn't understand my question, or she'd gotten irritated because I wasn't picking up what she was putting down, because she didn't answer me. Her attention was wholly focused on the girl, though, and I could feel her thinking deeply, ruminating over hundreds of thousands of years of memory.

Prue gently questioned Christine. "The doctors still don't know anything?"

"Not a thing." Christine shook her head. "It's got them stumped, but they assure me they are still working on it. All her bloods have come up clean. It's not drugs. They ruled out an infectious disease, but it might be a bacterial infection of some kind." She let out a quavering breath. "The good news is that her organs are functioning completely normally. And even though there is barely any brain activity, they know her brain is not damaged. She's just asleep." She shook her head sadly. "They don't know why."

"They'll figure it out," I said to her. Christine's distress affected me badly. I couldn't imagine looking down at Dexter in a hospital bed, unconscious, with no idea what was wrong with him, and no indication he was ever going to come back to me. "The doctors here are world-class. They'll find a way to bring her back."

From *where,* though? That was the question. Where was she?

Prue sat down on a chair on the other side of Christine. "Do you have any ideas?"

The older woman looked startled. "Me?"

"Sometimes, a mother's intuition is everything. That's what my mom says to me, anyway. Do you have any suspicions on what might have happened to Lexi?"

Christine sighed deeply. "I don't know. I'm... I'm not very good with gut feelings. I was hoping Oliver would have some sort of insight into it – he's Lexi's twin, you know. They were connected, once upon a time, but they became two very different people. I was hoping that by sending them to the same university, they'd get that bond back that they once shared, but they act like they hate each other most of the time." She frowned deeply. "He has no idea what's wrong with her. He's... upset. With Lexi being here. It's made him more unstable."

"*More* unstable?"

"Back in high school..." Christine pressed her lips together. "I don't want to gossip about my children's problems. It's not my place to say."

Chloe shrugged. "That's okay. Boys can be funny sometimes, I know that. They can take things way too seriously. I wish they talked about their feelings more, then they wouldn't get so angry."

Christine nodded. "Oh, yes. *Exactly*. Olly was the same. He had a girlfriend in senior year, but she dumped him, in quite a humiliating manner, I'm told. She left him for a girl."

"Oh."

"It wasn't done in my day, but I guess it's probably the same if she left him for another man," Christine went on. "He was so upset about it. He'd always had quite a...symbiotic relationship with his father." She dropped her eyes down, looking away, in a gesture that waved a red flag. What did it mean? Christine seemed to be a kind, loving woman, and if Olly was a bit of an asshole, then that would probably mean–

Her next sentence confirmed it. "Both of them are very similar men, so at first, they were fine, but as Olly got older, they started to clash a little. And when Olly's girlfriend dumped him..."

"They clashed more?"

She shook her head. "I've said too much. It's in the past, now, anyway. It's Lexi we are here for." She brushed the girl's hair again softly. "I'll be here for her."

We nodded. "Do you think something happened to her at that party she went to on Saturday night?" Prue asked her.

"Your cousin seems to think so, even though the doctors can't think of what it might be. It would make sense, though. I was told that she was found in her dorm, unconscious, the morning after the party. No one saw her come home." For a second, her eyebrows furrowed deeply. "No one can even tell *when* she came home. She doesn't appear on any of the security cameras on campus, which would be impossible. Campus security told me they've got cameras everywhere, but they can't get any footage of her coming home."

That was another clue, however mysterious it might be. Something magical happened to her. Someone – or something – snuck her back into her bed unseen. They were either invisible, or they somehow had access to magically erase the security footage.

Wait. It might not be magical. It might be someone on the security staff who did it. I frowned. This sleuth stuff was hard.

"They're sure it wasn't drugs?"

"My daughter doesn't take drugs," Christine said automatically. Then, her eyebrows pinched together. "Well, she probably does," she sighed. "Kids these days… I just don't understand them. In *my* day, we didn't do drugs. We just mixed every single spirit we could find in our parent's house into a forty-ounce bottle, chugged it like it was water, and blacked out. Like *normal*," she emphasized. Gazing down at her daughter's face again, she blinked back tears. "It's not drugs, though. The doctors couldn't find a trace of anything. There's no foreign chemicals in her bloodstream, and no unusual activity at all. She's just asleep." A tear escaped her eye and ran down her cheek. "All I can do is stay here, and read to her, and hopefully she'll hear me and wake up."

She can't hear her, Mavka whispered inside of me. *She's not there.*

But if she wasn't in her body… Where was she?

CHAPTER 5

We excused ourselves and left Christine to her reading. Chloe stayed for a few more minutes to listen, because she really loved that book, while we did a quick sweep to see if we could find the other girls.

We found them all on the same ward, in rooms all next to each other. As we suspected, the doctors were keeping them all together. Ginger didn't know the other girls well, so we didn't feel qualified to pretend to be their friends, although we did manage to offer our condolences to a father at one girl's bedside. Luckily for us, it was the girl who Ginger could not confirm was at the rave or not. Unluckily for us, her father had absolutely no idea if she had been there. Again, we left when he started crying.

God, it was sad. My heart felt like it was breaking.

Even more sinister, Mavka said the girls were exactly the same. They weren't there. Their spirits were not in their bodies anymore. Her feathers were well and truly ruffled.

We fetched Chloe, and went to go and find Dr. Herd, Aunt Marche's contact at the hospital. Prue got directions to his office from a roving bunch of students and strode off towards the stairs. "Maybe this doctor knows something. He should," she said. "Aunt Marche says he's an expert, apparently." She paused, and shuddered. "This whole thing is giving me the willies. It feels weirdly familiar to me."

"Is this because of your near-death experience? You were unconscious for a long time too, weren't you?" Chloe was under the impression that Prue drowned in the bath as a toddler, but her mother performed CPR and brought her back to life.

"Yeah." Prue was right, it was oddly familiar. For a time, her spirit hadn't been in her body either. But her body died, like it was supposed to. Therein lay her problem – her body was dead and had rotted away, but since her mom tethered her spirit back to her body, her corpse remained animated. Lexi's body, just like the rest of the girls, was still alive.

It didn't make any sense. I could feel Mavka inside of me, puzzling over the mystery.

We took the stairs up a couple of floors, and eventually found the right office. The name on the door read Dr. Oblix Herd, M.D. P.H.D, along with a few more lines of letters I didn't understand.

Tentatively, we knocked on the door. A deep, smooth voice called out immediately from within. "Enter!"

Pushing the door open, I saw immediately that it wasn't a normal office. Dr. Herd had designed his office more like a laboratory. Instead of a desk with a pile of papers on it, a long counter ran the length of the room, with test tubes, microscopes, and all other manner of scientific paraphernalia.

Behind the counter, an incredibly tall, handsome and very aristocratic-looking man stood, examining a petri dish with a hand-held microscope. His hearty welcome, the three-piece tweed suit, voice, and thick nerd spectacles screamed *I'm a distinguished gentleman.* But his thick, shoulder length golden hair, broad, muscular shoulders and towering height yelled straight back: *Romance novel hunk!*

We gaped at him, standing in the doorway.

"Come in, come in," Dr. Herd waved us forward. "Welcome, ladies."

He turned to Prue. "You won't remember me, but I met you as a little girl," he said, winking. "It's lovely to see you again, Miss Nakai."

"Hey, Doc." Prue gave him a casual wave.

I found my tongue. "Hello. I'm Sandy," I said to him, almost straining my neck to look up at him. The man was *tall.*

"It's a pleasure to finally meet you, Sandy. You must be Marcheline's niece," he said to me. "You look quite similar to her."

I smiled. Aunt Marche was in her seventies and looked like a cheerful white prune. I looked nothing like her now, but I'd seen old photos of my grandma, who was Marcheline's twin, and I supposed we looked very similar.

The doctor turned to Chloe, and hesitated for a second, blinking at her. After a moment, he smiled. "Hel*lo*." His voice grew deeper and smoother. "Welcome. Please, come closer."

Prue and I shuffled closer, up to the counter. He must have had it ergonomically designed for him so he could work comfortably, but because he was so tall, it almost reached my head. In an incredibly English Professor gesture, he took off his glasses and cleaned them with a little cloth, put them back on, and stared at Chloe again. "Please, I haven't had the pleasure of hearing your name."

I looked at her. Chloe was still standing in the doorway; mouth hanging open, eyes wide, the dumbest look on her face. Suddenly panicked, realizing we were all looking at her, she smacked her lips together like a goldfish. "Urgh. Um. I'm um.." Her eyes blinked frantically.

"That's Chloe," Prue said flatly. "My best friend. Say hi to the doctor, Chloe."

"Er. Huh. Huh." She swallowed, and tried again. "Hi."

"Ah," Dr. Herd said heartily. He walked closer to us, his movement smooth and confident. God, he was a hunk. Chloe was definitely, as Prue eloquently put it, cock-struck. He gazed down at us, moving as close as the counter would allow. There was a strange noise coming from behind the counter, too, which piqued my curiosity. An odd, loud hollow clomping sound. Maybe he was running some fancy lab equipment back there.

Prue, entirely comfortable, snagged herself a high stool and swung herself up on it. "Any news on the coma girls, Doc?"

He tore his eyes away from Chloe, still standing frozen in the doorway. "Not anything worthwhile, I'm afraid, Prudence. We've managed to rule a lot out. Unfortunately, all we're left with are more questions." He frowned deeply; it made his jaw seem more square. "It's not a virus or a bacterial infection." He walked over to the far side of the counter, picked up a piece of paper and brought it back. The odd coconut-shell clap echoed through the room again. I glanced over at Prue and raised my eyebrows. She shrugged carelessly back.

Dr. Herd brandished the paper, covered in incomprehensible numbers and letters. "All of the girls are the same. No drugs in their system, apart from a little marijuana and trace amounts of three four-Methylenedioxymethamphetamine."

I glanced at Prue again. "Molly," she explained.

"Oh. So, nothing that could cause a coma?"

"Not only that, but there's no sign of the kind of damage we look for in a comatose person," Dr. Herd said, taking off his glasses again. He ran a hand through his thick, golden hair. "The only thing I can confirm at this stage is that it's not a virus or a bacterial infection. My specialty is virology," he explained. "With a minor in epidemiology."

I nodded. "Well, I guess it's good to rule things out."

"We've questioned the family and some friends, of course," he said. "Nothing of note came up. Nothing suspicious, and nothing that can tie the girls together apart from the obvious: they are young females, and they're all freshmen and juniors at Georgetown."

"What about the raves?"

"We know for sure that four out of the five attended at least one of those parties," Dr. Herd said. "But from what I understand, almost the whole university has been to them. It might not be something that happened at the 'rave' at all." He put his hands up and made the quotation marks in the air with his fingers. It was such a posh-dad thing to do that I almost sniggered. "You also need to take into account the fact that the girls were all discovered in their own beds. They weren't discovered at the party."

"But it was something they picked up at the party?"

"I've already ruled out disease," he said. "And, I've, uh–" He shot a look at Chloe, still gaping at him. "I've done *other* scans, to see if it's something... metaphysical. An *outside* influence" He frowned again. "There are no traces of anything else lingering on their bodies."

I nodded deliberately. "I understand." Mindful of Chloe's status as a Normie, he was saying that he'd checked for spells and lingering magic, but found nothing. We knew that anyway; he'd already spoken to Aunt Marche on the phone. I assumed he was an old wizard friend of hers. Like Merlin, if Merlin was thirty-five years old and did Crossfit.

He cleaned his glasses again. "At this stage, we are monitoring the girls carefully, looking for any sign of change. The good news is that they all seem stable." He brightened. "And in a couple of days, I have an associate visiting from my homeland that may be able to…" he glanced warily at Chloe again. "Analyze their brain scans, check for consciousness, see if they can get a read on them. That sort of thing."

He had a psychic coming to try and read their minds.

I sighed. "I guess it's good that they're not getting any worse."

"Yes," he said, moving around the counter. That lab equipment he was running made an absolute racket, I could barely hear him over the echoing clomp sound. "I'm sorry I can't give you better news, but please know that I am doing everything I can to figure out what is going on with them." He reached the end of the counter, swung his torso around and came over to join us…

His bottom half was a horse.

A goddamn *horse.*

Doctor Herd was a centaur.

I inhaled in shock, choked on my own spit, and started to splutter.

Someone could have warned me, goddamnit. I'd never seen a centaur before. I had no idea they were actually real.

Of course they are real, Mavka murmured.

You should have warned me!

Pish, child. Are you blind? Look at him! Did you not hear his hoofs clomping? Inside me, she eyed the centaur haughtily. *Centaurs are boring.*

The centaur looked down at me disapprovingly. "Are you okay, Miss Montefiore?"

"I'm– I'm fine."

"As I was saying, the girls are all stable–"

I snorted. The doctor glared down at me; I clapped my hand over my mouth.

"And it's not a disease," he went on. "Hopefully we can rein in–"

Rein? I kept my hand over my mouth and bit my lip, trying desperately to keep from laughing.

"And we have yet to confirm the link with the rave parties, but it seems likely. Until the last girl is confirmed to have attended, I cannot say yay or–" He paused, and met my eyes, staring at me seriously. "*Nay.*"

Oh, shit. A high-pitched giggle escaped my mouth; I shoved my fist in there, bit it hard, and turned away.

My bad manners jolted Chloe out of her stupor, at least. She elbowed me furiously. "Don't be rude, Sandy."

"I'm sorry!" I squeaked. I bent over and took a couple of deep breaths, got myself under control, and turned back to face the mighty centaur standing over me. "Thanks so much for your time, Doctor. We really appreciate it."

He looked directly at Chloe. "It's my pleasure. Please come back and visit me anytime you wish. Although, I'll be away on Sunday. I'm giving a lecture on epidemiology in Atlanta."

"Epidemiology?" I squeaked again.

He gazed down at me through his thick professor glasses, serenely, almost daring me to say it out loud. "Yes. Virology and epidemiology are specialties of mine."

"That– that– that makes you–"

Prue stood up abruptly. "Okay, time to go. Doc, thanks. Nice to see you again, by the way. We'll come check in a couple of days, see if there's any changes." She grabbed me by the arm, hauled me out of the room, and shut the door behind us.

"You dickhead."

"He's the Centaur of Disease Control!" I was laughing so hard I couldn't breathe.

"Hah. Yeah," Prue sniggered. "I forgot he was a centaur."

"How could you forget? Can't you *see* him?"

"If I concentrate, I can. His projection is even better than mine." She squinted at me. "But after that demon possessed you, you couldn't even see my projection, could you? That's pretty unusual, you know. Most supes see the projection first, but if they flex their extra sight, they can see me as I really am. It's the same with Doctor Herd."

I snorted again. "Doctor *Herd*."

Prue rolled her eyes. "Stop being such a child. As I was saying, when I look at the good doctor, all I see is a normal looking man."

"I see a chesty-looking man-hunk with golden locks and a Clydesdale's behind. That man is *tall*. And quite gorgeous, too. No wonder Chloe–"

We stared at each other for one second. "Chloe," Prue muttered. She opened the office door. Chloe was still standing there, staring at Dr. Herd with the dumbest expression I'd ever seen on her face, which, for Chloe, is saying something. Prue grabbed her by the back of her shirt and gently pulled her out of the room, and shut the door.

CHAPTER 6

Despite our grim mission, I was determined to have a good time, for this part of the evening at the very least. We were at Chloe's house, in her apartment just a few blocks from me in Foggy Bottom, getting ready for the rave.

Chloe's dad, a super-conservative old-world, oil-rich billionaire, bought the apartment for her to assuage the vague guilt he felt in keeping such a delightful young woman a secret. Chloe was the result of a dalliance her father had with a young woman stripping her way through nursing school back in the late nineties. Harry wasn't bothered with having an illegitimate child. The problem was the woman he'd fathered her with.

Chloe's mom Linda was now a ferociously powerful ex-nurses' union rep who helped other industries unionize, and was the nicest ordinary human woman I knew. Despite having a political ideology completely opposite from Harry, Linda let Harry look after Chloe financially, and he'd bought this apartment for her, paying several million dollars. I was having the time of my life getting dressed up in her fancy apartment with its cutting-edge design, indoor/outdoor balcony areas, fern garden feature walls and hideously expensive Norwegian imported furniture.

Fortunately, Chloe decided not to come with us to the rave. Unfortunately, it was because she was sick.

*Love*sick. Absolutely, sickeningly, overwhelmingly lovesick for Doctor Oblix Herd.

"He's a dreamboat," she signed, chin wobbling, on the verge of tears. "So handsome. So intelligent. *So* out of my league," she sobbed. "My heart is breaking. I've met the man of my dreams, and he'll never even look at me."

"He *was* looking at you, idiot," Prue muttered. "He spoke to you. You were the one who stood there staring at him like he was a giant block of cheese."

"I do love cheese," Chloe whispered. "It's hopeless, though, Prue. He's a *doctor*. I'm a hairdresser. It would never work."

"Don't be silly, Clo." I rifled through the outfits Ginger had picked out for me so I wouldn't make a fool of myself. Everything looked… strange. I couldn't imagine how any of the pieces would work together. There were boxy cut-off hoodies covered with graffiti paired with bike shorts in what I thought was a horribly unflattering length, sequined granny undies under mesh flares to be worn with what looked like glittery nipple pasties… I cringed, and looked at the next pile. "You're a catch, you know," I said to Chloe while I rummaged through the clothes. "Have you forgotten you're a blisteringly-hot woman with a huge trust fund?" I picked up an oversized fluro-green t-shirt, which, apparently, I was supposed to wear with a strange black chain harness thing over top.

I giggled, held up the harness and shook it in front of Prue. "Maybe Chloe should wear this for Dr. Herd."

She snorted with laughter. "Stop."

"Why would I wear that?" Chloe looked confused. "He seems more like a Chanel kind of man. Classy. Distinguished."

"I wonder what his favorite dance is?" I sniggered, holding up a pair of orange parachute pants covered in zips. "I know!" I busted out my fist and sang. "Watch me whip, watch me neigh neigh."

Prue held her sides, chuckling. "*Ohhh,* stop!"

"I don't get it," Chloe whined. "Anyway, I think he's the kind that would know how to waltz, y'know? Maybe a foxtrot."

I decided on the orange cargo pants, which were comfortable and roomy, sat nicely on my hips, and had lots and lots of pockets. I slipped on the plain white crop-top that went with it and looked at myself in the mirror.

"Perfect," Prue said.

"I feel a little self-conscious baring my stomach." I circled my arms around my waist. "My mom would slap me."

"Your mom's not here. And you're lucky you've got such a flat stomach, having popped out that kid of yours. I tell you what, there's something to be said for having babies young."

"It did take a couple of years to go back to normal." I poked at my belly. My stomach was flat, mostly due to three years of a starvation diet and outright slavery, which I wouldn't wish on anyone. In the last few months, I'd been eating properly and I'd gotten stronger; I was still carrying Dexter around with me everywhere, and that kid weighed a ton. "Well, having Dexter is one thing I'll never regret," I said, staring at my exposed midriff. There was a hint of silvery stretch marks on my skin, but I thought they looked kind of pretty. "I'd go through all that shit with Terry a million times just to have my kid." I made a face. "But, if there was any way I could have had him later in life, possibly with a different man..."

"If wishes were horses, beggars would ride," Prue said dryly. "We can't change the past. We can't even change the future. We can only change the present moment." She upended her champagne glass into her mouth and swallowed.

"You look *amazing*, babe," Chloe circled me, making woo-woo noises. "You should dress like that more often."

"It's not something a mom wears, though," I muttered, pulling at the crop top so it covered more of my exposed stomach. It sprang back up again. My boobs weren't enormous, but they were too big for my little frame.

"Well, that's lucky," Prue refilled my champagne glass. "Because tonight, you're not a mom. You're a senior at Georgetown who loves electronicore."

I took a sip of champagne. "And who are you tonight?"

"A bad bitch, as usual. No one will dare talk to me, so it doesn't matter who I am. We're going to keep our eyes and ears open, and with your phenomenal people skills, you're going to charm whoever is doing this into telling us how to fix the coma girls."

Chloe blinked back tears. "You both look amazing," she said, sounding like a middle-aged mom sending her kids to the prom. "I wish I could come with you, but I'm just too sad." Her bottom lip wobbled. "My soulmate is in Georgetown. He's a star, just out of reach. The perfect specimen of manhood, one who I will never get to touch."

Prue winked at her. "Speaking of manhood, I bet he's hung like a horse."

I spat out my champagne.

* * *

SINCE THE RAVES WERE ILLEGAL, secret, and underground, we had to wait for Ginger to message us with the location. Every single one was in a different warehouse, all of which were based around the city. It seemed like a bit of a gimmick to me, but I guess it added to the atmosphere.

Prue's phone buzzed. "Okay, I've got it. Dupont Circle. Let's go."

We parked Chloe on her sofa, wrapped her in a blanket, shoved a tub of ice cream in her arms and kissed her on the forehead. "Have fun," she mumbled through a mouthful of Strawberry Sparkle.

Prue hailed a cab just outside and we jumped in. As usual, she looked amazing, wearing what looked like a tiny bra made of silver sequins and matching hot pants, with her long black hair swept off her face and braided with silver thread. Her own outfit was a magical projection – the clothes weren't real. Before we arrived at Chloe's, Ginger had flipped through an album of rave wear. Prue chose and willed it to appear. I was slightly envious at how easy it all was for her, until I remembered how hard it actually was.

She settled in the back seat of the cab and sighed. "I'm glad Chloe didn't want to come with us. If anyone was going to get led astray and end up in a magical coma, it would be her."

"Yeah. It might be easier with just the two of us, so we can look out for each other. I'd worry about Chloe slipping through the cracks."

"What's the plan? Are you going to wander around and play with people's hair until they tell you their secrets?"

"Well…" It was going to be a lot easier than that. I'd just have Mavka sniff around until she found some super-evil man-blood. Prue didn't need to know that, though. "Yeah, I guess. I've got pretty good instincts, so I'll try and see if I can find anyone behaving suspiciously, and give you a signal or something."

She pursed her lips. "I mean, I guess I can do the same thing."

I tried to choose my words carefully. "We have to be subtle, though, Prue. You can't just punch people until they admit they have anything to do with the coma girls."

"I *could*, you know," she said sulkily. "You have your methods, I have mine."

"We'd get thrown out. And we wouldn't get back in. It would be much harder to find out what's wrong with Lexi."

"Fine," she sighed. "You chat to all the men, get all flirty with them, and if you get suspicious of someone, just give me a signal."

"What's the signal?"

We agreed on a jerky finger-gun dance that Ginger, cringing badly, had taught us.

Prue checked her makeup in the cab window. "So, what's the deal with Aunt Marche? Is she teaching you?"

"What?"

"Are you studying witchcraft?"

"No... what gave you that idea?"

"Oh. It's just that she was really emphatic about how you could *definitely* find out what's going on with the coma girls. She made it sound like you had some sort of special talent for magical detective work, or something. I know you're good at figuring out mysteries, but I just thought that you were learning a little of the craft."

My heart pulsed when Prue said the word 'detective'. God, why couldn't I stop thinking about him?

I already knew the reason why. *He* was supposed to be taking me to investigate what was going on with the coma girls. I remember him quite clearly, sitting in the window of Scarlett's bar, asking me to help with tracking down a couple of rogue vampires who may have something to do with unconscious girls after frat parties.

And I never heard from him after that.

I knew he was okay. I'd even called the station twice, just to make sure. So far I hadn't stooped so low as to ask to speak with him. I still had a little dignity left.

It was probably for the best. If he ever found out about Mavka...

"Aunt Marche would only teach me the craft if I asked her," I said abruptly, forcing my thoughts back to the present. "And I haven't asked her. I'm not sure if it's for me."

"Yeah," Prue muttered, looking out the window. "I'm not sure if it's for me, either. It's so... so..."

"Your mom is still pressuring you?"

She nodded. "I don't want to end up like her, Sandy." Her voice sounded hollow. "I mean, I'm already a monster. Can you imagine if the temptation got to me, and I went down the path of blood magic?"

"You're not a monster, honey." I rubbed her bony knee. "Skeletons are normal, they're human."

"I didn't mean my body, dumbass. I mean, I'm already quite abrasive and prone to violence."

"Oh." I gave her a little smile. "You might be right."

She frowned deeply. "My mom insists..." She shook her head, exasperated. "She keeps pointing to an explosion in my chart. She thinks I'm going to need the magic. But... I don't know if it's... *safe* for me."

I could sympathize. I had a bloodthirsty demon inside of me who would eat a man for tax evasion if I let her.

"You're a good person, Prue," I said. "I can't imagine you doing awful things."

"Oh, of *course* I would. I'd burn the whole world to the ground to protect the people I love. I think that's the problem. If someone fucked with you or Chloe or Ginger, or the rest of my family, I'd be cracking skulls. I'm not sure if it's a good idea if I power up with magic. I don't even like talking to my mom about it," she muttered. "She'll use it as a conversation starter to harangue me into learning the craft from Aunt Marche."

"She's already got one acolyte at the moment. Maybe just tell her that Aunt Marche's books are closed?"

"Aunt Marche can take on fifty students and not lose breath. She loves to teach, more than anything in the world." Prue gave me a sly look. "Wait until Dexter gets old enough. Marche is obviously dying to get her witchy mitts on him."

"Dexter?"

"Didn't you see the way Marche spoke to him the other day? When she found out he already has a powerful familiar? She was positively giddy."

"A *what?*" I was flabbergasted.

"That damn cat."

I shook my head. "He's just a cat."

She let out a bark of laughter. "He's not just a cat, Sandy. You know that."

I didn't actually think about the cat that much, even though it was now Dexter's constant companion. "Huh." Now, I thought about how Gor'gamuth had slapped the magnet out of Dexter's hand before he put it in his mouth. "I thought he was just being an overprotective pet."

"He's a partner-in-crime, that's what he is. A mischievous little creature, at the very least. After you left the other day, I slammed the door behind you and all the cans and boxes fell off the shelves in my pantry. It gave me a hell of a fright. Those little bastards had lined up everything on my pantry shelves so they were right on the edge and would tip if they were jostled. That cat *pranked* me, Sandy. Him and Dexter pranked me."

"Noooo." I shook my head. "My kid? A witch?"

"Probably a very powerful one, just like Aunt Marche. It's a direct bloodline, you know."

"My grandma wasn't a powerful witch. My mother isn't either."

"They probably could be, but they rejected the craft for the Church."

I thought about it in silence for a few minutes. "Hmmm. Dexter was ridiculously insistent about bringing the cat home. He sleeps with him, too, and never leaves him alone." I frowned. "What the hell is a familiar?"

Prue smirked. "I'll let Marche explain." The cab came to a halt. "Come on, we're here."

We got out. The address for the party was deep in the city between tall buildings, and down a series of tiny lanes. As we walked, we were joined by other flamboyantly dressed young people, all headed to the rave. Soon, the thud of music reached my ears. We walked to the end of a short driveway where a ramp led up to a double-wide roller door, tightly shut. The little exit beside it, though, was open, and flanked by mean-looking bouncers in dark suits, wearing earpieces.

I nodded at Prue. "Don't you think it's a little strange that an illegal underground rave is being held in a corporate parking garage? And staffed with professional-looking bouncers?" I peered past the bouncers. There was even a metal detector just through the doors. The security was professional.

Prue shrugged. "I don't think they're illegal underground raves; I think it's just a gimmick. It's probably an events company putting these parties on, and they're pretending to be grungy and badass just to draw the kids in."

We joined the line of people waiting outside. "If the coma girls have something to do with these raves, then we should probably find out who is organizing them," I muttered in Prue's ear. "There might be a link." I bit my lip, mindful of what I hadn't told Prue about my 'date' with Detective

Conrad Sinclair. "I think I remember Sinclair telling me about one of his investigations..."

"That bastard," Prue snarled. "I can't believe he ghosted you after one date."

"Yeah, yeah," I waved my hand dismissively. We'd already spent a couple of weeks on the subject of Sinclair and the one date we'd had. I'd told the girls we had a nice time, but he was far too intimidating, and probably a little too old for me, which was entirely true. The last part was true, anyway. "I don't want to go over that again, and anyway, that's not the point. He told me he was investigating a couple of frat parties where girls were being drugged unconscious, and he thought rogue vampires were involved."

"Vampires, hey?" Prue looked thoughtful. "Well, I hope it *is* them."

I stared at her, aghast. "Why?"

"They don't bother me," she said simply. "They never have."

"I don't understand." I shook my head, confused. "How come vampires… oh. That's right. You don't have any blood to suck."

"Nope," she said cheerfully, as we moved through the honor-guard of incredibly intimidating security at the door, then through the metal detector inside. "Vampires have zero interest in me. They never pay me any attention at all. It's great. I have nothing they want."

"I guess that's a good thing." We paid the entry fee, which made my eyeballs bleed. I noticed the girls in front of us had custom-made snap bands they displayed for the cashier instead. It looked like you could pre-purchase tickets. Or someone was giving them away. Moving down the corridor, the music thumping louder and louder, I glanced behind me and saw another bunch of young women had snap-bands too.

I needed to find out who was running these parties. Someone was going to great lengths to make sure beautiful young women would be here.

The corridor funneled us out into a dark, single-level underground parking garage. The heavy bass of music pulsed through my entire body, suddenly overwhelming me. It took a while before I could dial down my senses and concentrate on anything else.

The whole place was pitch black apart from glow sticks and laser lights. At the far end of the parking garage, there was a stage set up, where the D.J. – wearing a Freddy Kruger mask – stood behind a vast deck, nodding in time with the beat, twirling knobs and pushing buttons. A laser light show blazed out from the stage, casting flickering neon-green lines on the pulsing throng of dancers.

On one side of the space, they'd set up a bar area, with high tables and stools arranged in daisy patterns in front of a bar, and bean bags scattered against the wall. On the other side of the cavernous space, they'd installed those fancy portable toilets. There were already lines snaking outside the stalls.

The whole place was packed, the atmosphere throbbing with excitement and danger. *Mmmmmm,* Mavka purred. *The air here is thick with the sweet scent of evil blood. There are several men here who reek of sadism, I cannot wait to locate them.*

We will, Mav. That's why we're here.

Urgh. Delicious scents, malicious thoughts, they're all here. It's a shame the crowd is so thick; it's going to be like finding a needle in a haystack.

Mavka sounded as overwhelmed as I was, maybe more so. She was as excited as a dog at the beach for the first time; exciting smells everywhere, she didn't know which way to look. I took a few deep breaths, trying to acclimate myself to the environment. Talk about sensory overload.

"I'm too sober for this," Prue yelled in my ear.

"I was just thinking the same thing," I shouted back.

She nodded towards the bar. "Want to get a drink? We're never going to find Lexi's brother in that seething pack of sweaty meat-sacks. Maybe we should hang there and see if he comes over. That might be easier."

I nodded, and we dodged some staggering zombie-like college kids, headed towards the bar.

A big group of young men were at the table closest to the edge of the crowd, and I ran my eyes over them carefully to see if I could spot Olly, Lexi's brother. He was still a key suspect. If I could get close enough to him, Mavka would be able to read him and find out what he knew.

He wasn't there. The men were young, probably freshmen or sophomores, and they eyed us back with interest as we walked towards them on the way to the bar. One of them; an arrogant-looking guy, shirtless, tight-muscled, with rippling long hair, tipped his chair back on two legs and whistled at us. Prue ignored him, walking directly past his table.

"Orrrr," the man made a weird noise, and I glanced at him. He waited until Prue was looking, too, and he smirked, and pulled the corners of his eyes with his fingers. "Kon-nee-chee-wahhhh," he called over.

Oh, God, no...

I waited for Prue's explosion, but instead, she gave him a huge smile. "Konichiwa," she called back.

Wait... what? Prue wasn't even Japanese, and the dude was making fun of her, obviously pissed that she ignored him. Why was she playing along? Was this her new passive-aggressive way of dealing with racist assholes?

She grinned at him happily and walked over towards his table. His friends, all perched on barstools of their own, smiled back at her. Reaching the racist dude, she hooked her foot underneath his stool and tipped it.

He lost his balance and fell into the guy next to him with a strangled yell, then, *that* guy's chair tipped over, too, setting off a chain reaction of young men falling off their high stools and slamming into a heap on the ground.

Oh. Not passive aggressive. Just normal aggressive.

Vampire, Mavka whispered to me. *Young stupid vampire, an idiot, almost brand new, his scent is thick with fresh evil, he's drunk on this new life.*

What? Who? That shirtless guy?

He is brand new, newly made, and made for the purpose of creating chaos, Mavka muttered, her attention bouncing around the dark cavernous space. I looked back towards the tangle of young men on the concrete floor, but Prue had already stalked off towards the bar, so I turned and quickly followed her.

Does he know about the coma girls, Mav? Is he a suspect?

He has a master, the master is here, his master will know more, she muttered. *I will find him and I will eat him, mmmmm.*

I could almost see her inside of me, head whipping everywhere, following the laser lights as they flickered and bounced off every surface, involuntarily twitching her hips to the thudding pulse of bass. She was far too excited. Just like me, she couldn't concentrate.

We both needed a drink. Luckily, Prue had already ordered a couple of tequila shots each and a vodka-tonic chaser. I threw back the first shot, then the second, and slowly sipped my vodka. Immediately, I felt less tense. More relaxed, but more excited. "Ahh." Prue chugged half her vodka. "That's better."

I squinted at her. "How… where… Um…"

"I've got an etheric storage relay in my mouth," Prue explained, taking another sip of her drink. "Everything that passes through me ends up in Fort Totten. The alcohol effects are all psychosomatic."

I smiled at her. "I did wonder how you manage to get high."

"Oh, I manage," she said. "I know we're on the job here, but I don't think we're going to get anywhere unless we get a little on the same vibe as everyone else."

A liver, a kidney a heart, my love, Mavka sang happily inside me, in time to the music. *I will consume thee, the blood of men, I drink to quench my thirst.*

I pressed my lips together so I wouldn't laugh. "Yes, but let's just stick to getting slightly buzzed, okay? I'm not going to be able to concentrate if we get wasted." And I had no idea what Mavka would do.

Dance, she murmured to me. *I shall dance.*

You can dance?

I love to dance. A ring of blood around a fire and fresh man-hearts on a pike, and I will stomp my feet hey-ho. Her attention ricocheted around the party again. *A flock of sheep, pure and innocent, with the wolves hiding amongst them, preying on them. I leave the sheep and hunt the wolves, oh yes, I will consume their flesh.*

I giggled. Prue shot me a look. "I was just thinking about that asshole," I pointed a thumb behind me, to where the group of men had gotten back on their barstools, muttering furiously. One of them had a smear of blood on his cheek. Another was shouting angrily, pushing his friend. "Good job, by the way."

She made a face. "We should check him out. He's a new vampire."

"You can tell? Like, without seeing the fangs?"

"Of course. I can See, remember? There's a slight luminescence over his eyes. That's how you tell if someone's a supe; it means they can See, too. Other supes have height-ened senses of smell, which is usually how they figure out what someone is, but I don't have that. I have to rely on checking out their eyes." She fixed her gaze on me. "You've got it too, but the color is different."

A tingle of fear ran through me. She could tell I was a supe? "I'm not following you," I said. "What color?"

"Most humans can't see the full spectrum of existence," she explained. "I've told you this before, dumbass. There's a veil over their eyes. You know, like how cats and dogs can see extra colors and hear things off the normal human spectrum? Well, when a human is exposed to the supernatural world and they can't happily ignore it, it's like taking wax out of their ears. They can See, and they can Hear. Usually, you can tell by looking into their eyes and you can see the dullness has vanished. Their eyes are clear."

"Yeah, I got all that. What do you mean about the color?"

"It's how I tell what kind of supe someone might be. To me, when I look at a vampire, I can see a silver luminescence over their eyes. Wolves have a golden sheen. Fae are pale green, but then again I've never looked closely, because whenever I'm in the vicinity of a fae, I'm hauling my ass out of there." She pouted and took another huge sip of her vodka.

"Do I want to ask why?"

"You don't fuck with the fae," Prue said darkly.

I met her intense stare, waiting to see if she'd elaborate, but she didn't. "Okay," I said finally. "Duly noted."

"Witches usually have kind of a browny-green shimmery thing going on in their eyes," she said. "Good ones do, anyway. When my mom turned, her eyes changed. They were glowing pale white. It was horrifying."

I looked into her eyes. "I can't see any color shimmers over your eyes."

"You might not be able to. It takes practice, anyway." She

squinted at me. "Usually most humans – the ones that can See, like you – don't have any colors at all. But you've got some kind of ultraviolet glow in there." She pursed her lips, looking closer.

Ultraviolent, Mavka sniggered. *Violence. Justice. Violent justice,* she sang.

"It might be the lights in here," I said hastily.

"No, I've seen it before." Prue frowned. "Not all the time, though. I just get little flashes of it. I thought it was a little odd."

"Hmmm. I don't know." I looked away. The bar was filling up. The table next to us was crammed with beautiful young women, all wearing similar outfits to us. More and more came in until they'd spilled over into our table, all chatting away dreamily to each other. Judging by the slurry conversations that were going on around us, none of them knew each other. We were just girls, swarming together, drunkenly admiring outfits and stroking each other's hair. It was quite nice. The flock of beautiful women blocked out the group of young men Prue had tipped off their seats, who'd been staring venomously at us the whole time.

"Vape?" A gorgeous blonde passed her e-cigarette to me.

I shrugged. "Sure." I'd never tried vaping before, but I knew all the cool kids were doing it, and I wanted to blend in. I took a deep inhale, expecting to cough and choke, but I felt almost nothing. Passing the vape to Prue, I exhaled a cloud of vapor.

"Like a dragon," I giggled. "Puff the magic dragon."

The girl laughed with me. "That's the one!"

Prue blew out her own big cloud, and smacked her lips. "Hmmm. Is that a weed vape?"

"A wahhhh?" Suddenly everything seemed quite foggy.

"Yeah," the girl giggled. "I get them on prescription. For my anxiety."

Weed? Oh, good grief. I put my hand over my eyes.

I'd been high before, only a couple of times. It was kinda fun, but I still carried around the vision of my mom in my head, berating me for smoking the 'devil's lettuce.' I was still a goody-two-shoes at heart, so I stuck to drinking if we were partying.

I shouldn't have done that.

I felt *niiice,* though. What was the harm? Falling into the dreamy sensation, I nodded my head in time with the music; a deep, pulsing throb with a hypnotizing melody. "How are you feeling, Mav?" Oops, shit, I said it out loud.

Prue didn't notice, anyway, she was sucking on the vape again and watching the D.J.

Let us take to the floor. Mavka pulled at me. *It's been a millennia since I've danced. The holy oil of calamus and the sweet liquor you consumed commands me.*

I poked Prue. "Dance?"

"Yeah."

She took my hand and we weaved through the crowd. "Pay attention, Mav," I muttered under my breath as we got closer to the stage. "We've still got a job to do. We've got to find out... something..."

In good time, child. The scions of chaos surround us, and they are not going anywhere. For now...

She started stomping her feet, her whole body leaning into the movement, echoing the thud of the base, a wild, tribal dance. Her arms flowed around her, vibrating with power and majesty. I danced with her, and in my mind's eye I watched her, a mighty goddess of vengeance performing her war dance. I followed her, mimicking her movements, letting my arms, which felt absolutely weightless, drift up towards the sky, waving in time with the music.

I loved to dance. It was one of the things I missed most

when I married Terry and moved back to Emerald Valley. Terry hated most music except for country, and he would never dance. On the very rare occasion we were out somewhere with country music playing and people dancing, he wouldn't let me dance in case another man got too close to me.

Before Terry, I used to go dancing with Prue and Chloe all the time. It didn't matter what type of music – pop, R&B, techno, even old-timey swing. It was always sweet, sweet bliss to get a little tipsy and lose myself to the music.

Mavka and I apparently had that in common. The magic running out of her almost overwhelmed me. I let the beat run through me, run through *us*, stomping our feet, swinging our hips and shaking our arms in time with the delicious thud of bass. Dancing with my vengeance demon.

The crowd thickened around us, young women surrounding us, dancing just like me. With deep stomps and arms to the sky, eyes closed, powerful shoulders thrown back and womanly hips shaking from side to side, I suddenly realized Mavka's magic had soaked into the air around me. An atmosphere of feminine power, of beauty and strength blazed around us as we danced together, women reveling in their magic.

I DON'T KNOW how long I danced for, but it was long enough for me to sober up a little and realize Prue was nowhere to be found.

A tingle of unease chased away the last of my buzz. "Where did she go, Mavka?"

Her euphoria, too, had ebbed away. Her powerful movements slowed, then ceased. I felt her push her senses out around the room. *I do not know.*

Glancing around the crowd, all I saw was a heaving mass of half-naked bodies. "Can you hear her?"

I cannot hear the thoughts of women, child. Mav's voice sounded a little subdued. *Perhaps we should locate her.*

"Good idea." I moved through the mass of people, first heading towards the stage in case she'd wanted to get close to the D.J. I vaguely remembered a couple of times I'd found her practically straddling the bass speaker at a club, but she wasn't there.

Moving back through the crowd, I zigzagged, wiggling past hot bodies and sliding up and down sweaty flesh, until I was at the edge of the dance floor.

"I don't understand." I bit my lip. "She wouldn't leave me alone. We never do that." Even without being undercover at a dangerous, illegal rave, we would never leave each other alone when we went out. It was Girl-Safety 101.

Mavka was worried, too. *There are evil thoughts abounding in here; I am finding it hard to separate them.* I felt her shake her head, trying to chase away the last of the drugs in my system, drugs that were probably clouding her powers.

"Fuck!" I never swore; the curse felt weird on my lips, but appropriate. I was furious with myself and getting more frightened by the second. "How could I be so stupid to get drunk and high? We had a fucking job to do, Mavka."

We were swept up by the power of the music. She sounded almost contrite. *Never fear, child, we will find your bony best friend, and I will flay the hide from whoever lured her away and use it as roti, and crush his innards to make the dipping sauce.*

The vision in her head was too visceral for me; a sudden surge of nausea made me retch. "Can you keep the mental images to yourself, please, Mav," I begged. "Can you hear anything about her?"

No.

I tried the bathrooms first; pleading with the girls in the

line as I skipped through. "I'm just trying to find my friend. Have you seen her? Skinny, in a silver sequined bikini and with long black hair braided with silver thread?"

The girls – most of whom were also in sequined bikinis and with their hair braided back with various color thread – shook their heads sadly, looking worried, offering suggestions as to where she might be. I ducked inside the bathroom, checking the stalls, but there was no sign of her.

"Hear anything, Mav?"

There are no men here, she murmured.

The girls around me patted my shoulders, offering suggestions. "There's a chill-out room just off the bar area. What about the corridor to the back exit? They've got a first aid room, maybe try there?"

"First aid room?" I grabbed the girl who spoke.

"Yeah, just in case of a medical emergency. Go through the sparkly curtain beside the bar, follow the sound of ambient trance and you'll find the chill-out room. Just through there, there's a corridor, and the first-aid room is the first door on the left."

I thanked her, and ran out of the bathroom into the heaving mass of bodies on the dancefloor. Fighting my way through the crowds, feeling more and more panicked, I headed back towards the bar. The group of young guys were gone, although the bar was almost empty now. Almost everyone was dancing, or slumped in a beanbag in the corner with their eyes closed.

For me, the buzz was long gone, the mesmerizing, seductive atmosphere had disappeared.

Only pure panic remained. The music, again, was too loud, the people too wasted, the darkness was too dark, the flashing lights were too bright. My heart thumped in my chest. I had to find Prue, *now*.

I ducked through the sparkly curtain next to the bar and

entered a different space. It was almost like going through a portal to another realm – the room was softly lit with gentle blues and greens, and a projector shot a swirling kaleidoscope of lights on one of the walls. Low sofas and beanbags were strewn across the floor. A handful of college kids slumped on them, watching the lights on the ceiling. The music was soothing; a gentle, calming beat, but it didn't make a dent on my panic. I quickly checked all the faces in the room, and darted through to the other exit.

Sweeping back another sparkly curtain, I found myself in a short corridor. At the very end, a green neon sign indicated the fire exit. The first door on the left was closed, so I opened it slowly and peeked inside.

It was empty. Just a couple of chairs and a hospital bed, but no one else around. I guessed everyone was being relatively responsible with their drugs tonight. Cursing myself again for being so stupid and losing Prue, I backed out of the room and tried the next door, which was just a little storage closet.

The next door was locked. I glanced down, staring at the lock, my heart thumping.

Suddenly, Mavka snarled. *In there.*

"What?"

They have her; she is trapped. They are arguing about what to do with her.

"Who has her, Mav?"

The vampire, she hissed. *I can hear them clearly. The young, foolish vampire. His pride was destroyed by your skeleton friend, so he decided to make her pay.*

"How? She doesn't have any blood!"

He did not want her for her blood. They want to take her spirit.

"That doesn't make any sense!" I stared down at the lock again. I could pick it; I had my tools. It might take a couple of minutes, though.

Unzipping one of my many pockets, I pulled out my picks. "What are they doing to her?"

She is trapped in a circle; one I have not felt before. Prue has been bewitched by the young vampire, he is holding her under a compulsion, but he is new, so he is concentrating hard. His master is berating him. The young one has–

The door rattled. I yanked my picks out of the lock and backed away.

He's coming, Mav warned.

Quickly, I walked backwards until I was near the first aid room door. There was no time to run; it would look suspicious, anyway. I slumped down, leaning against the wall and put my head in my hands.

The door opened; angry male voices spilled out. "You've fucked up, Harley. That one's no good."

"I don't get it," another man whined. "I know she's got no blood, but I thought since she was a supe, we could still use her. I thought we might get more power out of her."

"She's already broken, you idiot. The tether is too tight. We can't use her." The voice grew louder as the man speaking walked through the door. "Get rid of her," he snarled. He slammed the door.

I kept my head down, feigning a drug-fueled haze and I prayed, as the man stalked past me.

Mavka thrashed. *Let me loose,* she demanded. *Blood witch, he is a blood witch, the most evil, the most oppressive, a hater of women, he is a scion of chaos, we must consume him...*

I had to save Prue. God knows what the vampire was doing to her if she was under a compulsion. Besides, we were in a relatively public corridor; I couldn't grab this man and eat him now. Goddamnit, Prue was so blasé about the vampires because they couldn't drink her blood, but they could still compel her. She'd pissed off a young vamp and he was out for revenge.

The man stomped past me, hesitating slightly as he walked by, but he kept walking. Black suit pants, black leather shoes, a whiff of tobacco… that's all I got before he'd stomped away, down the corridor and out of sight.

I sprang up and ran to the door, checking the lock to see if there was any chance the man had left it unlocked when he left. He hadn't, but it was a simple cylinder lock. Frantically, I grabbed my picks and tension wrench, and got busy, trying to work as quietly as possible. "How many inside, Mavka?"

Two men, hideous, monstrous, with the sweetest evil blood, she seethed. *The young vampire and another, a human boy who dallies with blood magic. He is not a practiced witch; he is an evil man who has only just been introduced to the dark arts.*

I hesitated. "A human boy?"

They are arguing about how to best destroy your friend. They will pull her apart, bone by bone, until her spirit tether shatters.

The lock turned; I pulled the handle and rushed into the room, slamming the door behind me.

The room was almost bare. Just a long metal table– a workbench, by the looks of it – on one side, scattered with odd things; metal tools, sharp spikes, leather pouches, bottles filled with sludgey looking stuff…

Prue sat cross-legged in the center of the room, gazing blankly into the eyes of the young shirtless vampire from earlier. A circle surrounded her, black and charred, looking like it had been burned into the concrete floor with a corrosive chemical.

"Hey!" The other young man whipped his head around and glared at me as I slammed the door. "What the fuck are you doing in here? Get out!"

The vamp waved his arm, not breaking eye contact with Prue. "No," he snapped. "Leave her and lock the door behind her. It's too late; she's already seen us, and they're friends, I saw her with this one earlier. Fucking Mullins didn't lock the door," he muttered, his eyes glowing silver. "It's okay. This is good. If we can't use this one," he nodded at Prue. "We can use *that* one. Message Mullins and tell him to come back."

The new blood witch stomped towards me and grabbed me by the wrist. "Come over here, bitch."

The vampire smiled, still staring at Prue in the circle. "This one can watch while we pull her apart. Slowly."

I glanced at Prue. Her face was blank. It scared me more than anything I'd seen so far. My vibrant, bolshy, expressive friend was sitting in a circle obediently, waiting to be ripped apart.

It was my turn to do some ripping. "Have you got everything you can from them, Mav?"

I have all the information I can access, Mavka confirmed. *Switch with me, child. I am starving. I must feast!*

I didn't want to leave. I had to make sure Prue was okay. Steeling my stomach, I took a deep breath, slid my consciousness out of the metaphorical driver's seat of my body and let Mavka take control.

CHAPTER 7

Mavka

My hunger was too wild and expansive for Sandy's little body; the men inside the room were too close, their scent too enticing. I bloomed like a night lily, converting all the atoms and molecules of my host's body into my own mighty form.

Oh, the scent of evil blood! How I adored the smell, it called to me, my throat was parched; it demanded the sweet liquor of it. The young man who held my arm – the young acolyte blood witch – the scent of his burgeoning monstrousness was as clear to me as springwater. A newly minted evil witch, but a long-time oppressor of women, it seemed. The beatings, the rapes, the violence – it all flavored his blood, and it *called* to me.

My hair blossomed around me, no longer the rose-gold softness of Sandy's hair, but wild and black like a stormy night sky. I grew, bursting out of the tininess of Sandy's form, letting my powerful shape fill the room, six feet, then seven, then eight. I clicked my claws, savoring the metallic chime as they clashed together, razor sharp. And I watched, chuckling merrily to myself, as the man in front of me took in the sight of my magnificence. His eyes bulged, his mouth quivered, he gaped, and I laughed out loud at the sight of it.

He was still holding Sandy's arm, which was now *my* arm, bone-white and suffused with enormous power. I met his eye and tugged, sending him flying into the wall on the other side of the room.

The young vampire turned, breaking eye contact with Prudence, and he let out a shout of shock and outrage. I swooped like a great raven and gathered him up in my fingers, piercing the razor-sharp claws through his stomach. The sweet blood flowed.

Oh, he was young, and so evil, so delicious... Vampires were tricky, by nature, their bodies behaved like a humans until their heart was pierced or their head was cut off. Even after that, for a while they'd bleed and their organs would seep out of their wounds, but the older vamps would turn to dust quickly and there was nothing left for me to consume.

The young ones, though, they were fun. I reached inside the young vampire's body cavity, rummaging around in the same way my beloved Sandy looked for snacks in her own purse. I located his liver, my favorite, and pulled. It came loose, thick, tough and purple, and I shoved it in my mouth, gnawing off a chunk and swallowing. Delicious. Opening my mouth wide like a boa consuming a sheep, I gulped it down, shivering in delight.

The vampire screamed, shaking, helpless in my clutches. Stabbing my claws in again, I pulled out a kidney, and slurped it down. Mmmmm.

Sandy nudged me again; I was too entranced by the sweet flavors to notice she'd been trying to get my attention. *Get rid of the blood witch first,* she begged. *Prue will see you.*

I chuckled. It was probably too late for that. But I obliged anyway, dumping the young vampire on the concrete floor where he wrapped his arms around his wound, trying to gather up the entrails and organs as they slithered out of the ragged gash in his stomach.

I swept over to the corner of the room where the blood witch lay crumpled on the floor, panting desperately, trying to drag himself towards the door to escape. The thought occurred to me that he was rather odd – an evil man, a young one, already well practiced in human monstrosities and violent misogyny, and he'd been recently introduced to blood magic by another. It was forbidden by witches and vampires to reveal their nature to humans, I knew this, but someone had taken this disgusting slug, this rage-filled boy, and introduced him to the evil arts.

Too bad he hadn't had more practice, like the last one I consumed. Linus Brady had been a young witch, too, one born into a coven, though, and he possessed power enough to make me cautious.

This one did not. He had no skill, no resources of power to call on. I'd already broken his body when I'd flung him into a wall, his legs did not work anymore.

"Tsk, tsk." I waved a long black fingernail at him. He let out a scream of fright as I swooped down and grabbed his ankles, and pulled him back towards me. I yanked him up off the floor and brought his face near mine. "Who is Lord Seth?"

I knew my lovely hostess would appreciate me trying. So far, none of the evil men I'd consumed had thought about their master directly. In their thoughts, he was an endless black hole, a swirling pit of chaos, no doubt as a result of a geas on their minds. But he had a human form. I knew that; I could sense it in the tenor of their thoughts. He was a real man, not just a monster. He walked the streets of the capitol, with the rest of the city unaware he was a dark god who was stirring and scraping power towards himself.

But the man in my grasp just shook his head frantically, spit flinging from his lips. "I don't know! I don't know!"

There was a flash there; a tall man in his thoughts, but it disappeared as soon as I glimpsed it. I shook the boy by the leg. "You have been introduced to him, have you not?'

There it was again. A man, tall, with dark hair. He was faceless, though; I could not see, and then his thoughts displayed for me the black pit of chaos again. I was right; the boy *had* been introduced, possibly as he was recruited. When the boy's mind touched on the subject of Lord Seth, his thoughts screamed in terror and devotion. It was true. He *was* their god.

I sighed. I was not going to get anything else out of him. Dropping him to the ground, I sliced open his belly.

There was a blink in my mind as Sandy departed. She'd done well to last this long; she was so kind-hearted, but so soft and squeamish. Bending over the man's body, I buried my face in the bleeding wound, and sucked out his entrails like they were spaghetti noodles.

His consciousness left his body quickly; he was soon an empty shell, completely dead. I returned to the vampire, sobbing on the floor, and lifted him up by the neck. "Who is Lord Seth?" I demanded.

His thoughts told me nothing new. He, too, was wholly devoted to his master, the one who introduced him to his new life. All I got was the swirling black pit, not even a glimpse this time of the tall, dark-haired man. Sighing, I ripped off one of the vampire's fingers and stuffed it in my mouth, chewing thoughtfully.

How would I get the information Sandy needed? Perhaps there was something in the fact that the newer recruit showed me a man's form. Maybe it takes time for the geas to mature. Perhaps I could hunt a brand-new recruit, and his thoughts might tell me more.

The vampire's screams were distracting me somewhat, they were so high-pitched, like fingernails down a black-board. "Hush," I told him, breaking off another finger. "I am trying to think." I chewed the flesh off his finger, but his screams persisted. He was slightly annoying. I plunged my hand into his chest, grasping at the pulsing muscle inside, and ripped it out.

Ah, the heart. Not my favorite organ – I always preferred the liver – but there was something so primal about eating a heart. In my hand, it squirted blood, and I lifted it to my lips and took a bite.

Sandy twitched within me. "Hello," I greeted her happily. "I thought you checked out."

Prue!

Oh. I forgot about her. I paused, mid-chew, and glanced over.

Prudence was sitting cross legged in the circle, her eyes clear and bright. She was watching me, an expression of mild interest on her face. A lollipop stick hung out of her mouth. While I looked at her, she pulled at the stick, twirling it around on her tongue. She smacked her lips a couple of times, pulled the lollipop right out of her mouth and saluted me with it. "Hello," she said.

Don't talk to her! Maybe we can wiggle out of this somehow...

It was too late for that. Besides, Prue seemed to be taking all this in her stride. "Well met, child." I inclined my head towards her graciously.

She bowed deeply back; the sign of respect warmed me to her even more. “Are you the pontianak?” she asked me.

“I am,” I told her. “But I am much more than that, if you must know. I am an archetype, a powerful spirit from the astral plane. I am a goddess.”

My host had a habit of referring to me as a demon, which was entirely incorrect, but I understood her reasoning. Her rigid and quite inaccurate spiritual education branded everything it didn’t understand as demonic. That church she used to frequent would often call ordinary intelligent women demons. It did not bother me.

Prudence gestured at me with her candy stick again. “Have you been in Sandy the whole time?”

I inclined my head again. “I have.”

She made a fist and pumped it in triumph. “I *knew* it! I could sense it sometimes, I was sure of it. Occasionally when I’d look at her, I’d see a mighty and terrifying force staring out through her eyes.” She grinned at me, seeming absolutely delighted. “You never left her, did you? She told me about the possession.”

Don’t tell her about the banana!

I scoffed to myself. For some reason Sandy felt embarrassed about the fact she’d consumed the vessel I’d been trapped in after the first time I possessed her. I thought it was rather brave of her, but she was still coming to terms with the fact she’d deliberately tried to sic a bloodthirsty demon on her good-for-nothing-but-eating husband.

Prue shuffled up until she was at the edge of the circle, leaning forward, her eyes bright. “Can I just say – and I’m sorry to gush about this – but I’m a *massive* fan of your work. You’re amazing,” she sighed. “What you did to Terry? Scaring him senseless? Perfection.” She kissed her fingertips. “I thought he’d never loosen his clutches on my girl Sandy.”

“Well,” I said heartily. “I warmly return your admiration.

It was wonderful what you did – how you drove to the Valley and rescued her. It was lucky for Terry that you did," I added, winking. "If you had not done that, I dare say there would be a trail of blood and entrails from Emerald Valley to this nation's capital."

She chuckled dirtily and waved a hand over the floor, gesturing to the bloody chunks of the men scattered around. "And thank you for doing this, too." Suddenly, she looked a little sheepish. "It's not like me to screw up like this. That damned vampire caught me on the dancefloor and compelled me to follow him. Asshole," she snorted. "I guess he was out for revenge."

"It was more than that, child. These men were after something else. Can you not see the circle you sit in?"

She gazed around the floor. "I assumed it was a ward."

"It's not just a ward. This circle hums with black magic. It's not something I have encountered before."

Prue wiggled on her bottom uncomfortably. "I have to say, I'm not feeling all that great in here. I can feel something tugging at me, like leeches sucking at every part of my skin." She glanced up and met my eye. "I don't suppose you can get me out of here, can you?"

I eyed the circle carefully. Whatever magic was working inside that circle, it wasn't a spell the young witch had cast. If it was, it would have ceased when he died. It must have been the older witch, the one they'd referred to as Mulberry. Or Michaels. I couldn't quite remember. The one who had stormed out of here, anyway. What was it he said? *This one was broken.*

"A sucking sensation?" I stroked my chin. "Hmmm." They were trying to siphon off her magic, perhaps. That would mean there would have to be a vessel nearby, something to hold her magic.

I swooped down, gathering the torso of the witch on the

floor, and checked his pockets. He had nothing except little plastic bags filled with tablets, which I dumped on the ground. The vampire had even less; just some plastic wristbands.

Check the table, Sandy whispered.

I surveyed the scattered contents of the workbench near the wall. There were screws and scalpels and tongs – torture implements – as well as bottles filled with cat eyeballs and the tiny bones and skulls of ravens. Common blood witch paraphernalia. A leather pouch caught my eye; the texture of the fabric was suspicious. I snatched it up and examined it. As I suspected, it was human leather. It had been sewn shut, but the contents pulsed with dark energy. "This might be it. I held it up triumphantly.

"Oh, great!" Prue's eyes lit up.

"Catch!" I tossed it at her. A dirty white light pulsed through the circle.

Prue shivered. "Ohhh, that's better," she said, climbing to her feet. "That sensation was making me feel really sick."

"Are you free, child?'

She pushed her hand through the circle. "Yes. I can't thank you enough, my goddess," she said, bowing again deeply.

I tittered. "Stop that, child. You may call me Mavka."

"Mavka." Prue curtsied. "As much as I loved making your acquaintance, can I have my friend back?"

"Of course." Sandy was waiting patiently for me to hand her the wheel again, although she could just take it if she wished. She may not venerate me well enough, like Prudence did, but she did have very good manners. "It was lovely to finally make your acquaintance, Prudence."

"Likewise." She grinned at me. "Let's hang out sometime, grab a movie or something."

Okay, that's enough, Sandy wriggled inside me. *I'm sorry, but if I let you two go on, you'll be braiding each other's hair and getting sushi together. And eating popcorn made out of evil man fingernails or something.*

I sniggered, and let go of the metaphorical wheel, leaving the vehicle of Sandy's body back in her capable hands.

CHAPTER 8

Sandy

I came back to my body, standing in a puddle of blood and entrails. Again. "Eww," I lifted my shoe, inspecting the bottom. "Oh, thank God I wore my leather Cons. I'd never get the blood out of my canvas ones."

"Well, you don't go to a rave wearing canvas shoes, babe." Prue wrapped her arms around me and squeezed me hard. "Ahhh, it's good to have you back."

"Really?" I hugged her back and tugged on her braids. "Here's me thinking you were going to ask Mavka on a date or something."

She sniggered. "God, I'm buzzing about that. We're going to have a big talk soon, Sandy. But first–" She nodded towards the door. "Let's get out of here."

I hesitated. "Should we just leave it like this?"

"Yeah. We'll lock the door behind us. The only person

discovering this mess will be the assholes that set it up. They can do the cleaning themselves," she sniffed.

I opened the door quietly and took a peek out into the corridor. A couple of people were walking through, headed towards the chill-out room, so I ducked back in and waited for a second. When the coast was clear, I pulled her out of the room behind me. "Let's go." I flicked the lock and shut the door behind me, sending up a little prayer that it would be the blood witch from before that found the bodies, and not some innocent janitor.

We turned to head for the exit at the end of the corridor, but before I took a step, the exit door clanged and started to open. Panicking, we did an about face, and scurried back up the hallway, past the first-aid room, through the sparkly curtain, and back into the chill-out room.

The space was dark and inviting; the soothing music and trippy kaleidoscope light-show projecting on the walls and ceiling instantly enhanced the endorphins surging through me. The relief of getting Prue back almost made me feel as high as I was before, dancing on the dancefloor, deep in the grip of the magic of the music.

"Let's rest a while, babe." Prue pointed to a couple of beanbags in the corner.

I bit my lip. It was a little dangerous; the blood witch might come back and discover his minions ripped to pieces inside their makeshift ritual room.

It's a good idea, Mavka drawled sarcastically. *The blood witch might come back. We need to find him. He'll have more information.*

I let out a tiny sigh, and nodded. "Okay."

We picked our way over a couple of unconscious hippies and disappeared into the sea of beanbags, sinking into fuzzy suede cushions in the corner.

"So," Prue lay back and closed her eyes. She was more

wrung-out than I'd thought, and I was glad we'd stopped to rest. "Mavka, hey?"

"Yup." I let my head lol back and sighed deeply. "Sorry I didn't tell you."

"It's okay. I knew it, though," she hissed under her breath triumphantly. "I could sense her. Since you came back, you've had a wild power lingering just under the surface, and I swear I could even hear her at times." She raised her head and squinted at me. "Does Aunt Marche know?"

I nodded. "She sensed her too."

"Did she? Well." Prue let her head thud back behind her. "I guess my mom was right. I do have the talent," she sighed, making it sound like she had herpes instead of an innate magical gift.

"It's why Aunt Marche wanted me to help with this investigation," I told her. "Mavka isn't just a vengeance demon."

"She's not a demon. She's a goddess," Prue breathed out.

"Stop with the fangirling. It's embarrassing."

"I wonder if she'll take on an apprentice. I'd rather be her acolyte than anyone else's."

"Prue, stop. Mavka's... well, she's great, but she's no one to mess with. She eats evil men, for God's sake."

"That's why I love her so much."

I sighed. "Yeah, she's pretty cool," I admitted. "She does more than that, too. She's the reason why Aunt Marche was so confident in me helping out with this little mission. Mavka can hear evil thoughts," I explained. "She can sniff out dastardly man-deeds like a bloodhound."

"Oh, right." Prue's eyebrows pinched together. "How come she didn't pick up on the fact that that asshole newbie vampire lured me away?"

"We were both stoned," I said sheepishly. "And enjoying the dancing. Her magic was leaking out around us; did you see?"

"Yeah," Prue laughed. "It was amazing. For a moment, it felt like we were at some great coven gathering, dancing naked around a fire."

I giggled with her.

"Hang on," she said abruptly. "Is that why you went out with the Enforcer? Was Mavka helping him with something?"

The sound of Sinclair's title jolted me; almost painfully jabbing me in the chest. I rubbed it absently, trying to make that hollow feeling of longing go away. It was stupid, and I hated it. "He doesn't know about her," I confessed. "He thinks I'm a powerful psychic. Remember those guys who were hanging out with that leech in Scarlett's? That guy who we thought might be blackmailing Chloe?"

"What was his name again?" Prue wrinkled her nose. "I don't remember. The accountant. Keith, maybe? He was hanging out with a vamp, and a Russian gangster. They spiked those girls' drinks."

"Well, it turns out the vamp was a rogue, and part of a bigger conspiracy. Drugging those girl's drinks was only the tip of the iceberg. Mavka read all the details out of his mind like it was a grocery list and wanted to eat him."

"She didn't try to eat him?"

"I didn't let her. I thought… I don't know…" I shrugged helplessly. "I just thought they should face proper justice. A courtroom and a judge."

Prue looked at me for a whole minute, her face expressionless.

"Yes, I know." I rolled my eyes. "You agree with Mavka. But honestly, Prue… how will their victims get any closure if I just go around eating all the bad guys?"

"Bloody Pollyanna," she muttered under her breath. "It's a good thing Mavka chose *you* to set up shop inside of. If she were inside *me*, there'd be no men left in the world."

I chuckled uncomfortably. It was my fault Mav was inside of me. She didn't say as much, but I got the feeling she was trapped.

I'd done that to her. I ate the banana. I'm sure I'd have to face some consequences for that at some point, and the thought scared me.

"Anyway," I went on. "I gave a tip to Sinclair; that's why he was there to arrest them. He tracked me down at the salon the next day – thanks to you, I might add."

She shrugged. "Babe, I put *everyone* on the salon's mailing list. So, did he threaten you?"

"What? No!"

"He didn't blackmail you into helping him?"

"No, he came to see if I needed any help from *him.* He thought I was a gangster moll, desperate to get out."

"Oh. I guess he really *is* a good guy."

"He is."

"It's weird. He's such a huge personality on the supe scene – he's the human that makes supes shake in their boots. Everyone is scared of him. He's the monster under the bed for monsters. But he showed up to our salon to make sure you were okay."

To my horror, my eyes pricked with tears. I blinked furiously, cleared my throat, and changed the subject. "Anyway, remember Linus Brady?"

"Yeah. He was one of our suspects."

"I told Sinclair we were going after him to find out if he was the blackmailer, and he got real mad, said that Brady was too dangerous. I told him I was going to do it anyway, so he asked me to come with him instead. It turns out Brady was a suspect for a bunch of murders he was investigating. So I went on my 'date' with Sinclair to check him out."

She eyed me with interest. "Go on. What happened?"

"We checked him out. He was worse than we thought." I shrugged. "Mavka ate him."

Prue shivered with delight. "Oh, she's a bad bitch. I love her."

"Linus Brady was part of that conspiracy Sinclair was worried about. There's a group of supe men, banding together, calling themselves the Blood Kings. They've got some sort of evil agenda to put women back under their boots, take away all their rights, that sort of thing. Linus Brady's legitimate PAC was working towards legislation to put women's rights back to the dark ages. No voting, no owning property, no birth control – and certainly no abortion – no driving, etcetera, etcetera. Effectively, we'd be back under the ownership of men, handmaid-style. And as a blood witch, Brady was abducting and torturing woman for use in his blood magic rituals."

"Sheesh. Well, I'm glad Mavka ate him."

"Brady was just an acolyte, a scion. He was a symptom of the disease, and there's one person at the top pulling the strings. Their master's name is Lord Seth, he's a powerful entity of some sort, and that's all we really know about him."

Prue nodded thoughtfully, dissecting all the information. "So... what happened with Sinclair?'

I bit my lip. "Nothing."

"He really *did* ghost you?"

"It's probably for the best. If he finds out about Mavka, he'll have to kill me."

She blew a raspberry. "He wouldn't do that."

"He's the Enforcer, Prue. It's his whole job. He's supposed to keep supernatural creatures in line. He can't let a demon run around D.C. eating people. He'd kill me," I said again.

"She's not a demon."

"Yeah, yeah, I know. Not that it matters. She's powerful and *exceptionally* dangerous."

"She's a lot like Sinclair, in a way. She's taking out the bad guys. Queen Bad Bitch, ridding the world of evil men."

"Why don't you get T-shirts printed?" I muttered, sinking into my beanbag. "Mavka Fan Club."

"She's amazing, though." Prue closed her eyes, resting. "I wonder why she didn't eat Terry?"

"We made… boundaries. There's a Scale of Evil that we're following. She's not allowed to eat anyone less evil than a rapist or a murderer."

"That sounds fair enough." She opened one eye again and peered at me. "Although Terry, I think, deserves it more than anyone."

I nodded, thinking about Terry, and the last time I saw him, just after Father Benson's funeral. That girl, Kate, who had answered the door when I'd knocked… Her face kept swimming to the front of my mind's eye. She was doomed to my fate, I just knew it. As soon as I left, Terry immediately went out and found someone to bully and manipulate into a life of slavery.

And she didn't have a demon to save her.

Goddess, Mavka whispered to me. *At least your friend venerates me properly.* She was reclining in my mind, just like I was on the beanbag, digesting her meal of evil man-flesh.

We rested a little in silence, watching the colors and patterns swirl on the roof, listening to the soothing ambient trance music, breathing in the vapor from the fog machine.

"What now?" Prue breathed out. "What's our next plan of attack? We still haven't found out anything about the coma girls."

"We've got some clues. I've got that spell pouch in one of my pockets, Aunt Marche might be able to help us identify what its purpose is. We can describe the circle and see what we can come up with. We might be able to break whatever spell is on them that's preventing them from waking up.

Although–" I held up one finger. "Mavka says they're not in their bodies."

"What?"

"Their spirits are not in their bodies."

"That's not possible. Their bodies are still alive."

"That's what she says."

We lapsed into silence. "I'm wrecked," Prue said. "That circle really took it out of me."

"Maybe we should go home, call it a night. Take what we've got to Aunt Marche and see where we go from here."

"Agreed." Prue held out her hands and I helped her up with a groan.

"You know, for a pile of bones, you're really heavy."

"It's all in your mind. Everything's all in your mind, you know."

I pulled down my crop top, trying to get it to cover a little more of my stomach again, but it wasn't going to do much more than cover my boobs. "Do I still look okay? No blood splatter?"

She shook her head and smiled again. "Mavka is a very careful eater. You look amazing, babe." She brushed my hair back over my shoulder. "Let's go."

Holding hands, we left the chill out room, and walked back into the main space. The music in here had morphed again; it was less frenzied, the bass heavier, the melody more hypnotic. The crowd danced, blank faced, watching the lasers, as if in a trance.

My vision focused on a young man deep in the crowd. I smirked, nudged Prue, and pointed.

She followed my gaze. "Is that Antonio?"

Shirtless, glistening with sweat, twitching like a spider on meth, my brother had two glow-sticks in each hand and a lollipop in his mouth.

Prue frowned deeply. "Did you know he was going to be here?"

"No. I didn't know he knew about these parties."

I spoke to my little brother almost every day. He had a busy schedule as an EMT and a jam-packed social life, but he always made time to pop into the salon to see me or come over to the apartment for dinner.

I watched him for a minute. He appeared to be enjoying himself immensely. "I wonder where Ben is?" My brother's boyfriend was a cop, so maybe he was on duty. They seemed like they were joined at the hip: Wherever Antonio went, Ben went too.

He's behind you. Mavka sniggered. She seemed to be laughing at a joke I didn't get. It was probably some blood-thirsty pun, so I ignored her, and whirled around.

There he was. Ben was leaning against a pillar, slightly concealed from my view – he must have been watching Antonio. He was also shirtless, showing off his bulky muscled frame and hairy chest. His shirt was tucked into the back of his jeans. He saw me staring at him and he flinched. "Oh… Sandy! Heyyyy."

Mavka sniggered inside of me again, but I ignored her. "Hi, Ben!" I waved.

Prue turned. "What are you guys doing here?"

Ben hesitated for a second, suddenly sheepish. "Antonio loves to dance," he said, waving a hand towards the dance-floor where my brother was pumping his fists like a maniac.

We all watched him for a few minutes, and Ben cleared his throat again. "So, uh. What are you girls up to now?"

"We're heading home. We're beat," I said. "We'll leave you guys to it, maybe catch you tomorrow?"

Ben seemed relieved. Maybe he was embarrassed about being caught at a rave by his boyfriend's sister. He nodded. "Okay."

"Tell Antonio I said hi," I giggled, watching my brother dance like an idiot. "I don't want to cramp his style."

He gave me one more awkward nod, and I pulled on Prue's hand, leading her through the crowd.

"I wonder what that was about?" Prue glanced back, trying to catch a peek at Ben again. "Did he seem odd to you?"

I pulled at her, leading her through the edges of the dance floor. "I don't know," I said, looking back. "Maybe we're cramping their style." I turned and ducked my head, ready to charge through the crowd again.

I ran straight into a man.

A *hard* man.

A tall, hard, brutally gorgeous man, who'd planted his feet, crossed his arms, and was now glaring down at me with blazing eyes filled with barely controlled anger. His presence was like a beast, a mighty behemoth, pulsing with the promise of violence. The crowd withered around him, retreating, sensing even through their drug-fueled haze that someone incredibly dangerous was standing there.

I gaped up at him. "Sinclair?"

"Alessandra..." His voice was dangerously quiet, and vibrated with menace. "What the *hell* are you doing here?"

CHAPTER 9

I frowned at him. "What do you mean, what am *I* doing here? What are *you* doing here?"

He grabbed my arm and pulled me towards him, his blazing blue eyes fixed on me. My heart thudded violently. His hair was longer; it had been three months since I'd cut it and he'd obviously not had a trim since. The sandy blond locks were wilder, leonine, and touching the collar of his plain white t-shirt, which, in turn, bulged over his wickedly muscled chest. That body, damn it, I couldn't help but look – the tense, bulging biceps, his powerful chest; not deliberately sculpted like Antonio or shaped by heavy weights like Ben, no, his was a body built for killing, for violence. Speed, skill and phenomenal strength all coiled within those muscles, packed tight into his overwhelmingly masculine frame.

My heart thudded wildly. He was here, really here, and touching me.

"You shouldn't be here," he growled. "Why did you come here?"

I mouthed helplessly. God, he was gorgeous; I hated the feeling that surged through me when I looked at him, the wild longing, the desperate, pathetic star-struck devotion – it made me feel like I was a stupid little kid again, and he was the untouchable gorgeous movie star I was in love with, who just happened to be standing right in front of me. I took a breath and squashed the feeling down, and refocused on my anger. The crowd, sensing the power of an atom bomb about to explode, edged away, leaving us in our own empty space. I was still holding Prue's hand, but she was standing as far back as possible.

Ripping my arm out of his grasp, I took a step back. "It's none of your business what I'm doing here." My skin tingled where he'd touched me. My whole body, in fact, was trembling. Goddamnit.

He ground his jaw, stared down at me and crossed his arms over his chest again. "You shouldn't be here," he said, his voice low and menacing. "It's not safe. You have to leave."

I huffed out a breath in outrage. "Who the hell do you think you are? You've got no right to tell me what to do."

"It's not safe," he repeated, eyeing me meaningfully. He took a step towards me.

I knew it wasn't safe. *He* knew that *I* knew it wasn't safe. He thought I was a powerful psychic, so he had to guess I was aware of the dangers. "I can take care of myself." I thrust my chin up. "Anyway, why do you care?"

He closed his eyes briefly, and refocused on me with the intensity of a cobra about to strike. "Sandy, listen to me. Whatever you're doing here, you're in over your head. You need to leave. Now."

I let out a bitter chuckle. "I'm not leaving."

"Er." Prue was still standing well back. The Enforcer scared the crap out of her. She wanted to leave, and we *had* been on our way out the door, but… fuck this guy. God, I was mad.

"I'm having fun!" I gave him a fake, sunny smile. "The music's great, isn't it?"

He gritted his teeth, and growled low in the back of his throat, a noise that sent a red-hot rush of heat straight through my body. "Sandy…"

"This place is a bust." Suddenly, a tall, stunningly gorgeous brunette woman appeared and put her arm on Sinclair's shoulder. Willowy, with ridiculously long legs, wearing a black catsuit that plunged daringly down to her bellybutton, displaying a concave stomach and gorgeous perky boobs, she spoke directly into Sinclair's ear in such a casual gesture of intimacy it felt like an ice-cold knife to my chest. Sinclair stiffened, but didn't move as she leaned forward, her lips almost touching his earlobe, and murmured to him again. "The F.B.I. agents have done a sweep; there's nothing here. Squires and his partner are thinking of ordering the K9 unit, but I don't think there's any point. There's no link, Conrad."

Suddenly, she seemed to become aware that Sinclair had been talking to someone when she arrived, someone obviously unworthy of her notice. She blinked down at me, apparently noticing me for the first time. "Oh. Hi."

"Hi there!" I smiled at her perkily, wildly aware I looked deranged.

Prue wasn't quite as restrained as I was. "Who the fuck are you?"

The brunette shifted on her feet, edging away from Sinclair. She shot him a look.

There was an uncomfortable pause. Finally, he uncrossed his arms. "This is Detective Giselle Russo, a colleague from the homicide department," he said to me. "Giselle, this is… Sandy."

The gorgeous brunette looked down on me again, her expression inscrutable. Finally, she smiled. It was about as genuine as Prue's fake Gucci fanny pack. "Hello, Sandy. How *are* you?" She cooed at me in the same way as the staff talked to the babies at Dexter's daycare. "Are you enjoying the music? It's fun, isn't it?"

Prue, her ferocious overprotective nature winning the battle over her fear of the Enforcer, stepped up beside me, with one shoulder in front of me. "Why are you here?" she said rudely. "You're a bit old, aren't you? This is a college party. What are you, forty? Forty-five?"

Giselle Russo stared back at her, totally unruffled for a whole minute. Cool as a cucumber. She ignored Prue, turned to Sinclair, and raised one eyebrow. He ground his jaw again, clearly uncomfortable. "Sandy is… that contractor I told you about."

"Oh." She turned back to me and gave me another patronizing smile. "Nice to meet you, Sandy." In a stunning gesture of dismissal, she turned her back on me and Prue, and faced Sinclair directly. "I'm going to debrief with the agents, but I think we're done here. Meet you back at the station?"

He nodded once, his jaw tight. She stalked off without turning to say goodbye to us. We weren't important.

"Bitch," Prue snarled as she walked off. "Who the fuck does she think she is?"

His girlfriend, probably.

A former lover, Mavka whispered to me. *They are no longer involved. She is just a colleague.*

That didn't make me feel any better. It was easy to ignore the word 'former' and focus on the 'lover' part.

Of course they'd been lovers; that woman was insanely gorgeous, much more Sinclair's type; tall, like him, with a physique built from chasing bad guys through alleyways and rappelling off the side of buildings, probably. She was closer to his age. My bitterness was so tangible I could taste it on my tongue.

I had no right to feel like this. Sinclair wasn't anything to me. I was just a contractor. The bitter feelings surging through me, though, it was so hard to contain it, the burning, squirming jealousy that made me feel like tearing off my own skin…

I could eat her for you, Mavka said helpfully. *I'd make an exception to my diet, just this once.*

Sinclair's expression thawed slightly, the hard, furious stare replaced with an expression I couldn't decipher. "Sandy… please. Can you go home?"

I stared back at him. "Why?"

"This place is dangerous."

I gave him a tiny smile. "I know. That's why we're here."

The fury surged back into his expression, and he stepped forward, a hand outstretched, ready to grab me again, but he forced himself to stop. "Why?" His voice growled so deeply it vibrated through me. Even Prue took a step back. "What are you doing?

"Lexi Thompson is Prue's niece's best friend."

He shut his eyes for a second, exasperated. "So you're trying to figure out what happened to her."

"Of course." I squared my jaw.

There was another pause, as he stared at me. His gaze roamed around my face, dipping to my lips, my jaw and back up to meet my eyes. "I'll ask you one more time. Please go home. Leave this to me."

I shook my head slowly. "No can do. I'm sorry, Sinclair, if I can help, I'm going to." Suddenly, my anger surged within me again. "Besides, I thought you *wanted* me to help you with this case? I remember you telling me about the unconscious girls and a frat party a few months ago. It escalated, didn't it? You wanted me with you, you offered me a contract, damnit. Then you ditched me. Without warning. Without saying anything, in fact."

"It's too dangerous." His hand shot out and grabbed my wrist, he pulled me close. The heat from his body touched me; I flinched away, it was too much. "I wanted you with me on this, Sandy, I did. But this conspiracy goes deeper than I ever imagined. I can't risk it." He looked down at me, eyes blazing. "I can't risk *you*."

My heart skipped a beat, then plowed on as I dismissed his words easily. I remembered Chloe, and how both Prue and I wanted her close so we could protect her. Sinclair felt no need for that, obviously. He just wanted me away from him. "Yeah? Well, you might have said something. You could have told me that you were cutting me loose." I bit my lip. "I was worried I'd done something."

"No. No, of course not. I didn't cut you loose. I just– I just–" Exasperated, he ran his hand through his hair. My traitorous eyes followed the motion, and I melted at the sight of his biceps bulging as he lifted his arm and disheveled his hair a little more. "Goddamnit, Sandy. I just wanted to keep you safe."

I scoffed. "How would you know if I was safe or not? You ditched me, Sinclair. You haven't been in contact at all."

A guilty look flickered in his eyes. At the same time, Mavka sniggered inside of me.

There was something I hadn't realized yet...

"Oh." I took a step back, away from him; it was hard to concentrate when I was standing so close, but the truth of it hit me suddenly.

Ben, lingering behind me, just a few minutes ago. Dropping in to see me at the salon, bumping into me in the street. Dropping around for dinner almost every night, or running into us at Scarlett's or at the Dog and Bone.

I stared at him. "You put Ben on protection detail, didn't you?"

He took a deep breath in, and nodded, just once.

I almost laughed. The irony was staggering. Sinclair had no idea I could let the demon inside me rip apart every single person in this room within thirty seconds.

Mentally, I chastised her. You could have told me.

He is unworthy of my notice.

Liar. You thought it was funny, didn't you?

Well, yes. The idea that we would need him to protect us is rather amusing, is it not?

Sinclair tilted his head, watching me curiously. "You're doing that thing again."

I blinked. "What thing?"

"The thing where you look like you're listening to a conversation in your head. He leaned closer. "Are you listening to *me?*"

"It doesn't work like that," I muttered.

"Obviously not."

I frowned. "Why do you say that?"

"Because if you *could* hear my thoughts, you wouldn't be acting like... like... *this.*" He waved his hand at me, snarling the words out. "You'd be taking your friend Prue and going home, far away from here."

I knew I should feel flattered that he'd asked Ben to shadow me. I probably would have, if I'd not met Sinclair's ex-lover, the gorgeous Detective Giselle Russo. Meeting her was like a slap to the face, a reminder that he was so far out of my league we weren't even playing the same sport. They were the same; experienced, professional, hard-boiled detectives at the peak of physical fitness. He probably only had me followed because he thought I was going to do something stupid and get hurt.

"I don't need you to protect me," I said quietly. "You don't want my help, Sinclair, and I don't need yours. Let's just leave it at that."

Prue tugged on my hand, and led me away.

CHAPTER 10

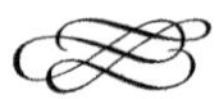

Three days later, we headed back to the hospital to see if we could find out more about the coma girls.

Aunt Marche had examined the leather pouch we'd brought her – she'd yelped in fright when I pulled it out of one of the many pockets in my orange cargo pants. She scuttled into her workroom, came out wearing a hazmat suit, picked the pouch up with long metal tongs, and disappeared back into her workroom. After an hour she reappeared, sweating, and declared the pouch was a fetish: a holding receptacle for dark magic. Luckily, it hadn't been filled, so it was just a nasty purse made of human skin, which she purified, blessed, and burnt to ashes. She buried the ashes in a pot and planted a Boston fern on top, and named the fern Trevor.

I didn't ask why.

We held long debates as to what the blood witch was doing with the circle, and what happened to the coma girls. It still didn't quite make any sense. Aunt Marche said that the fetish was used for holding siphoned power, but the spell attached to it was strange, and she wasn't quite sure what kind of power it was supposed to hold. The most obvious thing was that it was supposed to drain magic, but all the girls in comas were normies, and didn't *have* any magic.

"Unless, that's why they're in comas?" Prue furrowed her brow. "Maybe the blood witches are abducting girls at random, draining the magic ones, and somehow traumatizing the normies so much their consciousness leaves their bodies?"

"Mavka said the girls weren't in their bodies, so that kinda fits," I said hesitantly. "I'm not sure what it means, though. Maybe she *did* mean their consciousness. Maybe they're floating around the astral plane..." An idea flitted into the peripheral of my mind, but it disappeared before I could grab it.

Marche squinted at me. "Did she say anything else?"

"No. She just said they weren't there. And it didn't make sense. She'd never seen it before."

"Hmmm." She pointed at Prue. "Can you go over it again? What did the vampire and the blood witch talk about while you were in the circle?"

"I don't remember it very well; the compulsion filled my brain with fog," she said blithely, conveniently forgetting she'd been sucking on a weed vape like an asthmatic kid with an inhaler at a sports carnival. "I remember there was an older man, and he was absolutely furious. He was trying to get the circle to work, but it wouldn't, and he couldn't figure it out. He kept saying something like; "She's already broken." Her lips dropped into a frown. "Kinda mean, really."

I rubbed her arm. "The young vampire said the older witch's name. It was Michaels. I *think*." God, my memory was fuzzy too. "Sorry, Aunt Marche."

"It's okay. I get a little carried away when there's a fat bass and hot sweaty men dancing around me too," Marche snickered. "So, you threw the fetish at the circle, and it broke the spell?"

I nodded.

"At least I've got that to go on. I'll analyze the spell that I removed from the fetish, see if I can brew an antidote or something. Sage, wartlock, thin man's fingers…" she trailed off, muttering under her breath. "Maybe Oblix has found out more about the girls, too. Go and see him."

We nodded, and left her, and headed to Chloe's to pick up the car. On the walk over there, Prue was silent, obviously thinking hard about her experience in the circle. She didn't say it out loud, but I knew it had rattled her in the same way as the reference to the girl's spirits had rattled her. There was a connection there. We just couldn't quite figure it out.

I was deep in thought, too.

I hadn't heard from Sinclair, but Ben, apologizing profusely, admitted he'd been keeping an eye on me. Apparently it wasn't Sinclair who had asked him to do it, but his boss, who'd been given the brief by the commissioner himself.

It made me feel worse. The idea that Sinclair had asked the commissioner to send an order down the chain of command to have someone babysit me felt totally humiliating. Like I was a naughty girl that needed monitoring. Ergh.

Even more irritating, visions of Detective Giselle Russo curling her lithe, sexy body around Sinclair kept popping into my mind, unbidden. In my nightmares, she put her perfect, full lips close to his ear and whispered sweet things. And he smiled at her, the same way he once smiled at me.

I knew it was stupid. He wasn't with her, and he wasn't even mine. But I burned with jealousy anyway.

To make my week even worse, I'd gotten a letter from Terry, with notice that he was disputing custody of Dexter.

It totally blindsided me. It had been a creeping fear in the back of my mind that at a later date he might ask for shared custody, but I thought he'd have to manipulate that poor girl into living with him first. He would need someone to do all the heavy lifting if he wanted to have custody of a toddler. It wasn't that he didn't know how to take care of Dexter; he just didn't want to do it, so he wouldn't. He knew exactly what was involved, but he only wanted to do the fun stuff; playing catch, racing toy cars, watching Disney movies. But for all his faults, Terry did love his son, and I knew he'd want to see him, so I expected a scary letter demanding visitation at some point. Not this soon, though.

And, because my week wasn't bad enough, I'd gotten a message from my mother.

I'd been avoiding her calls ever since I left Emerald Valley. I felt like a coward, but I just wasn't ready to deal with her. At first, when I'd driven out of the Valley with all my gear in the back of Ben's car, I'd felt guilty about leaving without telling her. Then, I'd ignored her constant phone calls in a bid to protect myself. I knew she'd be furious with me, and try to guilt me into coming back. I told myself I just needed some space; a little time to get my head straightened out.

A whole month later, I finally got the courage to listen to a couple of her voicemails, and it was far more confronting than I thought it would be. It was the kind of stuff I expected, though: If I divorced Terry I would be damning myself to Hell, because the covenant of marriage was sacrosanct and I was spitting in the face of Jesus by leaving him, I must return, and repent, and beg Terry's forgiveness, blah blah blah...

For the very first time, her words shocked me. It wasn't anything new; she'd always been like this. She'd always said these things, and she'd always *meant* them. But after a tiny bit of distance from her and a month of radio silence, I was actually hearing her properly.

She wanted *me* to beg for Terry's forgiveness. Beg *him.*

My own mother wanted me to apologize to my abusive husband and beg him for forgiveness.

I'd walked around in a fog of confusion for a whole week, as the image of my own mother started to morph in my head to something more sinister, something far more real.

Another week went by, and I started to get really angry. She was my *mother*. She was supposed to be on my side. She knew what my life had been like; she knew I was working myself into an early grave at the salon, and she knew I'd waited on Terry hand and foot like a servant. She knew how miserable I was. She knew the stress had caused me to miscarry my baby.

But she sacrificed her only daughter's health and happiness on the altar of a patriarchal god who hated women.

It wasn't supposed to be like this. The Jesus of the Bible was *not* like that. None of the people from my stepfather's church behaved anything like what Jesus had told us – in fact, they acted completely the opposite. They were all judgmental, scornful, exclusionary, greedy, wrathful and full of pride.

Aunt Marche, comforting me while I struggled to readjust the image of my mother in my head, patted my hand and said: "If Jesus came back now and knocked on their church door, they'd probably call him a dirty communist N-word, have him arrested for loitering and thrown in jail."

I couldn't help but think that she was exactly right. My stepfather John, a pastor of the church, raged against anything that wasn't straight, white, staunchly conservative, and Evangelical Christian. And Jesus had been a middle eastern socialist Jew who hung out with hookers.

Emotionally, it was a tough time. I felt betrayed. My own mom had been betraying me for years and I just didn't know any better. So I sent her calls to voicemail, and deleted her messages without listening to them.

But yesterday, she sent me a text message, and I read it before I realized who had sent it. Her desire to persecute me must have reached fever pitch.

YOU HAVE the DEVIL inside you girl and HE WILL BURN YOU you must come back repent and beg forgiveness dont give into the temptation of satan and witchcraft IT IS THE ONLY WAY or you and your son will BURN FOREVER.

THE WORDS HAD STUNNED ME. I could handle being told I was going to Hell. She'd been threatening me my whole life with the fires of damnation if I didn't follow the word of her church exactly. Now, with a little distance, her rhetoric felt like a gunshot to the chest.

She thought my *son* would go to Hell if I didn't obey? She actually believed her own grandchild – her flesh and blood, the child she adored – would be sent to Hell by her god, and tortured for all eternity if I didn't return to his father and bring him back into the church.

The thought pierced my brain, and I couldn't stop thinking about it.

Why the hell would she worship a god who would torture her grandson? Why would she sing praise to a god that would condemn Dexter to eternal damnation for something *he had absolutely no control over?*

Who would worship something like that? I just didn't understand it.

That didn't sound like a loving god. That sounded like the devil himself. It sounded like she was worshiping an ancient pagan beast who demanded his followers throw their children into a pit of flames as sacrifice.

I groaned out loud, thinking of it.

"What's up, babes?" Prue punched me on the shoulder. We took a left at Lumiere Avenue, and headed west, where Chloe's apartment sat overlooking the river.

"Just thinking of my mom," I muttered. "I just don't understand her. She's so… so…"

"Evil?"

I breathed out a sigh. "Yeah. What she keeps saying… I mean, it *sounds* so evil. And it's my *mom* saying it."

"Moms are crazy. At least yours isn't murdering your sister's au pair and using her blood to bind your spirit to your dead body."

I squinted at her. "Is that what she did?"

"I don't know, maybe." Prue waved her hand carelessly. "I think she just ran away with her boyfriend, actually. Anyway, that's not the point. All moms are crazy."

"Chloe's mom isn't. She's awesome."

"Her dad is the crazy one."

"Yeah." I sighed, and chewed on my bottom lip, thinking. "I suppose I'm having trouble reconciling the person who brought me up with the woman I see clearly now. What is really unsettling to me is the fact that if I'd stayed in Emerald Valley, I might have ended up just like her."

"Babe. You would *never*."

"She's a product of her own upbringing, though," I explained. "My grandma Moira was even worse than she was. I remember my grandma thrashing me with a wooden spoon, literally drawing blood on my legs, because I'd done the sign of the cross backwards. It was a *mistake*," I seethed, seeing the episode in my head from a whole new perspective. "I was *six years old*."

Prue shook her head, disgusted. "I can't believe she was Aunt Marche's twin. I can't imagine her doing anything like that."

"Yeah." We reached Chloe's door, and buzzed. Chloe's

disembodied voice told us she'd be right down; apparently, she was coming with us to the hospital. "Something must have happened to Grandma Moira to make her like that," I went on. "Aunt Marche would never tell me, though. She says other people's stories must be told by them, and them alone, and Moira is not here to defend herself."

Prue brightened. "Maybe it wasn't something that happened to Moira. Maybe she was always like that. You said her adoptive parents were strict and devout too, weren't they? Maybe something happened to Marche."

I pursed my lips. "That's a good point. I might ask her again. She might actually tell me his time. She did say that she…" I trailed off, my attention diverted, as Chloe stepped delicately down the stairs and opened the door. I gazed at her in horror. "What the hell are you wearing, Chloe?"

She smiled demurely at us. She'd set her hair in rollers and brushed it out into a fifties-style wave, and was wearing a canary-yellow tweed dress and jacket combo. "It's Chanel."

"You look like my grandma," Prue snorted.

"Your grandma wears tie-dyed t-shirts and surfs on the weekends."

Prue shrugged. "You look like *someone's* grandma. Maybe not mine. What are you doing, anyway? Why are you dressed like that?"

She blushed. "I just… I just thought..."

"You're dressing up for Dr. Herd, aren't you?"

Her blush deepened. I patted her shoulder. "Honey, I don't think you need to do that." Besides, she looked ridiculous; like she'd stepped off the set of a movie set in the fifties. Surreptitiously, I combed my fingers through her hair, breaking up the hairspray and backcombing, and smoothing out the rigid wave. "He was staring at you last time we went there, and you were wearing ripped jeans and that shirt with a raspberry jelly stain on it."

"I just thought he'd like something like this, something more refined," she mumbled. "He's so distinguished and handsome." She blinked her big eyes at me, shimmering with unshed tears. "You don't understand. I *love* him, Sandy."

"You've met him once, idiot." Prue joined me on the other side of her, combing her ridiculous hairstyle out with her fingers. "You've never even spoken to him. You don't know anything about him."

"We spoke in more than words," she said dreamily. "We communicated in spirit. He's perfect."

"Of course he is," Prue muttered. "Of *course*. A horse is a horse, of course of course..."

I thumped her on the arm. "Maybe this time you could try and say something in words, Clo? Ask him something about himself?"

She froze, looking terrified. I took the opportunity to remove her jacket, so that she was just wearing a little chic tweed dress. She looked much more normal now. "I'll try," she finally said.

"Good girl."

We bustled into her Mazda and took off, headed towards the hospital.

The building was packed with students. We fought our way through the crowds, and went up to the ward where Lexi was being held to see her first.

"Ginger said there was no change?"

Prue shook her head. "She's exactly the same."

We found her room. The door was shut, so we peeked through the window to see if anyone was in there.

There *was* someone there. It wasn't her mother, though.

To our surprise, her brother Olly stood by her bed, looking down on his sister's unconscious body.

We'd been chasing him for a whole week. Ginger, still convinced he had something to do with the coma girls, had even given us his schedule so we could try and catch him and question him, but he wasn't at any of his lectures. We'd even dropped by his frat house, hoping to catch him, but he was never in. It was infuriating, considering I only needed a couple of minutes with him to find out if he was involved or not. Mavka would be able to pick the information out of him easily.

I'd seen pictures of him, but he wasn't what I was expecting. He was a big guy, carrying a bit of extra weight, with a shaved head that made him look a little thuggish. His face was pale, and he had dark bags under his eyes.

I glanced at Prue. "Should we go in?"

She narrowed her eyes at him. "Hell, yeah. This is the perfect opportunity."

I opened the door, and walked in.

His head whipped towards us. "Get out," he snapped.

I flinched. He didn't know us, so his reaction was a little extreme. "I'm sorry," I said tentatively. "I know this might be a bad time, but–"

"I said get out!" He flung his arm towards the door, his face quivering with rage.

Prue's mouth dropped open. "Dude, we're just–"

"Are you fucking *deaf?* I said, *get out!*" He screamed, and stomped around the bed like a raging bull.

All three of us were so shocked by the strength of his rage; we backed up, and he slammed the door in our faces.

CHAPTER 11

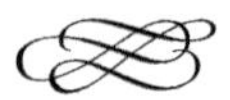

"Whoa." I watched through the little window as Olly stomped back to his sister's bedside, and continued to stare down at her, his expression blank.

"Fucking *rude*," Prue sniffed.

Chloe backed right away from the door, her legs shaking. She was more sensitive than me, and quite a bit more than Prue, who was as sensitive as a brick. "That was scary," she muttered, sinking into a chair in the hallway.

"He's just worried about his twin," I told her. "It's normal for him to be angry. We were just in the wrong place at the wrong time."

She shifted on her seat, clutching her Chanel purse to her chest. "I brought The Enchanted Wood to read to her."

"Next time, maybe."

"We should go," she said in a little voice.

I needed time to let Mavka read his thoughts. Turning back to the window, I gave Prue a little nod towards Chloe. Luckily, she understood immediately, and sat in the seat next to her, giving her a hug. "Don't worry about him," she said.

"If we hang out here for a second, he might come and apologize."

I looked at him. He wasn't going to move. His face was curiously blank.

His mind is a maelstrom, Mavka whispered. *A tempest, a whirling tornado. Underneath that frozen expression, his thoughts are whipping around so fast I can barely catch hold of them. There's so much anger, so much pain, the causes are many and varied...*

Do your best, Mav. We need to find out if he knows why his sister is in a coma.

She leaned forward in my mind, concentrating. *He is so conflicted,* she muttered. *He hates women, hates them with a passion, but he loves his mother and sister deeply so he cannot reconcile his love for them with this new hatred that has bloomed in his heart. A hatred that has been watered and tended by others. They've told him how the world should be, and he's committed to bringing about the vision... but not for his sister or his mother. He's torn, in pain, in agony...*

Who told him, Mav?

His friends... She concentrated, listening hard. *There's a face there, it's the face of the blood witch from the party we attended. The new one I consumed. He was filling Olly's head with nonsense about the world, how it's been broken, but they can fix it. The return to the old ways...* she snorted in derision. *Idiots. Keeping women in bondage was not the 'old ways.'*

The blood witch was in the process of recruiting him?

It seems so. His face keeps swimming in the maelstrom of his thoughts; the young vampire, too, and a handful of older men's faces. They are recruiting young men to their cause. Hurt men. Angry men.

I stared at Olly's face, remembering how his mother said he'd been so heartbroken when his girlfriend had broken up with him for a woman. Humiliated.

He loved her, Mavka whispered. *Now he's trying to convince himself that there's something deeply wrong with her; something perverted. She should not have been allowed to leave him. That's what his new friends are telling him. If they were in charge, in control, she wouldn't have a choice. She would be forced to be his girlfriend.*

I shuddered. How in the hell can he justify that in his head?

His friends have some terrifying rhetoric. How it's best for the country, for the planet, for women's own happiness because they need a strong man to guide them... But when he looks at his sister, he struggles, Mavka murmured. *His new friends tell him they can bring about the revolution, and create the world in the way that it should be. No woman would be able to do what his girlfriend did to him. He was seduced by these ideas; they punctuate every thought he has.* Mavka concentrated harder. *But when he looks at his sister, he remembers that he loves her, and he wants her to be happy. A small part of him understands that his girlfriend would never have been happy with him, because she was gay. He looks at Lexi, and thinks about her being forced to be with a man she doesn't like, and it unsettles him.*

Well. I'm not giving him kudos for not wishing sexual slavery on his sister.

As well you shouldn't. He is torn, though. Mavka's voice grew concerned. *He is on the verge of suicide. One part of him is screaming that it is Lexi's fault for being so stupid, she has obviously done something terrible, and she deserves to be in a coma....* She concentrated. *He is so full of pain. It is hard to separate the thoughts.*

Do your best, Mav.

A small voice in his head says that this is HIS fault. She focused, listening harder. *His friends told him about the rave parties and asked him to bring along as many girls as he could. When the rumors started to swirl that a handful had fallen uncon-*

scious and couldn't be woken up, his friends laughed about it. Said they'd got what they deserved; they'd obviously done something awful to one of the brotherhood. He'd laughed with him. Women are objects. Tools to be used. And if they do something to hurt a man, they deserve to be punished in the worst ways. But now... that's his sister, lying there. He loves her.

I waited for a moment. Can you get anything else out of him?

Some faces. She showed me. The face of the young blood witch and the young vampire swam into my mind's eye, but they were the only ones I recognized. There were a handful of other young men, as well as a haughty-looking blonde girl and a sweet-looking brunette with rosy cheeks, whom I assumed were Olly's ex-girlfriend and her new lover. There was one more, another man I'd never seen before, an older man with ruddy cheeks, and light-brown hair cut in a military-style fade. Could that be the mysterious Lord Seth?

No. Mavka showed me the vision she'd gotten out of the young blood witch. The glimpse she'd seen was of a very tall faceless man with black hair. *This Olly has not been introduced to blood magic,* she said. *He has not been fully recruited yet. He is merely on the fringe of the movement.*

I stared at Olly's blank face, at his empty eyes staring down at his sister. Mavka quickly showed me a glimpse of the rage and pain boiling beneath the surface of his expression, and I flinched. Sheesh. Should I do something? Slip him a card for therapy, or something?

The university offered him counseling, but the therapist was a woman.

Good grief. Men really are their own worst enemies, aren't they?

I believe Olly's fate is tied to his sister, Mav whispered. *If she awakens, he may be saved.*

Well. We'd just have to save her, then.

I turned around and faced the girls. "Maybe he's not going to apologize after all," I said sadly. "Let's go and see Dr. Herd."

We took the stairs down to the doctor's office, which took a little while considering Chloe was wearing the most ridiculous heels. "I'm not used to them," she said apologetically, clutching at the banister for support.

"Why are you wearing them, then?" Prue snapped at her, holding the back of her dress in case she slipped and fell down the stairs.

"Dr. Herd is so tall," she said dreamily. "I've never been allowed to wear heels; I'd tower over all of my dates if I did. This is the first time I've ever been in love with a guy who is way taller than I am, so I'm going to make the most of it." She wobbled, and clutched both hands to the banisters, steadying herself. "I wonder exactly how tall he is?"

"Sixteen to eighteen hands, I should think," Prue sniggered.

"What?"

I elbowed Prue. "I think probably close to seven feet," I told Chloe. "And anyway, honey, you've always been allowed to wear high heels. If any man feels weird about being shorter than you, that's their problem, not yours."

"I know that in theory, Sandy. In reality, it's just not like that. Besides, if I can make a guy I like feel more comfortable, then I'm going to do it." She hauled herself by her hands down the stairs. "Anyways, wearing high heels is not all it's cracked up to be. I thought it would be fun; I'd feel sexy."

"You sure do look sexy," Prue drawled, watching her teeter precariously down the steps like a baby giraffe, her knees knocking together.

"Gah. Fine." She kicked off the heels and stomped down the rest of the steps, coming out into the corridor of the second floor. We found Dr. Herd's door and knocked.

There was a brief pause. I could hear voices. There was someone in there with him. Finally, he called out. "Enter!"

Prue pushed the door open, and strolled in. "Hey, Doc, how are you–" She trailed off, and stared. "Well, fuck me sideways."

Detective Conrad Sinclair stood in the room, hard muscled arms crossed over his chest, square jaw tense, eyes blazing blue. He shifted on his feet and lifted his chin, staring directly at me.

CHAPTER 12

"Hello, ladies," Dr. Herd bellowed. "Please, come in." His hooves clattered loudly on the linoleum floor. My brain, refusing to acknowledge Sinclair, wondered idly why he didn't have carpet installed to muffle the sound. Probably because it was a lab, of course. It would be hell trying to get blood and urine samples out of the carpet. Easier to mop it up.

The centaur clomped right up to Chloe. "It's lovely to see you again."

Chloe's eyes were huge and round. Her mouth hung open; she looked like an idiot. Still happily ignoring the Enforcer, I nudged her in the ribs.

"Oof," she said, jolting. "Uh, hi." She licked her lips, staring up at Dr. Herd. "It's lovely to see you, too."

"I've been terribly popular today," he said heartily, tossing his beautiful golden hair back. "You girls obviously know Detective Sinclair? He popped by to ask about the patients, too. I mentioned you were on your way in, and he wanted to stay for a bit and say hi to you."

Chloe blinked, and turned to stare at Sinclair. Her wide

blue eyes narrowed. She glared – my sweet best friend *glared* at him. "No," said, her voice positively bitchy. "We don't know him."

"No?" Dr. Herd shifted on his hooves uncomfortably. "He said that you–"

"He's just an old client at our salon." She bared her teeth at Sinclair. "Nobody, really."

I cringed. Chloe was still under the impression that Sinclair and I had gone on a date, and he'd ghosted me. Bless her, she was defending my honor.

At least she was no longer struck dumb by Dr. Herd. Chloe turned back to the centaur and smiled sweetly. "I love your shirt, Doctor. Is that Burberry?"

"Uh, yes." Dr. Herd was still confused, but he brightened under Chloe's praise.

"It really brings out the violet in your eyes," she sighed, staring up at him.

"Thank you, my dear. And I love your dress. Butterscotch yellow is one of my favorite colors. Chanel, am I right?"

"Yes," she cooed. "I had the jacket to go with it but..." she looked around, suddenly perplexed. Then her eyes focused back on the doctor.

"It looks beautiful." They gazed at each other for a long moment. The silence grew like a tangible beast until it was almost unbearable, loaded with all the conflicting emotions building in the room. Chloe and Dr. Herd were locked in sickeningly sweet eye-embrace. Prue was looking at Sinclair, glaring at him and muttering under her breath.

And he was staring at me. My back was to him, but I could feel it. His hot eyes stabbed me, almost pierced my flesh, tearing at my skin like a wolf, desperate to get at the heart underneath, so he could smash it to pieces.

Your imagination is quite ridiculous, you know that? Mavka was bored. *He is just a man.*

I bristled. Coming from Mavka, that was practically a compliment.

Finally, Dr. Herd cleared his throat. "I suppose I should get to it," he said heartily, backing away until his horse-half was hidden behind the counter. "I have information to share with you ladies. I've just given the good detective a run-through of what I've discovered. We have had somewhat of a breakthrough, you know. I think I've discovered what the problem is."

I inhaled sharply. *Finally.*

Dr. Herd clattered back, holding a sheaf of papers in his hand. He gazed down at us all, his attention firmly back on Chloe. Hesitating for a moment, he shook his long hair back, suddenly awkward.

He knew Chloe was a normie. She couldn't See, and the Great Agreement forbade anyone directly introducing an unwitting human into the supernatural world. For a brief minute, I wondered what he'd say to get rid of her, so he could share whatever he'd discovered with us.

I braced myself to hate him for leaving her out.

Instead, he smiled at her. "My dear, would you like a tour of the hospital? I've been cooped up in here all day, I need to stretch my legs. The good detective here can share what I've told him with Prudence and Alessandra while we take a little stroll, if you like."

She nodded happily. "I'd be delighted," she said, in the exact same jolly English accent as Dr. Herd. She always did that when she was nervous, mimicking the accent of whoever she was talking to. It was mostly adorable, but sometimes super awkward if that person happened to be Jamaican or Pakistani. She blushed pink immediately, but he didn't seem to care.

He leaned down and offered Chloe his elbow. She took it,

and they clomped from the room, hooves and heels both making a racket on the floor.

Prue stuck her finger in her ear and wiggled it. "Gah. That bloody clomping did a number on my ears; I'll be hearing clip-clops for days."

"I wonder how long Chloe will be able to stand that for?"

"She can't hear it," Sinclair muttered.

Sighing, I turned to face him. He uncrossed his arms, but he'd never looked more combative. He looked like he was about to charge into an invading army and destroy them all with nothing but a broadsword and his fists. "So." I sighed heavily. "Are you going to tell us what Dr. Herd found out?"

"I'd be a fool if I did. You're better off staying out of this, Sandy."

"Yeah, well." I shrugged. "What are you going to do, arrest me?"

"I could, you know." For a second, his black mood lifted a tiny fraction. "I could put you in jail until all this is all over. At least that way you wouldn't get hurt."

I groaned in exasperation. "What makes you think I'd get hurt? Honestly, Sinclair, I don't understand it. You *know* what I can do. I *know* how to stay out of harm's way. Do you really think I'm that stupid?" My hands started to shake; I pulled them into fists. I didn't want him to see how upset I was. "You think I'll blunder around town, jabbing witches and werewolves and vampires with my hair clips, asking them if they're the bad guys? Do you really think I'm that dumb?"

He shook his head, confused. "What? No! I don't think you're *dumb*. No. God, Sandy, that's not it at all."

"Why are you behaving like this, then? I just don't understand. Why did you get Ben to shadow me?" A worrying thought occurred to me. "You're not... investigating me, are you?"

"I– I–" He paused, and pressed his lips together, clenching

his jaw together. "I just wanted to make sure you were safe, that's all."

Hmmmm. Mavka's ears pricked up inside of me. *That's... interesting.*

What?

There was a long pause. I could feel her straining. *Nope.* She shook her head. *It's gone. Your Detective Sinclair is very disciplined with his thoughts.*

My detective. Fat chance.

"Well, whatever your reason, it makes no difference to me. My best friend's niece's best friend is in a coma," I snapped, blisteringly aware I sounded like an idiot. "And I'm going to help her."

He glared at me for a whole minute. "I'm going to ask you one more time. Please. Stay out of this."

I stared back. "No."

Finally, he blew out a breath. "Fine. Goddamnit," he hissed. "If you're going to be involved in this, you have to listen to me, and you need to follow my instructions exactly, okay?"

Prue bristled. "Wow, control-freak, much? Who the fuck do you think you–"

He whipped his head towards her and glared.

She flinched. "Never mind."

"She's right," I said, lifting my chin. "I don't *have* to listen to you, and I don't need to follow your instructions." Prue cringed, but I plowed on before Sinclair could completely explode. "But I *will* listen to you, because it's a respectful thing to do, as well as sensible, because we should be sharing information. I can hear evil intentions, remember? So when I have valuable information to share, you'll listen to me."

He ground his jaw roughly. God, he was *terrifyingly* sexy; an absolute warlord of a man, the whole room throbbed with the force of his magnetism. I quickly went on before I lost my nerve. "And I *might* follow your instructions, if they're sensible, and I'll defer your combat experience when it's appropriate to do so."

The silence built again, as he stared back at me.

Prue backed into the counter and covered her head with her arms, bomb-threat style, and started whistling a funeral dirge.

It broke the tension. Finally, Sinclair uncrossed his arms, and exhaled heavily. "Fine."

I gave him a tiny smile. "Okay. So," I clicked my fingers, suddenly awkward. "What did Mr. Ed – I mean Dr. Herd tell you about the girls?"

Sinclair picked up the thick heap of papers on the desk that the doctor had dropped. "He's discovered the cause of the girl's comas. It seems that their spirits are not in their bodies anymore."

"We knew that already," Prue cut in rudely. "It just doesn't make sense." He raised an eyebrow. She flinched. "Sorry. Go on."

"You're right." He took a deep breath. "It doesn't make sense. There are only two times when a spirit leaves the body: First, during astral projection. Only a fraction of the population can do this, though, and travel on the astral plane is always a brief experience, only lasting a matter of hours. These girls have been unconscious for weeks."

I nodded. "Go on."

"Usually, the spirit snaps back to the body immediately if the body is in danger. The tether connecting the spirit to the body is sometimes drawn as a silver cord, and it's almost elastic. It pulls you back to your body, sometimes involuntarily."

"So… their cords are malfunctioning? Maybe the elastic has gotten a bit slack or something?"

He shook his head. "They're not in the astral plane. One

of the doctor's herd-mates is a powerful traveler – he attempted to locate the girls in the astral plane, but they're not there. Even worse…"

Prue looked at him sharply. She seemed… tense. "What?"

"The tethers aren't there.

"What?"

"There's no silver cord."

"That makes even *less* sense," Prue seethed. "If the cord is severed, the body dies. If the body dies, the cord is severed, and the spirit is released. These girls are *alive*. They're breathing, their bodies are still functioning…"

I reached out and grabbed her hand, and squeezed it. As much as she pretended she was fine, this case was causing her a lot of trauma. "Prue," I whispered. "It's okay. We'll figure it out."

She sighed out a breath slowly. "Yeah. Okay." She glanced up. "I'm fine. So." She stared directly at Sinclair. "What else?"

"Dr. Herd's friend discovered that the girls' spirit tethers have been magically severed. A blood magic ritual," he muttered. "The darkest of dark magic."

"Something else that doesn't make sense. Why are they still alive?"

"There's… another tether. A fake one; a fraud. He had trouble describing it, but he said where the spirit cord was silver, this one is the color of a worm. Pale. Dirty."

A memory nudged me. The color that had flashed when I threw the leather pouch – the fetish – at the circle where Prue was held. If I had to describe that color, that's what I'd say, too. Dirty pale. "So this fake tether… what is it tethered to?"

He hesitated a minute. "Are you familiar with soul theory?"

"Yep," Prue said, at the same time I said "no".

He turned to me. "But you understand the concept of reincarnation?"

"No." Sinclair's brow furrowed, so I clarified. "I mean, yeah, I understand the concept. But… it's not… it's not real, is it?"

They both stared at me. I rubbed my forehead and blew out a breath. "Okay. Fine." Mentally, I rifled through the filing cabinet in my head, brought out a thick folder labeled *Things That Are Blasphemous And Most Certainly Don't Exist And Even The Concept Is An Affront To God.* I flicked through the pages inside, found the brief labeled *Reincarnation,* plucked it out, and shoved it deep into the bottom drawer, where it mingled with other papers like *Werewolves, Vampires, Witches,* and the more recent addition, *Centaurs.*

I sighed. "Okay, yes. Reincarnation. Go on."

"Your soul is eternal, right? It's part of the collective consciousness of humanity, which, in turn, is part of the collective of everything. But at a personal level, your soul is made up of every piece of information about you, as well as containing a link to all the knowledge of everything about the collective. Are you with me?"

I nodded. I'd have to ask Mav about it later. I wasn't taking everything in. My mother kept popping into my head screaming *Blasphemy!* So it was a little hard to concentrate.

"So your soul is made up of every single one of your incarnations on Earth. When you're here, you're in a different body every time, right? If your body dies, the cord between your body and your spirit severs, and your spirit is absorbed back into your soul, which some people call your higher self."

I nodded. "Okay… so how does that fit in with these girls?"

"They've had their silver cords severed and their spirits removed," he said, his voice a low growl. "A dirty tether is tying their body to their souls, and it's keeping their bodies alive. And their souls are *screaming*."

Prue swore under her breath.

"The girl's spirits aren't anywhere to be found," Sinclair went on. "We can only guess they're being used somehow, in the same way blood witches use blood to power their spells. It's never been seen before, not in human history, so we don't know for sure, but the centaurs think that a human spirit, taken by force, might hold more power than the blood of the most innocent sacrifice."

"Oh, God," Prue exhaled heavily. "That's… that's…"

Sinclair turned to her, and spoke almost gently. "I know what happened to you, Prue. I know what your mother did. I've already spoken to her. What she did to you was so similar. The tether that she tied between your body and your spirit is similar to the one that is tied between these girls and their souls. She created one using dark magic."

"Except it was too late," Prue said, her lips bloodless. "My body was already dead and rotting away."

"It didn't work the way that she hoped it would," Sinclair agreed.

Suddenly, it occurred to me the reason her mother was so emphatic about Prue learning the craft. Prue's spirit was tied to her skeleton permanently. It meant she would probably never die.

Whoa. There was a lot to unpack here.

"That's not all," he said. "After you left the rave, we discovered something. A room filled with blood magic, with a circle burnt into the floor, and body parts scattered everywhere. We've I.D.'ed the bodies – or, the pile of ash and the body. It's a couple of students at the university. Boys, one a human, the other a new vampire. We think that they stumbled on the blood witch's set-up by mistake. One theory is that the room was ready for one of the Blood Kings to lure a girl into, but a couple of boys went in there instead, and the magic backfired and blew them up."

Prue and I glanced at each other.

He saw it. Goddamnit.

I cleared my throat awkwardly. "Okay, is there anything else?"

He thrust his chin at me. "What was that?"

"What?"

"Don't bullshit me, Sandy." His flinty blue eyes fixed on me. "You know something." He cocked his head. "You're really going to give me that speech about how we should be responsible and share information, and you're going to stand there and tell me you don't know anything about those two kids that were ripped to pieces in that storage room at the rave?"

"Fine," I sighed. Prue's eyes bulged, but I ignored her, and blinked up innocently at Sinclair. "I just didn't want you to be mad, that's all. Prue and I had a little run-in with those two boys at the rave. Then, I heard their thoughts, and they weren't good. The vamp was young, only just turned."

"We don't know who he is. I haven't had a sire claim him yet."

"You probably won't get one. Whoever turned him was a rogue. He's a Blood King. And the other kid was a witch, only recently introduced to blood magic. I followed them, I listened a little."

Mavka chuckled dirtily inside of me, but I ignored her. I wasn't lying. Not really. It wasn't lying if you just left out a few things.

Sinclair nodded. "Go on."

"They'd been ordered to find a girl to sacrifice, to put in the circle, but they hadn't found anyone suitable yet," I said, skating around the truth with the pizazz of Tonya Harding performing a triple axle. "I listened from the hallway, when they were in that little room. Their immediate superior – I think his name was Michaels–" I furrowed my brow. I couldn't exactly remember. "He was mad at them because they'd screwed something up. He was storming away from that room. I listened to him and I got as much as I possibly could, then, I went into that little room." Swallowing heavily, I looked up.

Sinclair gazed down at me; his focus intense.

I shrugged helplessly. "You saw the mess."

In the silence, I watched him fill in the blanks. The older witch, the one storming away, he'd killed the two younger ones for being stupid, or they'd messed up and the spell blew them to pieces, or something like that. In no universe could he possibly imagine that I'd done that to those men. But I'd seen the aftermath, and it was horrifying.

He let out a long, slow breath, and took a step closer. "I'm so sorry you had to see that, Sandy."

Have you ever thought about going into the theater? You'd make a stunning actress.

Mentally, I elbowed Mavka in the ribs. If I'm a good liar by omission, I learned it from the best. You can't lie, yet you seem to hide things from me all the time.

It's my nature to be dark and mysterious, she replied haughtily.

I hated lying. I especially hated lying to Sinclair, even if it was just by omission. It was nice to know I was good at it, though; even Prue was gazing at me in admiration.

Sinclair's brow was furrowed, he was thinking furiously. "This gives us something else to go on. There's not much of a lead on the young vamp; he's been a dead end." Ignoring Prue's snigger, he continued. "But the human kid had family and friends. Now that we know he was in on it, we can pursue that line of questioning. We might find a connection to the Blood Kings in his contacts." He nodded sharply. "Good work."

I blushed. "Thanks."

"So, what's next?" Prue, bless her, changed the subject. "We're both deputized, right? We're in on the case with you. What's our next assignment, Chief?"

He turned his full focus on her, and she cringed slightly.

"I know I've said it before," he said, his voice soft and rough. "But I need you to understand how dangerous this is. This goes deeper than I ever thought, and that's why I decided to cancel the contract the commissioner offered you. It's gotten too dangerous for civilian involvement. In the last two weeks, I've found two Blood Kings among the homicide squad at central." His fists clenched involuntarily; and I swear I felt a pulse of energy shoot out of him. The strength in those muscles was insane.

Prue squinted at him. "Did you get anything out of them?"

"No."

"What, they're just in lock-up, or something?"

He shook his head abruptly, just once.

It took a second for me to understand. "Sheesh. They killed themselves, didn't they?"

He inclined his head. "The department is in an uproar. They're worried about foreign agent infiltration, spies… no one really knows what's going on. I've had more officers assigned to the case, so I have more manpower, but it's tricky to keep the supernatural stuff from them. We're running on a theory that there's a satanic cult operating in D.C."

I found myself grinding my teeth at the mention of 'manpower'. He meant 'womanpower.' His ex, Detective Giselle Russo from the homicide squad, was helping him with the case. Prue had told me that Giselle still had the veil on her eyes, so she must be an unwitting normie. I wondered how much effort Sinclair was putting in to make sure his precious ex-lover stayed in the dark, and safe from harm. Jealousy ripped through me again when I thought about how her body looked in that catsuit.

Prue was nodding. "Standard normie behavior. Any time a human does something shitty, blame it on Satan."

Sinclair hesitated for a second. "There's more girls, too," he said, his voice dropping to a rough whisper. "More victims. This is classified information, okay? We're trying to avoid a panic."

"I thought there were just five?"

"There are twelve, in total." He swallowed roughly. "Twelve girls all in the same coma. Three of those girls just happened to come from supe families. One of them is a Prescott."

"Oh," Prue gasped. She obviously knew who the Prescotts were. I shot her look. "They're a powerful witch dynasty based up in Baltimore," she explained.

Sinclair nodded, and went on. "As soon as Irene Prescott heard that her daughter was in a coma, she visited her and communed with her higher spirit to find out what was wrong with her." His face darkened. "She killed her daughter immediately."

"Awwww, shit." Prue looked horrified. "That's bad."

"Irene Prescott won't answer any questions; she's in mourning, so she's not speaking. But she said her daughter's soul was screaming, her pain was sending shockwaves through our entire universe." He paused. A muscle in his jaw clenched. "Witnesses say that Irene stabbed her daughter in the heart with a butter knife. It was the only thing she had on-hand. She was sobbing and crying, and said she had to release her immediately, she had to stop her pain."

We lapsed into silence for a moment. The implication was horrifying. Whatever the Blood Kings were doing with the girl's spirits, it was torturing their souls.

Prue looked green. "I better not mention that to Ginger."

"We don't know if Lexi's in the same amount of pain. The other witch family – the Gardener's – their daughter is at home with them, they're monitoring her. They've said it feels like her soul is just lost and crying. The Blood Kings might not be using her spirit in any spells just yet. It's bad, though," he muttered, looking at the floor. "Whatever Irene Prescott heard from her daughter, it was horrific enough that she put her out of her misery immediately. She put her down like a horse with a broken leg. The Gardener girl isn't like that, but again, whatever is happening to these girls is unnatural; it's sending shockwaves through the universe – like pushing dark waves of energy through to our dimension, which is something else we need to worry about."

Goosebumps rose on my arms. Was that me, or Mavka? I checked on her; she was unsettled. This mention of unnatural occurrences in the spiritual realm made her edgy.

Prue shook herself and clapped her hands. "Okay, practical things. Let's talk about it. We know that the Blood Kings are using some sort of brand-new evil magic. They're luring young women into these circles, which cut their silver cords, and they are siphoning their spirits into some sort of fetish, and then they create a new dirty tether between the girl's bodies and their souls, so they can't die. And the blood witch can carry the fetish around and use it for whatever dickish thing they want, like an evil portable power bank."

Sinclair raised his eyebrow. "We're not sure on the method of extraction and what they'd be using to hold the spirits in, but a fetish sounds about right." He sounded almost impressed with her deductive reasoning. She shifted a little uncomfortably as he focused on her again. "I'm going to need you to speak to your mother."

"What? No."

"She didn't tell me very much about what she knew. I

need more information. At the very least, I need to know what ritual she used on you to create the tether between your body and your spirit."

"She's never spoken about–"

"We need to know, Prue. It's important."

She pinched her eyes closed for a second. "It's literally the most traumatic thing that's ever happened to her. And to me," she muttered. "She was almost lost to the darkness, and I was left as a monster. She's *so* filled with guilt. We don't talk about it." She pinched her lips closed, and looked away. Fear shone in her eyes.

Sinclair was edging close to her mom's darkest secret: In order for her to create such a powerful blood magic spell, she would have needed an innocent sacrifice.

And no one knew what she'd done. She'd never told a soul.

Sinclair was the Enforcer. He would kill a blood witch for human sacrifice.

He eyed her steadily. He knew. "Prue, I know that there are more skeletons in the closet–" He stopped and pressed his lips together.

Prue rolled her eyes. "*Dude*. There's no need for that."

Sinclair took a deep breath. It made his powerful chest expand, and my thoughts slid right back into the gutter. I hauled them out again and tried to focus. "Listen," he said. "I don't consider your mother a threat to humanity. She's recovered, and I assume she's remorseful about whatever she did to create the blood magic spell. If she helps us and tells us what she did to create the tether, I might be more inclined to be merciful."

Prue stared back at him for a long time; I could see the fear swimming in her eyes. If her mother admitted to killing someone...

She blinked, and bit her lip. "Can I have your word? If my

mom confesses, and she helps us… can you promise me you won't kill her?"

There was a long pause. Finally, Sinclair rubbed his chin thoughtfully. "You know what, I've never actually *had* a blood witch confess to a crime. Usually, I catch them in the act and terminate them immediately. Your mom is a rare case for me. Blood witches don't ever come back from the dark path, as far as I know."

"My mom did." Prue lifted her chin defiantly. "She's recovered. She'll never touch a grimoire ever again; she swore to it."

"I believe you." He nodded. "Okay, as long as she's not practicing, I give you my word that I won't kill her if she confesses to murdering someone to do the spell on you." He narrowed his eyes. "She may have to face some human legal action, you understand. There might be a family out there that's tortured by the disappearance of their kid, or a child who lost their parent because of your mom. At the very least, she'll have to pay restitution for whatever she did."

Prue let out a sigh of relief. "Okay. I can deal with that." Her relief vanished; she grew tense again. "Now I have to actually talk to her about it. Urgh."

"Good." He gave one short sharp nod. "Our next plan of attack is to find out about these raves. We need to find out who is behind them. They seem to have been set up for the purpose of luring in suitable victims, but they might also be a recruitment method for the Blood Kings."

"That should be easy," I said. "They're not illegal underground raves; that's obviously just a gimmick. It's a whole professional set-up. There will be an event company behind them."

He nodded, his expression softening, as if he were impressed. "You're right. It's an event company. I've already checked them out. They appear to be clean. They put on all types of huge events, weddings, sports events… They were hired by someone, though, and paid a fortune to put these parties on. We don't know who it is that did it. The communication was all done by email, and the raves are paid for by a shell company which has links to almost every single organization in Washington. It's almost impossible to untangle who might be responsible for hiring them."

"What about the locations?"

"The locations are scouted by the event team, and chosen by the hiring party. Again, all communication is done by email."

I bit my lip, thinking. "Well… what about the gossip?"

He looked at me.

"Gossip," I repeated. "What about the gossip?"

He leaned back, crossing his arms. "I'm not following you."

I huffed, exasperated. "Who is your contact at the event company?"

"A girl called Thea," he said, still not following me. "She showed me every single email trail from the shell company to her events team. There's no hint on who the individual is behind them." He cocked his head, peering at me. "Why?"

"Who does she *think* is paying for the parties? She must have heard some gossip. Event coordinators have both ears to the ground. She must have heard something."

Prue nodded. "Gossip is life."

Sinclair pulled his bottom lip through his teeth slowly in a gesture that almost made me groan aloud. "Well… She did say…"

"What?"

He met my eye. "She thought it might be some kid's dad. Some kid at the university. She said it sounded like it was some kid's rich, powerful dad, putting on these parties so his kid could go and have a good time, let boys be boys, that kind of thing. They're not allowed to hold these kinds of raves on campus, so she suspected it might be a parent doing it. There was no real evidence for her theory. It was just a feeling."

"Ask her again," I said. "There would be a reason she got that feeling. And that reason will be something we can check out."

He looked dubious, but nodded. "Okay."

"Women's intuition is a real thing, you know," I said sternly.

"Oh, I know." He rolled his eyes slightly. "I know that better than anyone," he added cryptically. He straightened up. "There's another party this Saturday night."

I eyed him back steadily. "We're going."

He ground his teeth, but nodded.

"This time, we'll even try and stay sober," Prue announced.

Sinclair whipped his head towards her. "What do you mean, *this* time? Were you… did you…"

"It's a rave, Grandpa," she said scornfully. Now that she'd gotten the promise that he wouldn't kill her mother, Prue had gotten decidedly braver. "We had to blend in."

"I don't think you should go, Prue." I took her hand and squeezed it. "He's right, it's too dangerous. I'll go, because I can listen out and find the bad guys. You might have to stay home and keep Chloe out of it, anyway."

Prue glared at the floor. "Chloe might be preoccupied anyway, since she seems to have found a new hobby. Horse-riding," she sniggered. "I feel a bit useless, though. I promised Ginger I'd help find a cure for Lexi."

"You're doing that. You have to talk to your mom."

Prue groaned. "Why do I get the shitty job?"

"Maybe your mom will know something that can help Lexi. Something to break the fake tether."

"Then she'll just die." Prue shrugged, then visibly brightened. "I mean, that is an option, I guess. We could just go and stab all the girls in the hearts, and their spirits will disappear, so they can't be used by the Blood Kings anymore. It would be like cutting off their supply chain." She stared at my disapproving face, and blinked at me. "No? Not into it? Okay, we'll call it Plan B."

"Just talk to your mom," I sighed. "Maybe you could go with Ginger and check out her boyfriend's fraternity. Jem, wasn't it? And Olly was in the same fraternity, wasn't he?" I quickly filled Sinclair in on what I heard from his mind. "Go check out his frat, see if you can get a sense of the place. If the event company girl thinks that someone's dad is paying for the parties, you might be able to find out more gossip."

"That's a good idea," she nodded thoughtfully. "Okay, I will."

Sinclair flexed his shoulders, but he didn't say anything. I almost expected him to growl at me, to insist that there was no evidence and no link and it was stupid to listen to idle gossip, but he didn't. Any other overwhelmingly powerful masculine man might bristle at my nerve; I was practically designing the game plan myself. "Our best chance is to catch the Blood Kings in the act, so I'll go to the rave and do my best to find the bad guys," I sighed.

"I'll take you," Sinclair said roughly. "I'll go as your date, and keep you safe."

Mavka surfaced in my mind, scowling at him. *Ruin my fun*, she muttered. *That's all you'll do. Cramp my style...*

Shush, you.

CHAPTER 13

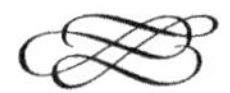

I stared at the letter in my hands, willing the letters to change, to rearrange somehow, to morph in front of my eyes to say something else – *anything* else.

Terry was suing for full custody of Dexter. Not just visitation, or shared custody. He wanted him back. Never in a million years did I think that he might do this.

The letter was horrific. Filled with scary lawyer terms, it accused me of abusing Terry, of abandonment, of absconding with Dexter, of denying Terry visitation, and of putting my son in an unsuitable environment for a child. The legalese was hard to decipher, and it was horribly untrue, but it hurt all the same.

I read the letter twice. A court date had been set to hear the arguments. My hands were shaking so much I couldn't hold the letter straight.

Prue, sensing my distress, wandered over, took the piece of paper out of my trembling hands, and ran her eyes over it. It was Saturday afternoon; we'd finished work for the day and had just locked the door after the last client left. Chloe was cleaning her brushes and sterilizing her combs, humming love songs to herself. Prue had been at the podium, finalizing the totals for the day, and I was finishing up some paperwork. I had a habit of bringing my mail to work and doing my admin there, so I could leave my home environment purely for relaxation and family time with Dexter. Plus, he and Gor'gamuth had developed a fun new habit of ripping every single piece of paper in the apartment to tiny pieces, so it was safer to read my mail at work.

And what I read made me sick to my stomach.

This couldn't have come at a worse time. In a few hours, Sinclair was picking me up to go to the rave. Prue was about to head off herself – Ginger was at the basin chairs having her green hair refreshed, then they were off to Jem's frat house to snoop around. We had work to do. There was a powerful, evil magical cult conspiring to legally enslave women, there were girls in comas, their souls possibly in horrendous, tortuous pain. These people, whoever or whatever they were, had to be stopped. And my good-for-nothing ex-husband kept popping back up and kicking me in the teeth.

I felt nauseous. Prue read the letter, her expression growing more and more thunderous as she reached the bottom of the page. "Babe," she exclaimed. "This is… this is insane!"

I wiped my face. "Yeah."

"He's accusing you of abuse? *You?* Domestic abuse? Talk about projection. The only domestic abuse you did was to enable him to be such an asshole." She let out a snort of derision. "Maybe that's what he's going to argue in court. Because *you* did all the domestic labor, and then left, he's feeling abused because he's got no one to do it for him."

I let out a trembling breath. "Lawyers have argued worse things," I told her. "There are judges who have awarded in favor of spoiled-brat children, because their parents didn't prepare them for the real world properly. I've heard of that before. Maybe that *is* the angle he's taking."

"Nah, Sandy." She shook her head violently. "Just... No. There's no judge in this world that would consider that an argument for abuse."

I shrugged. A tear escaped my eyelid, and I wiped it away. "It doesn't really matter. He's suing for full custody. He's going to try and take Dexter from me."

Chloe floated over. She was even more ditzy than usual, having spent the week in a love-struck haze, but my distress must have pierced her stupor. Dr. Herd was picking her up for their first date tonight – in fact, she was getting ready at my house. She descended on me and flitted around like a butterfly. "Sandy, it's okay. Everything will be okay," she murmured. "We'll make sure Dexter stays here with you."

Prue shook her head, aghast. "I don't get it. He can't handle his own kid for more than an hour by himself. How the hell does he think he's going to manage the workload?"

"Well, I think that's where the new girlfriend comes in..." Quickly, I told her about Kate, the girl who had answered the door when I'd visited.

"Hmmm," Prue stroked her chin. "Are they living together?"

"She'd have to be," I replied. "No way would Terry look after Dexter for a full night by himself. He's never gotten up to Dex, not once, and that kid is up at least twice a night to go to the toilet. I'm not even sure Terry can wake up, even if he wanted to. That man sleeps like the dead."

Prue squinted at me. "But you said this girl is from your mom's church?"

I nodded.

"They won't be living together, then. No way would they be living in sin."

Chloe held up her tablet. "Her Instagram has photos of

Terry. But this photo from her story this morning shows her in her bedroom at home. She hasn't moved in with him."

I gave her a quick smile. Prue and I were masters of social media stalking, it looked like Chloe was catching up with us. "You're right. Any girl that goes regularly to John's church would never consider moving in with a guy before marriage. I wonder what Terry's game is, then?"

Mavka stirred within me. *Another woman is doing the work for him, I guarantee it.*

I furrowed my brow. "Maybe the new girlfriend is *almost* living with him. Not officially. Maybe she's just there all the time. Not sleeping over. Just staying within the rules. Maybe she's a… a…"

Prue smirked at me. "Say it."

I shook my head. "No!"

"Say it!"

I sighed. "Maybe she's a Butthole for Jesus girl," I sighed, squirming uncomfortably. "Urgh, Prue. That term is *so* offensive."

It was a phrase Prue had coined one night, not long after we'd become friends. We'd been discussing our sexual experiences. I was raised as a strict Catholic, and then almost bullied into joining my stepfather's church – which was far more strict on stuff like premarital sex – and Prue wanted to know if there were any loopholes. I'd found myself explaining to her that the church only forbade vaginal sex, and a lot of young people in the church considered anal sex to be technically permissible, so they did that instead.

Prue had lost her mind laughing about it.

Apparently, this concept wasn't exclusive to Catholics or Evangelical Christians. When I started hairdressing, because I was great at gossiping about the juicy stuff, I'd heard it from some Muslim clients too. Apparently, butt sex was fine; it didn't count as premarital sex.

Some Mormons even had a practice they called 'soaking', where the penis goes in, but as long as neither of you move, it's not a sin. They even go as far as having something called 'jump soaking', where a couple will connect, then have a friend lie under the bed and kick at the mattress, jostling them. Again, as long as *they're* not moving, it's not considered a sin.

Prue thought it was insane, and teased me relentlessly about it.

I wasn't, as she put it, a Butthole for Jesus girl, because even with my blinding naivety, I knew how ridiculous the whole concept was.

When I was fifteen years old and just starting to have strong sexual impulses, I heard my stepfather giving a sermon about purity, and it shocked me. He directly linked the concept of purity with women's pleasure. That is, if a woman receives sexual pleasure outside of marriage, she is no longer pure.

There was never any mention of men's purity. Ever. It was the first time I'd understood the depths of my stepfather's raging misogyny.

When I realized that John fully believed that a woman's pleasure was sinful, but a man's was normal and part of God's will, I went out and lost my virginity to my friend Mateo from school. It was an impulsive fuck-you to my stepfather, and I paid the price in raging guilt. I'd gone straight to confession at my Catholic Church, where Father Benson, giggling like a schoolboy, told me to say three Hail Mary's and two Our Fathers, and I'd be right as rain.

"Will my sin be forgiven?" I'd asked in a trembling voice.

"It already has!" Father Benson exclaimed. Then, in a quieter voice, he added: "I hear Mateo Santiago's family are moving back to California in a month, so if you're so inclined, get another one in before he goes. Then pop back here and I'll give you a few more Hail Mary's, there's a good girl. Be safe!"

Father Benson was one in a million.

It was my secret, my little revenge, and I held it close to my chest, and brought it out whenever John started raging about the whores of Babylon. It was the only thing that stopped me from being a Butthole for Jesus girl, as Prue so charmingly put it.

Chloe giggled. "I forgot about that Butthole for Jesus stuff. It's so funny." Chloe, by contrast, having been raised by a pro-education, sex-positive mother, had lost her virginity to an Italian viscount at the age of twenty-one, in the royal suite of the George V Hotel in Paris.

"It's not funny," Prue frowned. "It's ridiculous. That's the whole point."

"You can't make fun of people's beliefs," I chastised her.

"When they're that ridiculous, of course I can! Maybe this girl *is* a Butthole for Jesus girl. Maybe she's all but living with Terry, and plans to help him out with Dexter."

Chloe patted my head absently. "Maybe you… maybe you could just ask him?"

We stared at her. "What?"

"Terry. Call him and ask him. See if you can work something out."

Prue snorted. "Chloe, you're being far too reasonable. Terry's a manipulative asshole."

"You might be able to find something out, though. See what his plan is. If he's planning on trying to look after Dexter himself, you might want to prepare for that, you know."

I furrowed my brow. "Yeah, you're right. Maybe he does just miss his son, and he wants to make a go of being a good dad." I frowned. Pulling my phone out of my pocket I wandered away, so the girls couldn't see how scared I was.

I dialed his number and waited. The phone clicked.

"Sandy." His voice was inflectionless. "What do you want?"

"I got the letter."

"Oh. That."

"I don't understand, Terry. I… I thought you didn't want custody of Dexter. Visitation, yeah, I knew we'd have to arrange that sooner or later, but I just…"

"She talked me around," he said, his voice tight. So the new girlfriend did have an influence over him. "She's gonna help me with Dex."

At least he had some level of self-awareness. No way did he think that he'd take Dexter and look after him all by himself. "She's right, you know," he added. "Dexter shouldn't be in a dangerous environment."

I froze. "What do you mean, a dangerous environment?"

"Living with you. In that building with that… woman."

I jerked my head, looking up at Prue and Chloe who were staring at me. "What woman? Do you mean Prue?"

He snorted. "No, not her. Fuck *her*." Terry had really taken his mask off. This was a version of my husband I'd barely ever seen before. Bitter. Nasty. "Not that bitch, although Dexter shouldn't be anywhere near her, either. I mean that witch, Marcheline. She's dangerous."

"She's not dangerous, Terry! What the hell are you talking about? She's my great-aunt, and she's wonderful!"

"She's a whore of Satan."

I was temporarily shocked into silence. "But… but… Terry," I said finally. "You don't *believe* any of that stuff, anyway. You always made fun of me going to church. You only went to John's church a handful of times, and only when there was a barbeque afterwards. You don't even believe in God."

"Yeah, well." He let out a harsh chuckle. "*She* does. And she wants to help me."

"Help you with what?" Good grief, I really did underestimate this new girlfriend. I'd thought she would be Terry's new doormat, not his enabler. "Terry, I want you to see Dexter," I pleaded. "I want him to hang out with you, he loves you! I'd be happy to share custody with you, if that's what you want."

"I'm taking him. Full time." His voice was ice cold.

My hands started to shake. "Terry… you can't."

"The fuck I can't. You left *me,* Sandy. You deserted me, left me with nothing. You took everything from me. Now, you're going to pay for it."

I inhaled shakily. "Is that why you're doing this? You're doing this to get back at me?"

He chuckled. "Of course. I love my kid, don't get me wrong, but he's a handful." His laugh had no humor, none at all. "She promised she'd look after him if I went for full custody. She'll do anything to get him back here."

"I don't… I don't understand."

"See you in court, Sandy." He hung up.

CHAPTER 14

I went home, picked up Dexter from Aunt Marche's apartment, and hugged him so tight he wiggled and protested. Damon had been keeping him occupied while I was at work; my Aunt's acolyte had been learning basic spellwork, and today's lesson consisted of aeromancy. He'd been working on forming bubbles with the force of will, so Dexter had a great time rushing around popping them with a flyswat. "Little dude is so fast," Damon ruffled Dex's hair. "Although, he kept asking to go down to your apartment to get Gor'gamuth and bring him back up here." Damon's huge, smiling wide mouth drooped down into a frown. "Sorry, Sandy, brah, but that thing gives me the heebies."

Dexter let out a little growl.

"I'm not having your familiar in here, darling," Aunt Marche told him. "I'm sorry, but Gor'gamuth scares the fur off of Winifred. She's not been the same since he moved in. Which, to be honest, is quite nice. Winifred can be an uppity bitch at times," she sniffed.

Then, she peered at me. "Are you okay, darling? You look a bit... pale. And shaky. What's going on?"

I briefly outlined the situation with Terry and his new girlfriend, using codewords so Dexter didn't understand what I was saying. No matter what happened between me and Terry, I didn't want to talk smack about him in front of Dexter. Terry was his dad, and he couldn't change that. Trashing his father would only make him feel bad.

When I was done, Aunt Marche looked thoughtful. "That's… odd. This new girlfriend really has her eyes set on the prize, doesn't she?"

"What do you mean?"

"If she's encouraging Terry to go for full custody, and telling him she'll take care of Dexter for him… she's obviously after a quick wedding and kids of her own."

"She's so *young*, though," I breathed out. "And timid. I honestly didn't think she'd have it in her. And, good grief, he's not a prize. He's a curse!"

Aunt Marche patted me. "It's okay, darling. It will all work out in the end. I have every confidence."

I scooped up Dexter and said goodbye to Damon. Dexter gave him a high-five. "I'll be seeing you later, little man." Damon would be babysitting for me again in a few hours, well after Dexter was asleep. I felt guilty enough about leaving my son to go to work for four days a week, so I'd planned to take him back to our apartment, read some books and play with his dinosaurs, then have dinner, bath time and snuggle into bed. Sinclair was picking me up late; the rave wasn't starting until eleven, so I'd have plenty of time to get Dexter settled and get ready for the rave.

Ginger supplied me with another outfit for tonight. This time she'd given me black silk cargo pants and a matching black one-shouldered crop top, which Prue ordered me to wear with my black platform Doc Martens. Laid out on my bed, the outfit looked so badass I was almost scared of it. No way was I going to pull it off.

Dexter ran into our living room and pushed the window open. "Gor'gamuth!" he hollered into the street. Immediately, the fat tortoiseshell cat bounced through the open window and landed gracefully on the carpet, eyeing me with his eerie glowing yellow eyes.

I stared back at him. He was supposed to be an inside cat. I had no idea he'd gone out. "I'm not going to ask you where you've been," I muttered.

Gor'gamuth frowned and flicked his tail jerkily at me; I swear I could almost hear him saying the words aloud: *It's none of your business where I've been, puny human.* Then, he turned his back on me and showed me his butthole. Dexter ran off into the bedroom; Gor'gamuth followed him.

I sighed heavily, and started hauling ingredients out of the fridge for dinner. We were having fish tonight, little filets deep-fried in hot oil, which Dex had specifically requested. I got busy, flouring and dipping the fish in the batter and warming the oil in a little pot, when suddenly I heard Prue slam the apartment entrance door and cuss loudly.

I stuck my head out. "Prue? Everything okay?"

She stormed into my living room, her face thunderous. "That was a fucking waste of time. Bunch of assholes."

Ginger followed her in. "I told you, didn't I?"

"Why are you even dating a guy in that frat?"

"His dad insisted! He said he wouldn't pay for his tuition if he didn't apply. It's his dad's old fraternity, and they need the numbers. Georgetown isn't big on Greek life; none of the fraternities on campus get any funding directly from the university. Apparently all the old boys have had to put pressure on their sons to join, and Jem's dad is as bad as the rest of them. Tradition, you know." She dropped her voice to a low rumble and thumped her chest. "Values. Family. Hoorah!"

"It's so stupid. And they're such assholes!"

I waved my hands. "Whoa, whoa. What happened?"

Prue threw herself on the couch and covered her face in her hands. "We went to see if we could find out any gossip about the parties, you know. They wouldn't even let me in."

I frowned, and gestured to Ginger. "You're allowed in the frat house, though, aren't you Ginger? To see Jem?"

She nodded. "The guys were real dicks about it when we showed up to visit. Said that I could come in, but not Prue."

"They were *so* rude," she seethed. "They called me old." She lifted her face out of her hands and glared at me. "Olly was there, too, on the porch. He told me to fuck off; called me a whore, a gold-digger trying to find a rich frat boy." She shuddered. "He's awful. Chunky little bastard, as if I'd be interested in something like that! Ha!"

Sheesh. I patted her shoulder. "So I guess you didn't find any gossip? No ideas on who is involved in putting on these parties?"

Ginger shook her head. "None. But it could be any of them, really. They all go to the parties. Everyone gets given free-entry slap bands." She glanced away; she looked worried. "Jem wasn't even there. The boys let me in, but he wasn't in his room when I went in to check. His roommate said that his mom called and he rushed off, some kind of family emergency." She scratched her head absently. "He's not even answering his phone." She wandered off, out the door, tapping her phone, heading upstairs towards Prue's apartment.

Prue was still trembling with rage. "Stuck up rich little fucks," she spat out. "They're so goddamn entitled. They seriously thought I was there to try and hook up with one of them."

I sensed movement out of the corner of my eye; Gor'gamuth padded out from the bedroom, where Dexter was fully occupied with using my bed as a trampoline. I watched him, because it was quite unusual for him to stray even a few meters away from Dex. The cat wove his way into the living room and lept gracefully onto the sofa, headed towards Prue.

Did he have something in his mouth? He did. He padded silently over to Prue and dropped a box of matches into her lap.

Prue picked up the little box and shook it, suddenly excited. "You know what, that's a great idea. I'm going back to burn down the frat house." She stood up abruptly. "I'll be back in an hour."

My mouth dropped open. "Prue! No!" Reaching out, I snagged the back of her jeans as she marched away. "You can't burn down the frat house."

"Of course I can. I should. They deserve it."

"Prue, no. You've got other things to do, anyway. You have to go and talk to your mom."

She sagged. "I'd rather burn down the frat house and go to jail."

"Babe, I know. Just... just stop for a second."

She whirled around and sighed. "Fine."

"I know you're scared. But it's going to be okay. Whatever your mom did, it's done now, and there's nothing you can do about it. She's clean, she's recovered..."

"–And the Enforcer has promised not to murder her if she confesses." Prue finished the sentence for me. She let out a slow breath. "I've been terrified my whole life that he'd find out what she did and kill her for it. Now that he's promised *not* to, I kinda thought I'd be less scared of him. I'm not, though. He still scares the pants off me."

"Me, too," I let out a slightly hysterical giggle. "How do you think *I* feel? This is the second time I've gone out with him, and I've got a man-eating demon inside of me. He makes me so nervous."

She cocked her head, staring at me. "I don't think nervous

is the word I'd use. You're not terrified that he'll find out about Mavka and kill you?"

"Of course!" I looked away.

She let out a snort of laughter. "Liar. You're not scared because you're worried he'll kill you. You're *nervous*," she giggled again. "Because you *like* him."

"What? No!"

She laughed again. "You do. Of course you do. And what's more, I think he likes you back."

"He does not."

"Of course he does. He showed up at the salon for a haircut with you because he wanted to make sure you were okay. He had Ben follow you around for months to keep an eye on you. Twice, now, he's suggested you go somewhere as his date, when he could probably just tail you there, use you as bait, and swoop in to grab the bad guys. Who knows what else he's done to look after you?"

"Prue, no." I shook my head firmly. "I went on that first date with him to find out about Chloe's blackmailer, and when we got there, I had to pretend we weren't together."

She looked at me slyly. "Why?"

"Because if Linus Brady saw us together, I'd be a target. A source of information." I remembered how I bristled at being reduced to an object.

"Bait," she nodded. "You would have been bait. So tell me; why didn't he use you as bait?" She leered at me. "He wanted to keep you safe."

I glowered at her. Sinclair had been so insistent on us not being seen together. Then, when Linus Brady saw me and approached me, Sinclair appeared out of nowhere and ripped Brady's hand off my thigh. He blew his cover so he could defend me.

I wasn't going to tell Prue that, though.

"And now," she crowed triumphantly. "He suggested going to this party as your date."

"His lover is probably otherwise occupied," I muttered sulkily.

"I bet you anything she didn't go to the last party as his date. They would have gone in a group, as colleagues, or something. They had a whole team, remember? She said the F.B.I was there, too. But this time, it's just the two of you, headed undercover, again. On a date."

"It's not a date," I snapped. "We'll be working. And if he gets even a slight, tiny whiff of the demon inside me, I'm dead, Prue! He'll kill me."

"Whatever, drama queen," she sniffed, then smirked at me again. "But you *do* like him."

"No!"

She eyeballed me steadily.

I blinked innocently back.

"You're a terrible liar, you know."

"I'm an amazing liar. Shut up." I pushed her away again. "Of course I like him. I have eyeballs, Prue. He's so gorgeous I feel like I might explode just from looking at him," I admitted. "Now, go and talk to your mother. Find out what ritual she did to create your tether, then come back here and do my makeup. This might be a fake date, and the Enforcer might have to kill me at some point during the night, but that doesn't mean I shouldn't look good."

CHAPTER 15

I made dinner, and we ate at the table. Gor'gamuth seemed to suddenly have his own little high seat at the table now, and had also somehow managed to procure a placemat with a picture of a fishbone on it. I eyed him suspiciously, wondering where it came from, while Dexter chatted happily to him over dinner. Damon or Aunt Marche must have given them to Dexter for his new best friend.

I couldn't stop thinking about Dexter. There was far too much going on in my head right now; I couldn't make room for everything. Normally, I'd be nervous as hell about heading out with Detective Conrad Sinclair, but my worry for my kid was canceling everything out.

I couldn't imagine not having him with me. He was everything to me; the idea that he could be ripped away from me forever made me feel so sick I could barely move.

With my heart aching, I gave him a bath, and settled him onto the sofa in his pajamas to watch a movie. When bedtime came and he started yawning, I let him fall asleep on the couch, clutching Gor'gamuth to his chest like a teddy bear. I wanted him close by. I'd transfer him to his cot later on, and

I'd have to move Gor'gamuth too. The damned cat purred so loud he sounded like a jackhammer in my living room.

Chloe arrived with a bottle of champagne. I took it off her and poured her a tiny glass, and we started to get ready. Dr. Herd was taking her to the opera, of all places, so she'd showed up in a deep-red velvet strapless ballgown with a silk sash.

"How are you going to sit down in that thing?" I asked her, eyeing the enormous ruffly hoop skirt.

"That's the beauty of it, Sandy," she giggled, waving the gown gently from side-to-side. "He's got a box seat, and he warned me that it was standing-only. He said leaning over the balcony is the best way to watch the opera, because you spend most of your time watching everyone in the audience, anyway. Seats are useless because you're always having to get up and peer over the railing. Because we'd be standing, I came prepared." She slipped her foot out from underneath the enormous skirt; she was wearing Reeboks.

I chuckled back. Of course Dr. Herd's box was standing-only. Horses didn't sit down.

Chloe was almost ready, so she bullied me into letting her style my hair. We decided on a slicked-back wet-look, which was far more dramatic than I was used to, but she insisted it would go with my outfit. I was struggling into my Doc Marten boots when Prue arrived, wheeling her make-up case behind her, scowling viciously, with tears staining her cheeks.

"Prue! Are you okay?" Chloe gave her a hug, which she almost accepted.

"I'm fine," Prue muttered. "I just had a talk with my mom, that's all." She eyed me meaningfully. "She told me something quite upsetting."

"Oh no! What is it?"

Prue sighed. "We used to have this old lady who lived

upstairs from us when I was a kid; she was really nice. Well, she was batshit crazy, didn't remember her own name half the time, but she always had candy and she never cared that I only visited her so she'd give me some. She'd slip me money sometimes, too. She had no family around; she was Albanian, and barely spoke any English. I didn't care. I just liked her candy." She sighed heavily again. "One day, when I was four, I snuck out of the house to visit her, and she wasn't there. She'd moved out. Mom only just told me what happened to her."

Chloe gasped. "What happened to her?"

Prue looked me in the eye. "She fell over in her kitchen and stabbed herself in the throat, and bled to death."

Ah, so that's what Prue's mom had done. She'd killed an elderly neighbor. "Oh," I said softly. "Well… I guess… she *was* old…"

Prue's eyes hardened. "I *liked* her. She gave me *candy*."

"Well," I said, choosing my words carefully. "If she was that nice to you, I'm sure she wouldn't have minded giving you a little more than just candy…"

"It wasn't her choice."

"She had a long life," I said gently.

"She didn't deserve to die like that," Prue snapped.

"I'm confused," Chloe said in a little voice.

Prue let out an enormous sigh, and closed her eyes. "They didn't find her for more than a month," she finally said. "When the super got a whiff of a funky smell coming from her apartment, he got the police to do a wellness check. They found her in her kitchen. Her cat had eaten her whole face off."

I recoiled in horror. "Good grief."

"Yeah," Prue muttered. We lapsed into silence. Gor'gamuth's purr inexplicably grew louder, and more resonant. It sounded like he was going *mmmm mmmm mmmmm.*

I pointed a finger at him and glared. "Don't get any ideas, mister."

He gazed back at me, blinking innocently.

"I can't help but feel guilty about it," Prue muttered. "I *liked* her. She was a really nice woman. And... and..."

"Her cat ate her face off." Chloe rubbed her arm sympathetically. "It's sad. That's why I haven't got any pets. My dad got me a dachshund as a pet when I was seven – he bossed me around so badly, used to bite me and everything. We took him to a trainer who told me that my dog had decided he was the alpha and I was his bitch." She frowned. "No more pets for me. Apparently, I'm too submissive."

"I don't know," I said thoughtfully. "You strike me as more of a horse girl."

Prue held back a snort. She wiped her cheeks and shuddered, apparently ready to shelve her emotional upheaval for the night.

She looked at me, and tugged on my black crop top. "You look badass, Sandy. I thought you'd look too sweet for this outfit, but with the slicked-back hair, and with a little makeup, you'll look perfect. You've got a whole Lara Croft thing going on."

I squirmed slightly and blushed. It was *so* not me; the outfit was very badass warrior-woman; I looked like I'd marched straight out of a video game. "I feel like an idiot. The insides do not match the outsides."

Hah. Mavka stirred. *With me in here, the insides do match the outsides.*

I'd already made her promise to try and take a backseat tonight. No eating anyone. Listening only, if possible. I couldn't give Sinclair any indication at all that I was anything other than a psychic. My life depended on it.

Pish, child. Your life doesn't depend on it. His does. I could see her inside me, pursing her lips and staring at me peevishly.

Do you really think I'd let the Enforcer murder my host? Not likely.

I froze, and turned away so they couldn't see my face. That's a big bomb to drop on me, Mav. Would you really kill him if he tried to kill me?

Of course. She inspected her fingernails. *I wouldn't even break a sweat. I wouldn't eat him, though. I doubt he'd be very tasty.*

If he killed me... wouldn't that mean you'd be free? Don't you... don't you want that?

That's not the point, my dear. It would be quite rude of him to try and murder you. I would not stand for it.

Thanks... I guess?

Prue set up her makeup kit and started working on Chloe, who was getting picked up first. I pottered around, cleaning up dinner, wiping the benches and pouring champagne for Chloe and Prue, trying not to let the avalanche of thoughts in my head overwhelm me.

For the millionth time, I passed Dexter, still fast asleep on the sofa, and I ruffled his hair gently. I'd have to move him to his own bed, soon, but I couldn't bear to have him any further away right now. He was the most important thing in my life. Ever. My beautiful, hilarious, hellraiser of a kid. I felt like Gollum, skulking over my Precious. The idea that he could ever be taken away from me was unthinkable. I didn't want to face it, but I had to.

The court date was in a month's time. I'd have to take the day off work and drive back down to Emerald Valley. I'd need a lawyer of my own. Maybe Aunt Marche knew someone who could help, someone not so expensive...

Hang on. I paused, halfway through sweeping a little bit of dust from the kitchen floor. Where was Terry getting the money for a lawyer?

He didn't *have* any money; he earned less than I did. He

refused to work any more than four days a week. His dad was on disability. He didn't have any money, either.

The new girlfriend, perhaps? I racked my brain, trying to think. If Kate was so determined for Terry to get custody so they could all play happy families, maybe she was forking out for a lawyer. Except, from what I remembered about her family, they were desperately poor, too. She was one of seven children. There was nothing spare at all.

Then where..?

A cold chill ran through me. My eyes fell on the lawyer's letter, folded neatly, sitting on the kitchen counter. Tentatively, I picked it up, and scanned it again.

There was only one law firm in Emerald Valley. The letter had been signed by Steven Briggs, the family law specialist at the firm. He can't have been cheap. I bit my lip, thinking.

One of the partners was an old client of mine, the founder of the firm, an elderly gentleman called Rupert Knoxville, who should have retired years ago but enjoyed the prestige of being a big fish in a very, very small pond. He was an asshole too, obviously. He had barely any hair on his head but he enjoyed his three-weekly trips to see me so I could rub his bald pate gently and snip off a fraction of an inch from all three of the hairs on his head. Even worse, he'd been a friend of my stepfather. They played golf together.

I had his phone number. Jenny, my old salon owner, made us confirm all our clients ourselves, on our own phones.

Before I could back out, I dialed his number.

The phone rang twice, and picked up. "Knoxville."

I cleared my throat, and put on my most polite, posh phone-voice. "Good evening, Mr. Knoxville, I'm–"

"Ah, Catherine. Hello, dear. Everything is fine, I take it?"

I froze for a second, as my head metaphorically exploded. "Yes," I managed. "Fine."

"I believe that Briggs sent the letter out, and delivery has been confirmed. The court date has been set. Mr. Becker is in full compliance. Everything is proceeding smoothly."

"Okay," I squeaked.

"Now, madam, I understand your distress," he boomed over the phone. "There is nothing to worry about. I know the judge personally, he's a good Christian man; he will be sympathetic to your cause. We'll have little Dexter home in no time at all."

There was a long pause. My heart hammered against my ribs, trying to escape the nightmare I'd just been plunged into. "Yes," I mumbled.

"Never fear, my dear! The forces of good will prevail. The prodigal daughter may be lost forever, but we will save whomever we can. No!" He suddenly screamed in my ear. "I said I wanted the chowder served on the *Royal Doulton china*, not the *Corelle!* Take it back, now!"

I flinched. He didn't bother to take the phone away from his mouth as he shouted at whoever was delivering chowder to him. Maybe he had a housekeeper. "I must dash, Catherine." His voice quivered, promising violence. "I need to see to something." He hung up.

I lowered my phone, looking at the screen.

Catherine was my mother.

CHAPTER 16

"That...fucking...*bitch!*"

Prue and Chloe snapped their heads towards me, their expressions shocked. "Sandy!"

"It was my *mother*," I snarled. "Not Terry's new girlfriend. My own *mother* is encouraging Terry to take Dexter off me." Viciously, I stabbed at my phone, bringing up my mom's number and hitting the dial button. "My own *mother* is conspiring with my ex-husband, offering to do all the heavy lifting just so she could force me to come back to Emerald Valley. My own damn *mother!*" I slammed the phone to my ear, listening to the dial tone.

She didn't answer. "Gah! I'm going to kill her!"

"Sandy... whoa..." Prue held up her hands and backed away from me. "Take it easy, girl."

"I've never seen you like this." Chloe shook her head, watching me pace back and forth. On one of my trips I scooped up my son and tucked him into bed, so I could rage at my mother without his sleep being affected.

I felt like I could rip off my own skin, I was so angry. I barely even noticed Gor'gamuth jump up on the kitchen bench, where he was most definitely not allowed to be. He padded lightly along the counter and batted at a carving knife with his paw, pushing it towards me.

I glared at him. "Don't encourage me."

Chloe sighed. "Babe… come over here." She took my hands and led me to the kitchen table. "If you're going to go and kill her, at least get your makeup done first."

"She's right," Prue declared. "The hair and outfit suit the vibe, but you're too rosy and fresh-faced for a jolly evening of murder and matricide. You need a smokey eye and a touch of nude shimmer on the lips for that sort of thing."

I sat down, practically vibrating in anger. "I should have known," I muttered as Prue dabbed serums and primers on my face. "I should have known she'd do something like this. I haven't spoken to her in months – I was afraid of hurting her feelings. I've only just started to realize how toxic she actually is… and she goes and does *this*," I ground out.

Chloe squeezed my hand. "It's going to be fine, honey."

"It's *not* going to be fine, Clo," I snarled, trying to keep my lips still as Prue slightly overlined them, giving me a shimmery soft-pink pout. "I'm going to kill my mother. I'm going to kill her."

"If you need a lawyer, I'll take care of it," Chloe offered. "Daddy's got an entire firm on retainer; one of them must do family law."

"There's no need, Chloe, but thanks. I am just going to murder her instead." The churning in my stomach was reaching a fever pitch.

As Prue was putting the final touches on my makeup and giving it a spray with setting spray, both my phone and the doorbell rang at the same time. I snatched up my phone. My mother was calling back.

"Clo, can you get the door? I'm going to take this." I

stomped into my bedroom and shut the door. I hit answer, and put the phone to my ear. "Mother."

"Alessandra..." Her voice sounded as haughty as ever. "It's nice to see you *finally* calling me back, my darling."

I clenched my teeth. "Why do you think I am calling you, Mom?"

"I'm sure it's because you have finally seen the light, dear. You're going to come back to us, back to Jesus."

"I am not coming back."

"Come now, darling." She let out a chuckle. "We've gone over this before. You cannot turn your back on the Lord. You cannot drag your son into eternal darkness. Your soul – and his – are at stake. I will not allow you to spit into the face of God." Her laugh was cold, totally mirthless. "I mean, *really*, Sandy."

I was speechless with rage.

My mother waited a moment, then filled the silence. "So when should we expect you? I've told Terry you will come back; he's prepared to forgive you, as long as you apologize for your willful and sinful behavior."

"Mother..." My voice was low, trembling. "Do you know how Terry treated me?"

"Well, marriage can be tough at times, darling. It's a heavy burden for a woman to bear, but it is our role. The Bible says–"

"Did you know he expected me to wait on him hand and foot? Did you know he would scream at me if I dared ask him to help me with anything around the house?"

"It's your role as wife, dear. You can't expect–"

"Did you know he wouldn't let me have access to our bank accounts? He gave me cash for groceries, never enough, of course, and he'd shout at me if I couldn't afford something he wanted. Did you know he forced me to work six days a week, while he only worked four, and he expected me to look after Dexter single-handed while he played Xbox on his days off? Did you know that I miscarried our second baby because of the stress?"

"Alessandra–"

"Do you know how many times he threatened to kill me? Every time he got drunk… which was at least a couple of times a week. He'd cry about his mother abandoning him, and he'd tell me every time: Sandy, if you ever tried to leave me, I'd kill you, he'd say. Then he'd lock the bedroom door so I couldn't get out, and… and…" I choked on my words, the memories suddenly overwhelming me.

Men have needs, I'd told myself, repeating what my mother had told me over and over, while I left him to do whatever he wanted with my body. Men have *needs*.

I felt like I was going to throw up.

"Alessandra." My mother's voice was firm. "That's none of my business. The covenant between you and Terry is unbreakable. Regardless of what he's done in the past. Sometimes, men can be… unpleasant, yes, but we all have our burdens to bear, and I know that you're not exactly sinless yourself, are you? Now, I'm sure you can *both* find room for improvement. We have marriage counselors at the church who will be able to help you. I've made the appointments for you already."

I took a breath. I wasn't going to get through to her. "Mom, Terry is a monster. He's a manipulative, abusive, narcissistic liar who made my life a living hell. Do you understand that?"

She was silent.

"Now tell me, Mother. Please answer me honestly. Do you want your only daughter to live like that? To live in Hell? To be stuck, living with a man who treats her like an object and a slave?"

"Well," she huffed. "I'm sure you're exaggerating…"

"*Mother.* Do you want me to come home and live with a man who abuses me? Answer me." I put steel in my tone. "Yes or no."

"I want you to come home." Her voice was equally as firm. "It does not matter what Terry has done in the past. He is your husband, and you cannot defy the will of God."

"So that's a yes." I chuckled bitterly. "It's nice to hear you say it out loud. You'd sacrifice your only daughter… oh, wait! That's right. You sacrificed your only son, too, didn't you? You threw Antonio out when you found out he was gay. You turned your back on him, too. You'd rather us live bitter, twisted, miserable lives than be safe and happy, just because some warped asshole told you that it was what God wanted."

"You don't understand!" Mom suddenly screeched at me. "It's not just the word of God. You have the devil inside you, the potential for the greatest evil! He *must* be kept chained. It's in your blood, Alessandra! The potential for great evil, the worst evil!"

For a fraction of a second, I was shocked out of my anger. Did she mean Mavka? How could she possibly know...?

She raged on. "You have no idea of the discipline, the strength I've had to have, what I've had to endure to keep the temptation at bay. But I did it! I kept the evil from my heart, when others in our family reveled in it!"

I blew out a breath. "Are you talking about Aunt Marche?"

"Our whole family, Alessandra! We're cursed. Our blood is cursed… You and Antonio, we all have the same blood! The blood of the Most Evil! And you're living there, with her, right in the path of temptation. The devil will find his way in and steal your heart!"

Okay, she definitely wasn't talking about Mavka. It was just her Evangelical babble. I was losing my patience with her nonsense. "What the hell are you talking about, Mom?"

I could hear her panting on the phone. She'd lost control,

but she was rapidly clawing it back. "Come back to God, Alessandra. Come back to the light. You *must*."

Was it her normal Evangelical babble? Maybe not. I ran her words back through my head, examining them carefully. After a moment, I spoke. "What blood, mother? What curse? Tell me."

"I will not speak their names." Her voice was firm. "It's not for you to know the sins of the father. It's only for you to avoid them."

"Fine." I ground my jaw. "If you don't want to be straight with me, if you don't want to be honest and open and loving… *fine*. You don't have to say another word. You'll listen to me, though." I dropped my tone low, letting my anger vibrate through my voice. "I know what you've done."

She didn't say anything, but I could hear her soft pant on the phone. In the near-silence, there was a soft knock at the bedroom door. I ignored it. "I know you paid for a lawyer to help get Terry full custody of Dexter," I went on. "I know you plan to support him. You – my own *mother*, the woman who is supposed to *love me* – you've chosen to side with my abuser. Not only that, but you've chosen to take steps to rip the most precious thing away from me, the thing I love most in the entire world. You're trying to take my son away from me."

I paused, so she could hear the weight in my words, and I opened the bedroom door. If there was any way Dexter was awake and could hear me, he probably shouldn't hear this part, so I better leave the room just in case. "You've betrayed me in the worst way. *You* are evil," I snarled. "It's you. You. Are. Evil." I stomped into the living room. "And if I ever see you again, I promise you, I will rip out your throat, *and dance in the puddle of blood next to your dying body!*"

I stabbed my phone, cutting off the call, and looked up.

My living room was full of people.

All of them were staring at me.

Chloe stood in the corner next to Dr. Herd, her blue eyes wide and startled. Damon was sitting on the sofa next to Prue, his big mouth wide open, goldfish-like. Aunt Marche stood in my kitchen, frozen, a piece of leftover fried fish halfway to her mouth.

And Detective Conrad Sinclair was leaning against my door frame, smiling at me.

CHAPTER 17

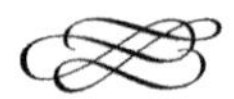

I swallowed roughly. "Oh. Hi. Hey, everyone." I waved weakly.

Prue sniggered in the awkward silence that followed.

Dr. Herd, resplendent in a tuxedo on his top half, and his chestnut brown hide brushed to a glossy shine, took up almost a quarter of space in the room. He blinked at me awkwardly, and deliberately glanced at his watch. "Is that the time? Oh, my, Chloe, we should get going. First bell will be sounding soon."

"Have a great time, guys," I said lamely as they clomped out.

"Darling." Aunt Marche stuffed the piece of fried fish in her mouth. "What was *that* all about?"

I squirmed with embarrassment. Sinclair was lounging so easily against my door frame, casually dressed in a light blue fitted T- shirt and perfectly faded, slightly distressed denim jeans, with his arms crossed over that perfectly muscled chest, so ridiculously masculine and so heartbreakingly handsome it almost hurt to look at him. I waved at him awkwardly. "Hi. You're… uh. You're early."

"Yeah." He looked me up and down, the faint smile still on his face. He was handsome when he wore his signature scowl, but when he *smiled*... Good grief, it was like the sun rising for the first time. I was surprised that some vain, jealous god hadn't smited him yet. "You look great," he said to me.

My face felt hot. Thank God Prue had toned my usual rosy cheeks down with green concealer. I was blisteringly aware of what I looked like right now; like some sort of badass female assassin, stomping through the room threatening to rip out people's throats. It was so *not* my style. "Thanks," I muttered, looking down.

Sinclair straightened up; the smile disappearing from his face. "I'm here early because I've got information to share." He turned and spoke to Marche, still stuffing her face with fried fish in the kitchen. "I'm glad you're here, High Priestess. We may need your help."

She inclined her head regally. "Enforcer. I shall assist in whatever way I can." A little flake of fish was stuck to her lips. It did nothing to detract from her dignity.

"It seems you were right about Thea," Sinclair began, moving into the room and shutting the door behind him. "I went back and asked her about her suspicions, and asked her to elaborate on why she thought it was a rich parent putting on these parties for their kid. She gave me a whole list of reasons. First, the person who hired her used a fake name: Tyler Durden. We already knew that it was a fake name, so we didn't look into it any further. Well, Thea googled it, thinking it was his real name and wanting to find out more about him and found it was the name of a character from a movie that was huge in the late nineties. She figured if you were a big enough fan of that movie back then – enough to use it as a fake name – chances are you'd be in your forties now and you might have university-aged kids of your own."

"Makes sense," I nodded.

"Also, the fact that she was directed to give extra free-entry wristbands to the fraternities and sororities on campus. Additionally, she said certain D.J.'s were chosen over other, more popular ones. She said that it seemed like someone was catering to a kid's specific tastes. Finally, she said the locations that were chosen from a list she provided all happened to be owned by the same shell company. She thought that was a little weird, too." He frowned. "I'd already tried to dig into the shell companies. It's like trying to untangle your grandma's knitting after your kitten has been at it."

That was a weird, oddly cute analogy. "But you found something...?"

He nodded. "I finally convinced the commissioner to let me contract a couple of hackers, so they could trace the I.P. address on the emails between the hiring party and Thea at the event company. We narrowed the address down to a block of commercial buildings upstate. Cross-referencing the list of kids in the Greek houses on campus, we came up with two suspects, one who was a prominent businessman."

His expression darkened, he looked at the ground.

"It was Jem's dad, wasn't it." I said softly. "Jem Tucker's dad. Ginger's boyfriend."

Sinclair looked up sharply. "How did you know?"

I glanced at Prue, who'd put her head in her hands. "Ginger told us Jem's dad was so pushy about him joining the frat, and going out and having a good time, sowing his wild oats and all that. Jem also told her that his dad was possessive and domineering, and wouldn't let Jem's sister go to university, so we already pegged him as a misogynistic asshole. And just before, Ginger tried to visit Jem, but he'd gone home for a family emergency, and she couldn't get hold of him..." I looked back up at Sinclair. "He's dead, isn't he? He killed himself before you could question him."

To my surprise, Sinclair shook his head. "No. It's worse than that. Roger Tucker – that's his name – he died before we even left to go and pick him up. He was found in his office, with his skin turned inside out."

Sheesh. I didn't need that mental image. "So he was assassinated?"

Sinclair nodded.

"Right after you found out his identity?"

Another nod.

"That means you have a mole in your department."

"Another one," he growled. "We already rooted two Blood Kings out of the department, but it looks like there's more. This conspiracy goes so deep, every time I think I've cut off one of Lord Seth's tentacles, another one pops up. I can't figure out who it is, though." A muscle ticked in his jaw.

Prue pursed her lips. "Who knew about Roger Tucker?"

"Just me and a couple of F.B.I. agents."

I frowned. "F.B.I?"

"I brought them in to help root out the Blood Kings in our department. I've got a handful of them helping with the case."

"But one of them could be a Blood King."

"Anything's possible, but it's unlikely. The vetting process for the F.B.I is far more rigorous than the police department," he added wryly.

"When I was in the hallway, and the blood witch passed me..." I began hesitantly. "I didn't look up at him. I was pretending to be wasted; I didn't want him to see my face–"

"Good," Sinclair cut in roughly.

"He was wearing black suit pants and black leather shoes. Quite formal, for a rave. Too dressy for staff. What was his name?" I remembered the young vampire saying it out loud. "Michaels, I thought, but that didn't feel right. Mulberry... something like that. He was the one who was activating the circles. He could be a double agent."

Sinclair rubbed his face in his hands. "There will be a small handful of agents at the rave tonight, although none of them know that I'm going. I told them that since the man who organized the parties is dead, there should be no more victims. They think I'm going after Roger Tucker's associates."

I nodded.

"And..." Sinclair hesitated a moment. "Gina Gardner is dead," he said softly. "One of the earliest coma girls, one of the girls from a witch family. Her parents killed her. They said her soul started screaming this morning, and they couldn't bear her pain."

Shit.

"They started using her spirit," Prue muttered. "Goddamn. Maybe they used it to destroy Jem's dad."

Aunt Marche whispered a prayer. She stepped forward, her face pale but determined. "The good news is that thanks to Prue, I've figured out how to restore the victim's silver cords, so I can bind the girl's spirits back to their bodies without using blood magic." She pointed at me. "But we need to find their spirits first. They will be held in those fetishes. You'll need to find them." She took my hands. "Find the witches who did this; find those fetishes. Rip the information out of their heads if you need to," she added savagely. Then, suddenly, she brightened, and gave me a cozy smile. "Okay, darling. Off you go, head out to your party. Have fun! Oh, and take this." She pressed a little packet into my hand and closed my fingers around it.

"What's this? A protection spell?" I glanced down at the foil packet.

"Yes. A protection spell! *Exactly.*" She giggled.

It was a condom.

CHAPTER 18

I could hear the bass pumping from down the street. "Well…" I gazed up at the big, dark building – the only one left intact in the street. All around us, the old crumbling buildings were boarded up and fenced off. "This is… different."

"It's an old abandoned dental school." Sinclair held the door of the Uber open for me. "This whole block was bought by a development company; they're planning on tearing everything down and building a movie studio. Sound stages, media buildings, that sort of thing. I heard they're going to leave the old dental school for movie sets."

"Creepy." I peered up at the big building. Bone-white in the dim streetlights, huge and imposing, it gave off a distinct horror film vibe. I felt like I was looking up at the creepy resort in The Shining.

"Thea gave me the run-down for this party. They've gone for an escape-room theme. There's a different D.J. set up on all three levels, in the main lecture room on each floor. The smaller surrounding rooms are themed, too. There's a make-out room, a chill-out room, a smoking room, even a themed first-aid room. She told me she's hired off duty first responders to wear creepy old nurse's outfits, so they treat suspected overdoses and scare the kids at the same time."

I gave a tight smile. "That's actually kinda cool."

Mavka inhaled the cool night air. *Mmm. I taste the delicious scent of evil blood on the wind.*

That's good, too.

She chuckled. *You thirst for evil blood as I do, child? With that, and you threatening to rip your mother's throat out, we'll make a good vengeful spirit of you yet!*

I groaned inwardly. No, Mav. I mean it's a good thing that there's at least some Blood Kings here. We need to find those spirit fetishes, and we need to do it now, before any other girls are tortured into madness or put out of their misery by their parents.

She nodded, inhaling the night air deeply. She was hungry, I could feel it; a slight hint of mania colored her thoughts. *Evil blood everywhere,* she hummed. *Oppressors, liars, cheats... That one is sleeping with his younger stepsister, his lust for her borders on obsession.* She nodded towards two older students joining the line ahead of us. *They are not students. Both are married, with wives and young babes at home. They come to these parties to try to sleep with drug-addled young girls.* She inhaled through her mouth deeply. *They are scoundrels, cowardly, immature, selfish, dastardly creatures who think only of their members and satisfying their own dark cravings. Mmm. I would like to eat their members.*

Yeesh. That's another visual I didn't need. Mentally I slid a divider between us so I didn't have to hear her licking her lips.

As usual, two enormous security guards stood on either side of the entrance. Ignoring Mavka, I glanced up at Sinclair as we joined the line of kids waiting to get in.

Suddenly, Sinclair seemed to be preoccupied, shooting

murderous glances at the group of boys ahead of us. They flinched, startled, and wisely turned around and faced forward, looking anywhere but at Sinclair.

I didn't blame them. He was quite dangerous-looking; it was like staring at the sun. There was no way he'd pass for a college kid. "What's our cover story, anyway?" I asked him out loud.

"What do you mean?" He looked away again, obviously distracted. I followed his hard stare; he was staring behind me, at yet another boy, who hastily looked away.

They are looking at you, Mavka whispered to me. *You look like a strong, powerful, incredibly desirable female, and they are subjugating you in their thoughts. Sinclair is violently aware that these boys are having sexual thoughts about you, and he does not like it.* She sniggered. *He is better at controlling his impulses than I am. He would like to break bones.*

Good grief. I should probably try and distract him; we had work to do. "A cover story. You know..." I lowered my voice, leaning closer, trying to ignore the thump of my heart. "I don't want to insult you or anything, but you're a little old to be going to a college party."

"I'm your date," he said roughly. "That's all the cover story we need."

"... Okay... But–"

"I'm not too old for you." Suddenly, he was staring down at me, looking directly into my eyes.

I blinked, trying not to tremble. "No. No you're not. Uh... you're not too old for me. How old are you, anyway?" I had to look away. His gaze was too intense, and he was too close, the heat from his body and his whiskey-and-fireworks scent was turning my brain into mush.

"Thirty-seven."

It was an eleven year age gap. "I guess that's not too bad."

"It's not bad," he said stubbornly. "It's fine."

I glanced at him. "You're not going to blend in, though."

"I don't need to. As long as I don't look like a cop, we'll be okay."

He definitely didn't look like a cop. He looked like an invading warlord; like a viking warrior, striding into battle wearing a T-shirt and jeans. His energy, as always, was blisteringly volatile; you could smell the danger wafting off him at twenty paces. Even now, standing in the line to get into the rave, we had a five-foot invisible barrier between us and the college kids surrounding us. Leggy, catsuited girls – and some playsuit-wearing boys – were all gazing at him with expressions of naked lust on their faces.

But they wisely kept their distance.

We approached the bouncers, who waved us through without even looking at us. The girl at the door, taking tickets and checking snap bands, came forward and led us around the metal detector, not saying a word. She gave me a ghost of a wink as we walked through.

"Was that Thea?" We walked down a corridor towards the main lecture room. The sound of trance music weaved a seductive spell around us, luring us in.

"Yeah," he nodded. "I asked her to smooth our entry. I'm packing."

"Of course you are," I muttered.

"Hey." He grabbed my hand, and pulled me aside, letting the kids behind us pass us by. "I've been meaning to tell you something. I wanted to apologize."

I backed up against the wall, trying to keep some distance between us in case I lost control and threw myself at him. "What for?"

"For not calling. It was a shitty thing to do, and I'm sorry. I– I just–" He clenched his fists, suddenly frustrated. "I had my reasons."

I stared back at him. "Of course you did." Like not

wanting to babysit a silly girl like me. Or not wanting to date a young single mom. Or, the fact that I was just not his type – judging by his ex-lover, the stunningly beautiful, sophisticated, mysterious, highly trained homicide detective, Giselle Russo.

He glared at me suddenly, almost like he could sense what I was thinking, and he thought it was stupid. "You don't understand. I've seen things in the last few months that would make your skin crawl. I've been deployed a bunch of times, Sandy, and I've seen horrible civilian casualties in war, but this…this…" He shook his head. "This stuff is *evil.* The things that they're doing to these girls. I just couldn't stop thinking about the chance of that happening to *you.* Someone very close to me–" He cut himself off, shook his head and looked away.

I waited patiently. Was he going to mention the ex? The sexy, sophisticated Detective Giselle Russo? Maybe that was why he broke up with her. He couldn't stand the idea of her always being in danger, so it was easier to cut her off. "Go on," I said. Rip that Band-Aid off.

He put both hands on the wall behind me, boxing me in, and leaned in close. I shivered as he put his lips close to my ear. "I have a very close family member who has a similar gift to you," he murmured in his ear. "She *knows* things."

I froze. My heart literally stopped beating.

"Before they happen." His voice was a rough whisper in my ear. "She tells me things, sometimes, important things. Before they come to pass. It helps me prepare."

Oh.

So *that's* why he always seemed to be in the right place at the right time. Why he always seemed to know where to go, and who to shoot, or where to stick the stake. He was famous for it, for his gift of knowing what weapons to pull and what door to kick down. *That* was why. He was completely human, but someone close to him had the gift of precognition.

It was why he'd been at the Dog and Bone, the night I saw him for the first time, I *knew* it. He'd been waiting for someone. I remember feeling the anticipation and expectation wafting off him. He was waiting on an important tip.

He'd been waiting for *me*.

He was human, every supernatural in the city knew that, completely, utterly human, but he appeared to have a sixth sense. Now I knew why. It wasn't him. It was someone else. Someone very close to him. A sister, or a cousin or something, although it was hard to imagine a god like him having normal siblings.

He leaned back, and stared me in the eyes, making sure I understood exactly what he was telling me.

Nobody knew about this.

And he couldn't tell *anyone*.

I might be new to the supernatural world, but I knew what happened to anyone who had the gift of foresight. Cassandra, the Oracle, even the ones who only had a touch of the Sight were either burned as witches, kept as slaves by megalomaniacs or locked up in mental asylums forever.

She was his secret. And he'd told me.

Mavka was as shocked as I was. I didn't know if she could hear any more than he was telling me, because she stood, with her mouth open, staring at Sinclair, just like I did.

His gaze dropped to my lips, just for a second, and back to my eyes. "My…" he swallowed roughly. "She said you'd be caught in the net of the Blood Kings. She told me that two months ago. When she told me that… I decided to do whatever I could to keep you out of this. So I cut you off."

My lips felt numb. "Oh," I finally stammered.

His expression grew furious. "Then I found out you were hunting the Blood Kings yourself." He looked away, and chuckled darkly. "Of course you were. As if I could ever get a moment's peace from worrying about you."

"I have to. I can help."

"I know. I just wanted to apologize. I was trying to keep you safe, but as it turns out, you don't need me. But I need *you*."

My mouth went dry. "You… you…

"You found out about the circles, and about the fetishes. You were the one who managed to get the blood magic ritual from Prue's mom."

"Prue did that. Not me."

"You were the oil that greased the machine," he murmured lightly. "And you were the one who suggested going back to Thea and getting more information from her. Because of that, we tagged Roger Tucker as a Blood King."

"Yeah, that didn't do any good, though," I muttered, looking away. "He got killed immediately, just like all the other scions of Lord Seth."

"Well, he's gone, and that's nothing but a good thing," Sinclair said bluntly. "The less Blood Kings there are, the better." Suddenly, the ghost of a smile touched his lips. "Besides, you were totally right about Thea. Event coordinators know an insane amount of gossip. She gave me a tip about a cocaine baron which I passed on to Narcotics. They busted him an hour ago during a drug drop; they've been after him for years but couldn't catch him doing anything. Thea is a goldmine for information. People tell her crazy stuff."

"That's nothing," I said. "I once had an old lady confess to murdering her neighbor while I was setting her perm." At his sudden alarmed look, I rolled my eyes. "Yes, yes, I called it in. She died before the investigation even started, but the neighbor's family got some closure. Apparently, they'd been feuding for years, all over a stolen pecan pie recipe. Honestly, once I get my fingers on someone's scalp, they'll tell me anything."

He tensed slightly. I remembered the sensation of running my fingernails over his scalp, and suddenly I felt hot.

I moved back. "We should go."

We walked into the lecture room on the first floor, which took up the whole side of the ground floor of the building. On the other side, smaller rooms branched off the hallway. We glanced inside as we passed. Some were designated vape rooms filled with dim lights and disco balls, with kids reclining on beanbags, puffing out clouds of fog, giggling and chatting. Others were small cocktail bars; one had a bartender dressed up as a mad scientist, serving bright colored shots in test tubes. In the next room, a vampire surrounded by dry ice served blood-red cocktails with swirling vapor in the glasses.

I peered at him as we walked past. "Is that a real vampire?"

"No." Sinclair peered sideways at me. "Can't you tell?"

I shook my head. "Not always. Sometimes the information comes to me very slowly." Mentally, I jabbed Mavka in the ribs. Look alive, Mav. We've got work to do

She seemed... annoyed. *This place does not work for me,* she sniffed haughtily. *I do not like all the separate rooms; it is messing with my senses.*

I could feel her concentration, but her attention wasn't on listening to the college kids round us. She was focused on Sinclair.

What are you doing? I jabbed her again.

I am trying to find out more about his Seer, of course. She sounded almost shocked. *He is stubbornly disciplined with his thoughts; it is most annoying. He is only focused on you, and keeping you safe.*

A rosy glow warmed my core. I tamped it firmly down,

and mentally told Mavka to stop snooping. He'd tell me more if he wanted to. I felt enormously privileged that he'd told me at all.

There's something there... Something familiar... I just can't catch it...

Stop. Leave him alone. We need to find the Blood Kings, and the fetishes. Concentrate!

We wandered down the corridor on the first floor, checking all the rooms, ducking and weaving through the crowds. The kids at this rave seemed far more unhinged than at the last party. It could be the almost labyrinth-like nature of all the separate rooms, or the jarring experience of going from one themed room to the next. You could go from mingling with Alice in Wonderland and puffing on a weed vape, to psy-trance and test-tube cocktails with the mad scientist. In the main lecture theater on the ground floor, a D.J. pumped out hardhouse music while half-dressed young people flung themselves around on the auditorium floor.

Sinclair leaned in close to my ear. "Anything?"

I shook my head. "Nothing. Let's go upstairs."

The second floor was similar. The main lecture theater was packed with sweaty people, almost invisible in the thick fog pouring from the smoke machine. On the other side of the hallway, the smaller rooms held a space-themed chill-out zone, a small bar staffed by a steampunk bartender riding a tricycle, and an almost pitch-black room entirely filled with fuzzy cushions. A few kids were in there necking. A sign on the door read *Thirty Seconds In Heaven.*

A dreamy looking girl wearing a crocheted bikini top tried to pull me inside as we walked past. "Come on," she tugged my hand. "It's the makeout room. Come make out with me."

"Uh... no..." I gently disengaged her hand from my wrist. "I'm here with my date, sorry."

"He can come and watch." Her pupils were so dilated her eyes were almost black. I peered at her, wondering. She looked like a demon.

She's not evil, Mavka sniggered. *She's just high.*

"Sorry," I told the girl. "Another time, maybe."

An equally wasted-looking boy joined her. "He can't be your date. He's too..." He looked at Sinclair, and quickly glanced away again. "Nah, dude. He's your bodyguard."

"What? No," I chuckled awkwardly, not looking at him. "He's my boyfriend."

They laughed like hyenas, like it was the funniest thing they'd ever heard. Another couple joined them at the doorway, watching me. "No way." They swiveled their heads, first looking at me, then looking at Sinclair glowering beside me. "No *way* is he your boyfriend."

A girl with long braids stabbed a finger towards me, trying to focus, her eyes crossing. "I bet you're some billionaire heiress, or a Danish princess, or something... and he's your security detail, come to keep you safe while you take a walk on the wild side." The others whooped with laughter.

"He's my boyfriend," I protested weakly. Sinclair crossed his arms over his chest, glaring at them. The kids collapsed with laughter.

"You're not fooling anyone, you know," the boy with the floppy hair said, waving his vape in Sinclair's direction. "He's got active combat written all over him."

"If he's your boyfriend, prove it," the blonde girl said, giggling. "Kiss!"

I flinched. I felt Sinclair tense beside me. "What?"

"Kiss! If he's your boyfriend, kiss him! Go on..." She gave me a wobbly nudge. "Make out with him. Or we'll know you're lying."

I blinked, hoping the floor would swallow me whole.

"Kiss him! Kiss him! Kiss him!" The circle of faces chanted.

I turned to face Sinclair. He reached out, grabbed me by the arm, and then–

"We don't have time for this," he said gruffly, pulling me away. "You kids need to make better choices." Holding my arm tight, he marched me back down the hallway.

CHAPTER 19

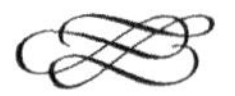

Every love story I'd ever read would have gone differently. Two people, a man and a woman, undercover, faking a relationship, pressured into sharing a kiss so they wouldn't blow their cover.

If this was a love story, he should have turned to me, the circle of faces would have faded into the background. The music would swell, and he'd lean in slowly, tentatively, and he'd kiss me. A little fake kiss to keep up appearances at first, but soon, the gentle press of lips would morph into something more. A deeper, more passionate kiss, revealing intense emotions, unlocking feelings that couldn't be stuffed back down again when the kiss was over. We'd break apart, staring into each other's eyes. It would change us, change our relationship, and we'd go from fake boyfriend and girlfriend, to passionate, all-consuming lovers.

This wasn't a love story.

My heart felt like it had been stretched like a rubber band and snapped against my gut. It stung. I knew it was stupid, I knew that Sinclair was out of my league... but for a second there, I'd hoped against hope that he'd take this opportunity, and kiss me.

He didn't. I was a fool.

I couldn't look at him as we marched away.

He leaned closer, and murmured in my ear as we walked. "The last two doors at the end of the corridor were locked."

"Were they?" My voice was inflectionless. "Maybe you should check them out."

"We need to see the other levels. Are you picking up anything yet?"

I wasn't getting anything from Mavka, but she was still sniffing around, getting restless, itching to find someone to eat. For a wild moment, I considered checking out of my own body and letting her take control. I felt humiliated. And so stupid.

She finally heard me. She'd been so busy sniffing for evil blood, she only just noticed my distress. *Child, stop. It is not what you think.*

I didn't care. I was dangerously close to tears, which made me feel even worse. I was just a stupid, foolish girl, a sucker for love stories. But they weren't for me.

I tugged my arm out of Sinclair's grip. "I have to use the bathroom."

"Okay." He nodded towards the other end of the corridor. "Thea said the bathrooms are on the west side of every level. I'll wait." He moved with me, but I walked fast, almost running towards the bathroom. I felt him behind me, pausing at the door to the ladies. I ran in and locked myself in a stall.

You're being foolish, child.

"I know that," I muttered to her. "That's *literally* why I'm crying in the bathroom, Mav. I behaved like a fool, and now my feelings are hurt."

Pull yourself together. Oh! Suddenly, she inhaled deeply. *I can smell the blood of one who is corrupted. An evil man, a blood witch.* She licked her lips. *He is here; he is close.*

"What, in the girl's bathroom?"

No. She rolled her eyes. *Directly above us, in a small room upstairs. I can hear him... he is checking the preparations. The circle has been burnt into the floor; the ingredients have been assembled; everything is in place. He will bring a victim in soon.*

I cursed under my breath. "Soon?"

Now. She growled softly, listening to his thoughts. *The Blood Kings are aware that these parties may not yield them anymore female flesh, there are more circles hidden in this building, they plan to take as many victims as possible... He is leaving the room,* she said abruptly. *He will be back very soon, with a victim, and it will be too late to stop him once she gets in that circle. We must go now.*

Oh, God. I need to get Sinclair.

There's no time! Once he has a victim in there... She urged me into action, tugging at me. *We do not know which room it will be upstairs. There are many small rooms, some of them are locked. We might be running around for too long, and this witch will have a victim in there very soon, they already have her subdued by a spell, they just need to bring her to the circle. Very soon, they'll be severing her spirit, draining her, using her...*

Mavka's uncharacteristic panic was contagious; my muscles felt tense and itchy. I had to act now.

Right above us. Right up there.

I looked up. There was a grate just above my head. Before I could really think about what I was doing, I leapt up on the toilet seat and climbed into the cistern, then balanced on top of the stall, mentally thanking my eight years of childhood gymnastics training.

I pushed the grate up silently, sliding it aside, and hauled myself into the air vent. I only just squeezed through.

In the small claustrophobic air vent, I saw another grate

just above me, slightly ahead. Wiggling like a worm, trying to stay as quiet as possible, I inched across until I was directly below it.

"Anyone in there, Mav?"

I cannot sense any men.

That was as good as I was going to get. I pushed the grate up with my fingers, slid it aside, and wriggled through the tiny vent.

I emerged into absolute pitch blackness. The change was almost frightening, like being born into a world of complete darkness – until I realized that the lights were just turned off. The rooms on the back side of the building had no windows at all. This place was constructed before building codes had specified the need to have an escape route in case of fire.

I straightened out of my crouch, and put my hands out in front of me tentatively, trying to feel my way around, but there was nothing in the room to touch. Edging forward slightly, shuffling my feet, I felt nothing but concrete under my shoes.

I needed light. I patted my pockets, found where I'd stashed my phone and pulled it out. Turning on the flashlight, I swept it around the room.

It was just a plain, boring utility room, with nothing but a workbench in the corner. The cinder-brick walls were bare and looked very sturdy. The door was thick wood, with a slide bolt lock that would be tricky to pick. For a wild moment I was grateful I'd broken in straight away.

I swept the light over the floor, and groaned. "Oh... fuck."

I'd stepped into the circle.

CHAPTER 20

Mavka was seething. *How could you be so stupid, child!* She admonished me like I was a naughty schoolgirl. *Now, we appear to be trapped here.*

"Come on, Mav." I was close to tears again. "I feel bad enough as it is. I kinda thought… I thought that *you* would have warned me about it, or something."

Well, I can't think of everything, she said sulkily. *I am too busy concentrating on finding the blood witches. It is difficult to scent them through so many walls. I am wholly preoccupied with my job. You are the one who is driving this body,* she added unnecessarily.

I held out a hand and tapped the air in front of me experimentally. My palm smacked against hard air; an invisible barrier. I sighed. "We're stuck."

Your genius is unparalleled, Mavka muttered dryly. *The circle is spelled with a synx.*

"What the hell is a synx?"

It's the opposite of a charm. It's a trap, like a fae circle. One way in, no way out, until you are released by the spellcaster.

I patted my body. "I don't feel anything. It's not sucking my spirit out."

It hasn't been activated. This circle is layered with multiple spells, like a tiramisu.

We'd had tiramisu for dessert a few nights back, and Mavka had declared it almost as delicious as an arms dealer's kidneys. *The first synx is designed to trap you in the circle, the next will start creating a dirty tether to your higher self, and the next will cut your silver cord. Finally, the last curse will suck out your spirit and trap it in the fetish.*

I squirmed. "Is it trying to create a tether to my soul right now?"

She nodded. *It won't do anything. The tether is superfluous, as long as your silver cord remains intact. I can remove it easily.* She sniffed around the circle, examining it. *The magic in this circle isn't as sophisticated as the previous circle I examined,* she declared. *The one from last weekend. It is a different caster; a less experienced one.*

"Hmmm." I remembered the man with the suit pants and jacket striding down the hallway, annoyed at the young witch and vampire for grabbing Prue, who was already broken. Mullins.

Wait, that was it! "Mullins!"

Have you lost your mind, child?

"That was his name! The blood witch who was activating the circle last week. The one who stormed out of the room. Remember? You desperately wanted to eat him as he walked past, but we were in a semi-public hallway."

She frowned. *Oh, yes. I thought it was Michaels.*

I stabbed at my phone. "No, I remember now. Mullins. I have to tell Sinclair." I put my phone to my ear.

Sinclair answered immediately. "Sandy. Are you okay? Do you need anything?"

"Mullins!"

"What about him?"

"It was *Mullins*. The blood witch from last week, the one with the suit pants and nice shoes who stormed out of the room because that young vamp and new witch screwed up. I was in the hallway when he stomped out, remember! It was Mullins. I *just* remembered his name."

There was a pause. "Are you sure?"

"Positive. I heard his name twice. He was the senior Blood King that night, the one activating the circles. I wonder if he's here?"

"He's not." Sinclair growled.

"How do you know?"

There was another short pause before he spoke again. "Mullins is one of the agents from the F.B.I that was helping with the case."

"Oh. That's not good, is it?"

"It most certainly isn't." Sinclair exhaled heavily. "I don't know where Mullins is now. He and his partner, Agent Squires, were called away on another assignment – something big, apparently. He's not here."

"Can you find him?"

"Of course. He won't be able to hide from me." Sinclair's tone promised violence.

"Good." At least I'd done something right tonight. I'd blown the cover of another one of Lord Seth's spies.

"Sandy…" Suddenly, Sinclair's tone was hesitant. "Are you okay? Do you need me to… uh… get anything for you?"

The uncharacteristic hesitancy in his voice confused the hell out of me.

He thinks you need feminine hygiene products, Mavka snickered. *I can hear him; he's almost directly below us.*

"Oh. Oh! No," I chuckled awkwardly, a blush rising on my cheeks. "I'm fine."

"Good," he blew out a breath, sounding relieved. "You've been in there a long time, so I thought…"

"Uh… um… Sinclair… I'm not in the bathroom."

A loaded pause. "I'm standing right outside. You haven't left yet."

"I'm…" I cringed. "I'm upstairs. I crawled through a vent right above my toilet. There was a blood witch up there, I was trying to listen to him."

"Sandy! God*damnit* Sandy!" He sounded furious. "Why didn't you come and get me?"

"I was worried I'd lose the trail. This place is like a labyrinth; I can't see the layout, but I can hear the evil thoughts, and I wanted to catch him. The blood witch was right above me, he left to go and get a victim. I had to come up here."

"I'm on my way."

"The door is definitely locked." I could see the bolt from here.

"Come back down, then. Now."

"Uh…."

His voice grew inexplicably deeper. "Sandy…"

"I'm… I'm kinda stuck. In a circle." I barreled on, getting all the bad news out at once.

"I'm coming up." I heard a bang below me, and a high-pitched feminine shriek. Clearly, he'd kicked in the door of the girl's bathroom. There was another crash, probably the stall door.

"The vent is too small," he snarled. "I can't get up there. Hold on."

Mavka strained her ears. *He's no longer below us. He's taking the stairs up.*

"How is he going to find which room we're in?"

Judging by the tenor of his thoughts, he's going to break down every single door until he finds us. Mavka sounded impressed.

I glanced at the lock again. It had a deadbolt as well as a sliding lock, and the bolt went straight into the thick door frame. He'd have a hard time smashing through it, even with his enormous strength.

Just then, while I was watching, the lock turned. "Oh, he must have gotten Thea to–"

The door creaked open. I froze. It wasn't Sinclair.

A burly, thick-muscled man with a full head of white-blond hair walked in, leading a blank-faced girl with a pixie cut and a nose-ring in by the hand. Behind her, two other young men slipped through the door, and it slammed closed behind him.

A shifter, Mavka whispered. Rogue wolf, the witch who was in here before, and another young blood witch.

Oh.... shit. Two witches and a werewolf.

They noticed me immediately. I cringed.

The shifter's lips curled up into a smirk. "Oh, lookie here. We got us a little birdy caught in the ol' snare already. How did you get in here, little birdy?"

"I... I..." Mavka, help me!

She wasn't listening. In my head, Mavka was pulling the scent from the Blood Kings towards her and rubbing it on her body like a dog would roll on roadkill. *Delicious,* she moaned. *Oh, the flavors! I've not scented this evil in a rogue shifter in eons. He is sublime. And the two! Oh, Hekate spare me, the combination is sublime. Two evil human boys turned blood witches, oooh, and the shifter is older, the rank scent of his festering spirit more mature. His kidneys are thick with sweet vice. I ache to consume them.* She squirmed inside of me, lost in the sensation of deliciousness.

She'd clearly lost her mind. My legs started shaking.

The white-haired shifter turned to his companions. "Looks like we've got a two-for-one. Jethro, put the other one over there, we'll get to her shortly."

The one he called Jethro, a pale kid with terrible acne, wrinkled his nose. "Why don't I take her down to the other circle and do her there? Tommo can get this one started. I need the practice."

"The vamps are out getting a girl for that one now. Warnock's running that circle. They won't appreciate you butting in." The shifter's eyes glittered with avarice. "But we can get two fetishes stuffed in the same time as they manage to get one done. This might be our last chance to charge up for a while, brothers, so let's make the most of it. Tommo, activate the circle, get this one going. Jethro, put the girl in the corner. She can wait."

Jethro waved his fingers at the girl; his fingers trailed a dirty white smoke. She didn't blink; she was deep in a trance. He pointed into the corner. "Sit," he ordered.

She marched into the corner, blank-faced, and sat down.

The other witch, Tommo, pushed his greasy black hair out of his face, tucking it behind his ears. He crept like a little weasel over to the table behind me, leering at me while he skirted the circle that held me. I watched him as he plucked what looked like pre-prepared herbs and bones and stuffed them into a dark leather pouch. He was getting the fetish ready to hold my spirit.

Mavka… I pleaded with her. Concentrate! What do we do?

Ahhh, so delicious! She inhaled through her nose deeply. *Let me savor the scent, child. If I cannot consume the flesh, I must delight in the smell of that oozing blood, thick with dark magic.*

She almost sounded like she'd given up. Desperately, I stepped right up to the edge of the circle. The creepy Tommo turned and held up the fetish, and started muttering under his breath. The other witch, Jethro, watched carefully, his lips moving, echoing the spell, as if trying to memorize the lyrics to the song.

New blood witches, oh, they smell so good! Their hearts are black and packed with sin. The atrocities they imagine themselves committing. Mmmmm.

Mavka! We need a plan! We need to do something.

She chuckled. *Not this time, child.*

I frowned. Tommo chanted louder, his voice growing deeper and deeper. Suddenly, I felt a strange, sickening tugging sensation, right at the base of my spine. Goosebumps rose on my skin.

Wheee! Mavka crowed. *Hee hee. That tickles!*

Have you lost your damn mind?

Of course not. I am merely savoring the moment, that's all.

What moment? I seethed at her. I'm about to get my spirit ripped out of my body, Mav!

THIS moment.

Suddenly, the door smashed in. The deadbolt ripped right through the door frame, and, like a furious avenging angel, Sinclair stormed into the room, filling the space with the presence of a hurricane.

The shifter whipped his head towards the door and howled. "Enforcer!"

The three Blood Kings leapt into action. The shifter flexed his hands; wicked looking curved spikes grew out the ends, fur dusted his knuckles. Half changed, he leapt at Sinclair, springing with superhuman speed towards him. Sinclair ducked under the wolf's charge easily, moving with grace and phenomenal speed. The shifter flew through the air, smacking into the door with a thud. He landed roughly, and squirmed on the ground, skin bubbling in a horrendous way, fur rolling and tendons popping as he started to fully change.

The witch Tommo was chanting furiously. Greasy hair flying out around him, caught in a blustering wind I couldn't feel, he whirled his hands around and pushed, sending a foul-scented curse directly at Sinclair. Eyes blazing, snarling like a lion, Sinclair swiveled on his feet and held up his hand as if to push back the curse with his palm.

I screamed. Oh, God, not a curse, a curse that might turn Sinclair's skin inside out and leave him looking like shark chum all over the floor, the same as Jem's father...

A flash of light shone from Sinclair's palm a fraction of a second before the curse hit.

A mirror? Yes! Sinclair was holding a mirror in his palm. The curse ricocheted off the reflective surface and smashed back into Tommo, and with a wet popping sound I'll never be able to forget, suddenly his body disintegrated and flopped red and wet to the floor like a hefty bag filled with tomato soup.

I shuddered, squeezing my eyes shut for a second, not wanting to see the bloody remains of the young witch on the floor, but not wanting to take my eyes off Sinclair. He was outnumbered, fighting two witches and a werewolf at the same time, but at least one witch had been taken out.

The pimply witch Jethro let out a high-pitched battle cry, and flung a red haze towards him. At the same time, the shifter, fully changed now into a light-colored wolf, bared his fangs, growled, and sprang towards him, nails scrabbling on the concrete floor as he tried to get purchase to leap up and rip out his throat.

Sinclair moved. The grace and power in his movements stunned me. Every strike was well-practiced, every step rehearsed like a macabre ballet or an ancient war dance. He swung himself down, sliding on his knees with the red hazy curse drifting above him, and he whirled back up onto his feet in front of Jethro, punching him in the face as he rose, pulling him back in one smooth movement, gripping his head in both hands and twisting his neck with a sickening crack. Before the witch's body had even dropped to the floor, he turned to face the wolf as it leapt towards him, a SIG Sauer suddenly in his hand. Five shots rang out, and the wolf fell to the floor mid-leap, like a puppet with his strings suddenly cut.

The room was silent. Sinclair flickered his expert eyes quickly over the bodies lying on the floor, assessing the dead, making sure the threats were eliminated. Then, he turned to me.

I panted, desperately trying to get my breath back. I'd been so scared...

"Sandy." He strode over, quickly examining the circle on the floor. "How do I get you out of here?"

I pointed a shaking hand towards the work bench. "The fetish, I think. It breaks the trap spell."

"Where is it?"

"It will be there somewhere..." I peered over. It wasn't on the table anymore. "It's not there."

He paced the room, his frustration spilling out and whirling like a tornado. "Where is it?"

"I think the witch had it."

Lightning-fast, he pulled Jethro's body up and started rummaging through his pockets, dropping random things on the floor.

"Not that witch. The–" I swallowed roughly, looking at the mess on the floor. "The other one."

Sinclair kicked at the goopy pile of bloody organs and bones on the floor, then snarled and clenched his fists. "What do we do if it's missing? Is it the only way to get you out?"

The thought of being stuck in here made me feel even worse. "It's okay," I muttered. "I've got snacks. I'll live."

He whipped his head towards me. "You've got... snacks?"

"Sure. I've got two protein balls and a Capri Sun in my cargo pants." As the mom of a toddler, I never left the house without food and drink. Patting my pockets, I also found my little medical purse. I had a scrape on my upper arm from sliding through the air vent, so I unwrapped a Band-Aid and popped it on.

Sinclair was looking at me oddly. I pulled out a protein ball and held it up, showing him. "Do you want one?"

"No. Uh, no thank you." He ripped his attention away from me, suddenly frantic again. "I've got to get you out of there. *Now.*"

I pointed. "He was wearing jorts. I think that's them, over there."

Sinclair was on the blood-soaked fabric in a flash. He stared down at the gore at his feet, pulled on a glove, and picked out the brown leather pouch from the mess and held it up.

I let out a sigh of relief. "Throw it at the circle."

He tossed it towards me. There was a flash of gray light, and the sick pulling sensation at the base of my spine disappeared.

We were free.

I sagged with relief. We were safe. Thank God, we were safe.

Inexplicably, Mavka rolled her eyes at me. *Pah. We were never in danger, child.*

What?

She didn't answer me. Instead, she did something I'd never felt her do before. It felt like a blink, and then, she was gone.

Mav? Mavka? What the hell?

She was gone in the same way as I disappeared when she was driving my body, when the blood and gore got too much for me. She'd checked out in exactly the same way.

That was weird. Something must have spooked her. Why had she done that?

Suddenly, Sinclair was beside me. He grabbed me by the hand and tugged me out of the circle, into his arms.

The heat of his body was indescribable; he was so hard, so *hot,* I melted against him, shocked into silence. He looked down at me in his arms, and suddenly, I realized.

He swallowed roughly. "Sandy..."

Oh. *That's* why she left.

The Enforcer, Detective Conrad Sinclair, bent his head and kissed me.

CHAPTER 21

If this was kissing, I'd never been kissed before. Not like this. This was something else; an explosion, a tsunami, washing away everything in my whole reality, stripping away the ugly landscape of my past, showing me a glimpse of pure heaven. Never in my life had I felt this rush of energy, the blinding white-hot burst of passion flaring through me.

He wasn't gentle. The kiss was intense right from the start, explosive, almost desperate. His hand grasped the back of my neck, pulling me towards him as he buried his lips in mine. I fell into the kiss head-first, smashing myself against him, diving into his hot breath, the sweet taste of his mouth. I moaned, melting completely, my body on fire, and he made a low, male noise that sent a pulse of pleasure shooting down my spine. His tongue, oh, my God his *tongue,* it tangled with mine, exploring; the strength of it made my head whirl as I thought of where else it might go, of what else it might taste.

Too soon, he pulled back, and he stared at me, his blue eyes blazing. "Goddamn it, Sandy," he growled softly. His hand cupped my face. "Don't *ever* do that to me again. I was about to rip this whole building apart."

I mouthed helplessly, blinking. For a moment, I was truly speechless. His kiss had stolen all the words away from me.

Deep in the background of my mind, I felt Mavka pop back in. *Are we done yet? Ergh.* She saw Sinclair's face above mine, his delicious mouth still just inches from my lips, and with a little shudder, she was gone again.

My legs couldn't hold me up. If he wasn't holding me right now, I'd be crumpled in a mess on the floor. Bewildered, I blinked up at him. "I... I..."

He waited patiently, a slight furrow in his brow.

"I thought you didn't *want* to kiss me."

He let out a harsh chuckle. "Sandy, I've been wanting to do that since the second I laid eyes on you," he said. "Since that day, three months ago, when I saw you at the door of the Dog and Bone." He shook his head slowly. "I was headed to that pub because I was told someone would give me something I desperately needed. When I saw you standing by the door, I remember thinking so clearly. Why couldn't it be *her?*"

"But it was." My lips were numb. "It was me. I gave you the tip so you could take down the rogue vamp nest."

He nodded, and looked away. "I wonder if that's what she really meant, though. It was just a rogue vamp nest, anyway. I wonder if I was right after all."

My breath caught. "What do you mean?"

He glanced back at me, the fire in his eyes blazing. "I haven't been able to get you out of my head, Sandy."

I swallowed roughly.

"I tried. God." He let out a harsh chuckle. "I tried. You have a knack of popping back up and driving me crazy. I've been running all over the city, trying to keep tabs on you. I told the Vampire King about you this afternoon."

The segue took me off-guard. "What? The *what?* The Vampire… King?"

"I had a meeting with him about the Blood Kings conspiracy."

"You had a meeting with a King?"

He nodded, unperturbed. "There's too many rogue vampires involved, and he needed to be briefed. I left him halfway through the meeting because I was worried about you. For some stupid reason I got it in my head that you were planning on heading off to take on Lord Seth yourself."

"I'm not that stupid," I muttered. Gently, I disengaged myself from his arms. "Look, I don't want to be a burden. I don't want to be a target or a bargaining chip or whatever you think I am…"

"What?" He shook his head. "Sandy, no. That's not what–"

He just wants to protect you. Mavka was back.

"We need to get going." I was seriously in danger of bursting into tears. I felt like a fool. The pure bliss of the kiss had ebbed away, leaving my fears as fresh as ever, but now, the tempest of emotions sweeping through me was messing with my head. God, I wanted him, I wanted him so badly. Pulling away from him now felt like a sin. Being close to him was so dangerous; pulling away felt like blasphemy. I shook my head, trying to pull myself together. "We have to get back downstairs, to the other circle room. They've got one down there, a couple of vamps and a blood witch are running it. They might have a victim in it now."

He nodded sharply. "We're going to talk, though," he said firmly. "After this is all over. I get the feeling we both have a few secrets to share."

I nodded, swallowing down my fear. I couldn't tell him about Mavka. No way.

He'd kill me. It wasn't the best way to begin a relationship.

He took my hand and led me out of the room, muttering into his earpiece as we walked out into the hallway packed with hot bodies. Smoke machines poured vapor out of every room, clouding everything. Half-blind, we ran down the steps back to the second level, past the vape room and the velvet padded make-out room, where half-naked young people of indeterminate gender wound their bodies around each other so tight I couldn't tell where one finished and one began. I blushed, remembering how desperate I was to enact the Hallmark movie fantasy of him kissing me in front of those kids to prove we were a couple, so we wouldn't blow our cover.

My way was better though, Mavka said smugly. *The blood, the fight... the rescue. It was much more romantic, wasn't it?*

What? I stumbled, tripping over my feet. Sinclair caught me, holding me upright. He wrapped me in his arms, shielding me slightly while he examined the two locked doors at the end of the hallway, while I seethed at Mavka.

What the hell did that mean? I spoke to her internally, through metaphorical gritted teeth. What do you mean, my way?

A man like that is hardly going to bend to the whims of a few drug-addled schoolchildren and playact for their benefit, she sniffed haughtily. *He is a warrior. He does not do anything unless he wants to. No, my way was so much better.*

I ground my teeth. Did you… set that whole thing up?

Of course. Do you think I am stupid enough to let you wander blindly into a blood magic circle, child? We weren't even stuck. I probably could have broken that circle if I'd put a little effort into it.

You said we were stuck! You can't lie, and you did!

I said we APPEAR to be stuck. Appearances can be deceiving.

You let me think we were stuck in a blood magic circle,

about to have my spirit ripped out, just to let Sinclair storm in, kill everybody and rescue me?

Yes, she said blithely. *And he loved it. Bursting in, killing the bad guys, rescuing his damsel in distress, sweet evil blood dripping on the floor... Now THERE'S a love story. I could have done without the kiss, but the blood and gore was most appealing.*

I was speechless. There was no time to chastise her, though. Sinclair pulled out a set of keys from his pocket and tried to open the first locked door. "Thea gave me the master set," he murmured. "It's the set she got from the development company. None of these keys opened the door of the last room, though. I had to break it down."

I bit my lip, thinking of how he'd ripped that deadbolt right through the wooden doorframe. "I hope you didn't do any damage to yourself.

"I might have a bruise," he admitted. The door clicked, and opened.

We peered inside. It was just a storage space. We moved on to the next one. "They're down here somewhere," I said. It must be here.

He checked the lock. "The same as upstairs. None of these keys will fit it." He scowled, and cursed under his breath. "We've got to get in here." He backed up a couple of steps, and took a breath, visibly bracing himself.

"Sinclair, no!" I hissed at him. "You're not breaking the door down."

"We have to get in," he said stubbornly.

"You'll break your shoulder."

"It will heal." He squared his jaw, and took another few steps back.

I grabbed his arm. "*Conrad.*"

He glanced at me, with shock and a strange, electrified excitement reflected in his eyes. He liked me calling him Conrad.

No time for that, though. I pointed at the lock. "There's no door frame. The lock bolts straight into the brick. You'll break your shoulder, and we still won't get it."

He looked down, and cursed again. "I'll have to get the ram from SWAT."

There's no time, Mavka murmured, listening through the door. *They have a victim. A senior blood witch is in there, a... oooh... mmmmmm.* She started drooling in my mind, hiding the witch's worst atrocities from me.

Is it Mullins?

No, he is not here. I do not know this one, but he knows the secrets of the Blood Kings. He is filthy with sin. Vengeance will be so sweet.

I huffed out a breath, and turned to Sinclair. "Don't worry. I'll pick the lock."

He glanced at me. "You can do that?"

"Sure. Just give me a minute or two." I pulled out my picks and tension wrench, and got to work. It was lucky I didn't have to keep quiet; the bass from the hard house music was shaking the whole building. Even if we shouted through the keyhole that we were coming in to kill everyone, I doubt they would hear us.

Hurry, child, Mavka hissed. *I must feast.*

"Actually," I added, desperately trying to ignore Mavka inside of me as she started pacing back and forward like a tiger in a cage. "I'm kinda surprised that *you* can't pick the lock. Don't they teach you that at Enforcer school?"

He gave a tiny shrug of his huge shoulders. "I'm out of practice."

"You're more of a bust-down-the-door kinda guy, aren't you."

"Exactly."

I got the tension wrench in the bottom of the keyhole and applied a tiny bit of pressure. "How do you know how to do this, anyway?" Sinclair asked me. He'd gotten down on one knee, so he could watch me while I worked.

"Necessity," I said shortly, concentrating on the lock. "I found myself locked out of my own house on quite a few occasions."

"How come?"

I slipped the rake pick into the keyway and pushed it all the way in, and started to scrub. "I was married, you know. My husband was... not the greatest. There were quite a few occasions where I found myself locked out of the house with my son, unable to get back in because Terry was asleep or playing Xbox with his headphones on or whatever and he couldn't hear the door." I bumped all the pins and kept up the tension. Almost there. "Mostly, he locked me out on purpose because he was mad at me. He'd lock me outside, sometimes with Dexter, and I'd have to find my own way back in. When Dexter was smaller, I'd climb up the gutter pipe with him swaddled on my back and sneak back in through his window and sleep in his room for the night. When he got bigger, it was too dangerous to climb, so I learned how to pick the lock to get back in."

The lock clicked. I'd done it.

I looked at Sinclair's face. He looked horrified.

"Oh, shit. I didn't mean to tell you all that."

"He... he locked you out of the house? To punish you?"

"Uh. Yeah." Why the fuck did I tell him that? I was spoiled goods, a single mom, used up, damaged... "See, I haven't told you this yet, but I used to be married..."

He put his thumb on my lips, silencing me. "I'm sorry. I know all about Terry," he muttered. "I know about your son. I know you had a miscarriage and I know you ran away from Emerald Valley to live with your aunt here in D.C." He shook his head roughly. "I'm sorry," he said again. "I wasn't trying to invade your privacy. I did a full background check on you after you gave me that tip. I found out everything I could about you. I even went through your high school transcripts. You got prizes for gymnastics."

I didn't know what to say. The silence stretched on between us, until I almost broke.

Suddenly, his earpiece buzzed. He frowned, then swore viciously. "Giselle's here. She followed a suspect in and they found a spirit circle on the ground floor." Just then, in the gap between the thump of bass, I heard a distinct sharp pop, the telltale sound of gunfire. Sinclair's head snapped towards the sound. "She needs backup."

"Go," I told him. "I'll wait right here."

He stared at me, then put his huge hands on my arms, drawing me closer. "Promise me you won't move from this hallway."

"Go," I pushed him. "She'll need your help. I'll be right here when you get back, I promise."

Another pop of gunfire rent the air. Sinclair gave me one last hard stare, then whirled and ran, flying down the stairs.

Mavka cracked her knuckles. My turn.

CHAPTER 22

He was only gone for three minutes. I was leaning against the wall when he came back, in exactly the same spot. "Everything okay?"

"She wasn't supposed to be here." He was breathing roughly. "Now we've got three dead witches downstairs and an hysterical girl who is convinced she's been drugged with hallucinogens."

"You got her out?"

His expression was stony, but he gave me one short, sharp nod.

"And your friend Giselle is okay?" I almost tripped over the word 'friend.'

"Not exactly." He looked distracted, and absolutely furious. "I told her not to follow me," he muttered under his breath. "Now she's hurt again."

"She's hurt?"

He nodded once, not meeting my eyes. "A break-bones spell; her collarbone is fractured. She's waiting for backup, but we've got to take this one down *now*," he said, nodding towards the door, his eyes hard. "Can you hear them? Are they still in there?

I nodded. The last part was true, anyway.

"I'm going in. Stay out here."

He drew his gun, pushed the door open with a bang, and ran inside.

I kicked the door frame awkwardly behind him, waiting, and heard him inhale sharply. "What the... *fuck?*"

I waited for one tenth of a second, then called out. "What is it? What's going on?" I stuck my head through the door.

Sinclair stood in the middle of the room, in an inch-deep pool of blood. Body parts littered the floor, a hand here, a gristly piece of shoulder over there. The overhead halogen lights were festooned with intestines, like decorations for a serial killer's birthday party. "Oh!"

Sinclair's eyes darted around the room. As we watched, some body parts started to lose their vibrant color, and slowly turned to ash. All except one chunk of arm, hairy, thick-skinned and liver spotted – the arm of a middle-aged man.

"Vampires," Sinclair let out a low hiss, watching the bloody carnage dissolve into a flaky mess. He pointed to the arm. "And an older blood witch, probably." He turned to look at the burnt-in circle, half obscured by the pool of blood. "There's no victim."

There had been. She was fine now, lying down in the chill-out room, sandwiched in between sweet young people who called themselves 'trip guardians'. She was easily convinced that she'd gone down a k-hole and had a near death experience.

Sinclair ran his hand through his hair, looking at the mess on the floor.

Mavka sighed happily. She was content. *Mmmmm. They were delicious.*

I turned away. I had a head full of information that I couldn't share with Sinclair. I had the location of the Blood King's chapter house, the place where they kept the spare fetishes. I knew where to find Agent Mullins; I knew what his new assignment was, too. He and his partner, Agent Squires, had gone to kill the Vampire King.

We had a busy night ahead of us.

You're not going to share all this with the detective? Mavka asked me.

I shook my head. No.

I understood him. He was a protector. It's what he was built for; for protecting, for destroying the bad guys. He'd never rest, he'd never stop worrying about me, in the same way he would always worry about his gorgeous ex-lover, the beautiful Giselle Russo, downstairs with a broken collarbone.

There were two fundamental truths I was beginning to realize; something Sinclair would never understand, and something he wouldn't ever suspect in a million years.

I wasn't going to tell him about Mullins and the chapter house and the fetishes. I was going alone.

I didn't want him to worry. And I didn't want him to get hurt.

The second truth was, *I* was the bad guy.

CHAPTER 23

The police officers escorted me right up to my door. They waited until I'd gone inside the building before they turned around and left. Standing in the entrance to my apartment, I watched them get into their cruiser and drive off, then, I stepped back outside and sat down on my stoop, sighing. I just needed a second alone, then I'd head back out and finish this.

Sinclair was working. Dead witches looked human, and Detective Giselle Russo had called it in, so the rave was overrun with officers in a matter of minutes. Sinclair was busy coordinating with homicide and tending to his injured ex-lover, so I excused myself, telling him I'd take a cab. But he gruffly ordered a couple of officers to escort me home, threatening them with dismemberment if they took their eyes off me for even one little second.

I took another big breath of the night sky in and sighed it all out. It was four in the morning, and I knew I'd never sleep. Inside my apartment my precious little angel slumbered, and I didn't want to sully his dreams with the stench of blood and gore which was bound to be sticking to my clothes. Experimentally, I sniffed myself. I smelled like marijuana, too. Like a fresh puff of smoke from a joint–

A cloud of smoke drifted past my nose. "Ah," Aunt Marche breathed out slowly. "Nothing like the cold night air at witching hour."

"I thought midnight was the witching hour," I muttered, waving the smoke away.

"When you're a witch, every hour is witching hour." She nudged me with her toe. "Scoot over."

I shuffled my butt across, and she sat down next to me on the stoop. "Should you be smoking?" I asked her.

"I shouldn't be smoking *here*," she said, taking another puff. "I should be smoking in the comfort of my own apartment, but I have a grandniece with a stick up her butt who gets cross if I smoke inside anywhere near her son, so I'm out here, aren't I?"

I squinted my eyes against the smoke. "Why aren't you asleep?"

"I'm waiting for you, of course. I take it you didn't need my little protection charm." She let out a giggle.

I looked away, gazing down the street. It was so quiet. "No."

"The date didn't go well?"

"The *operation* went well, if that's what you're asking. We took down all the circles and brutally murdered a bunch of the Blood Kings." I shrugged. "I got some extra information on where to find Mullins, the head blood witch. He's got all the fetishes. I'll head off in a second and go and get them."

She peered at me closer. "You're doing it by yourself?"

I shrugged again.

"Ah. I understand." She took another big puff of her joint and blew it out slowly. "You know, everyone has their demons. I'm sure Detective Conrad Sinclair has his."

"Most people have *metaphorical* demons, Aunt Marche. Sinclair's demons are the ghosts of people he couldn't save. His demons are the constant worry that someone he loves will get hurt, and he won't be able to protect them. He's fighting a battle he'll never win, and he'll never be happy." I turned so I could look her in the eye. "I can't tell him about my demon, because she's *real*. And I like her," I added. "She's a bloodthirsty monster, but she's a monster for worse monsters."

Aunt Marche gave me the ghost of a smile. "Just like Sinclair."

I groaned. "We're not the same."

"You're more similar than you think. And I know you, darling. There's more to it than that." She nudged me. "You know he likes you. Apart from the fact that there's a vengeance demon in your body that eats evil men, and–" She held up a finger. "You think Sinclair will kill you if he finds out about her – what's the problem?"

I sighed, and slumped in on myself. It took me a moment to get my thoughts into words. "I'm not the person he thinks he likes," I said finally.

"What do you mean?"

"This," I said, waving my hands over my sexy warrior-princess outfit. "It's not me. I remember him smiling at me when I broke Chloe's boyfriend's wrist, which was a total fluke. And again, just tonight, when he heard me on the phone telling my mother I was going to rip out her throat and dance in her blood, like an insane badass-type girl. *That's* the girl he likes, and well… that's not me. I'm not like that. I'm a hairdresser. I'm a single mom, I wear flannel pajamas and I like Agatha Christie and up until very recently, I was a stupid doormat for a manipulative, abusive asshole." I cringed again, remembering how I told him the story of Terry locking me out of the house consistently enough for me to learn how to pick a lock. I'd thought that was a normal thing for a husband to do to his wife…

I shuddered, trying to rid myself of the horror of it. "Anyway, it's not me. He likes who he *thinks* I am. Not who I really am."

Mavka rose up from the depths of my mind, outraged. *What tosh! That IS you, foolish child. You did those things that made him smile – breaking bones, threatening murder, looking sexually pleasing. That part of you was always there, it was just suppressed. You're a warrior. A fighter,* she snarled. *How could you look at yourself and see anything less than that?*

I blinked. Whoa. Okay.

And besides. She settled down slightly. *That's only part of the reason he likes you. He also adores the girl who packs protein balls and a Capri Sun into her cargo pants at a rave, and the girl that always has Band-Aids on her. He respects the girl who can give him the best haircut he's ever had in his life, although he found it slightly annoying how much more attractive it made him because he had to be meaner than normal to fend off admirers. And he especially likes the girl who scrapes her nails over his scalp in the way that makes him groan out loud...*

Okay, stop. I put my hand over my own mouth, and I turned to face Aunt Marche who was peering at me through narrowed eyes.

"She's giving you a talking-to, isn't she?"

I nodded.

"Good. It means that I don't have to."

I huffed out a long, long sigh, and tipped my head back, trying to see the stars. You could never see them in D.C. but it was nice to know they were there. Aunt Marche leaned back, too, putting her head close to mine. "Love is a funny thing, darling. It makes us all crazy." She wriggled down, getting comfortable. "Sometimes, it kills us. Sometimes we're forced to kill a part of ourselves, just so we can have the little scraps of love. And other times, it can kill everything."

"I'm feeling a story coming on," I said dryly.

She let out a weary breath. "It's something I should have told you a long time ago, but I didn't think that the past would affect you. I was hoping it was best that our ancestors stayed dead and kept the hell away from us here in the present. But the cards and the smoke and the tea are all telling me the same thing. This is important, and I have to share it with you."

My skin prickled. Was this what my mom had been talking about? A family curse? A demon in our blood? I waited patiently.

Aunt Marche took a big drag on her joint and began the story. "When Moira and I came over here from Italy over fifty years ago, we were looking for our mother's family," she began. "We knew nothing about her, not even her name. She died in an asylum not long after we were born. All we had was her notebook, covered in scrawl." She chuckled softly. "We were both so headstrong and willful, we were sure we'd find our lost family. We traveled around the country, getting into trouble, so many close calls, so many last-minute rescues. It's a surprise we lived long enough at all. Finally, piecing together some coordinates from our mother's notebook, we found ourselves in Emerald Valley. We hitched a ride into town with a couple of traveling salesmen, and were greeted in the main street by a girl called Maureen the minute we got out of the car, who seemed as if she were waiting for us. She knew our names," Marche said. "She told us she was our cousin, and we were blown away. Then, she told us she was a witch, our mother's name had been Monica, and we came from a family of witches. I was delighted, but Moira lost her damned mind."

Aunt Marche paused and took a drag of her joint. "Turns

out," she puffed the smoke up into the sky. "Our mother succumbed to the temptation of blood magic, turned evil, and almost killed everyone in the entire town."

I blinked. "Not the news you were expecting, huh?"

"It was a bit of a surprise. Maureen told us the whole story. Our mother, Monica, loved a local boy; they were friends, but he was a confirmed bachelor and wouldn't marry her, he wouldn't even make a move. She grew desperate and sacrificed a lamb to construct a powerful love spell. It worked for a while; they were together a few weeks, at least, but something was wrong. He was always distracted, acting like he was haunted by something. Then, they found him dead, hung by his neck in the barn. He'd killed himself."

"Whoa."

"Whoa, indeed. Monica went crazy. She'd already started down the path of evil, and now that her only love had been ripped away from her, she was convinced another witch had interfered. She accused her sister of casting a counter-spell on him, another love spell to confuse him, maybe. There was more blood sacrifice, more spells, more power, and more lives lost. Finally, the coven banded together and performed a powerful binding, sealing her magic away from her, so Monica couldn't fight anymore. She lost her magic, and ran away. They never heard from her again."

God, that was tragic. "But she was pregnant. She was pregnant with her dead lover's baby."

"They didn't know. No one did. Not until Moira and I drew closer to Emerald Valley. Our Great-Aunt Mildred – Monica's sister – saw our arrival in the smoke. She was so happy to see us; she wanted to take us in and train us to be witches just like them." Aunt Marche frowned deeply. "My sister Moira was horrified. She went a little mad herself, and I didn't realize what was going through her mind until it was too late. Turns out, she'd known for a long time that something was wrong with her."

"What do you mean?"

"Well, when we were kids, our neighbor's boy got sick. Moira, with the confidence of a nine-year-old girl who had no idea she was a witch, brewed him a soup with an odd mixture of herbs, and told him that it would cure him." Marche gave a sad smile. "And it did. Our neighbors came to talk to my parents, and my parents beat Moira senseless. Said they were 'beating the devil out of her.' It was horrific."

"Oh. Poor Grandma..." My stomach ached. That kind of senseless violence made me so sick. And to a *child*. A child that had helped save someone else.

"So when Great-Aunt Mildred told us we were actually witches, Moira lost her damn mind. She convinced herself that we had to be stopped, so she stole Mildred's grimoire and created a curse that would prevent us from ever being in love with a man. She wanted to avoid her mother's fate, you see. She was already a little crazy, and she had a modicum of self-awareness, after all."

"She cursed you?" I couldn't believe it. Not my uptight, devout grandmother.

Marche nodded. "She tried to curse the whole coven, but it only worked on me and her. She cursed both of us, so we'd never love a man."

I breathed out slowly, literally speechless. It explained so much, but it was so fantastical and extraordinary that it took me a while to fit these new jigsaw puzzle pieces in my head.

"That's... that's..." I'd always wondered why Marche never married or had children. "That's horrific, Aunt Marche."

"Yeah, well. The joke's on her. I loved a few women in my lifetime instead." She winked at me. "It's no big deal, Sandy. And anyway, she only cursed our romantic love, not sexual love or familial or fraternal. I found that I could love my friends and family and my students with my whole heart, so I did that instead."

I nodded. Aunt Marche was deeply beloved by her community, so that love was returned three-fold. She really did find the silver lining in everything.

"Moira tried to bind our powers too," she went on. "So that we could never do magic. To her, our mother's tragic story was evidence that the craft was evil, an affront to her God. She cursed me, bound me, and never spoke to me again. She clung to her faith like it was a life raft, and glued herself to that monster of a priest, Father Sampson, the witch hunter."

I just couldn't imagine my uptight, stoic grandma doing all of this – cursing her sister, binding her powers. "But my grandma got married and had children."

"She never loved Gilbert. She never loved her kids either." Aunt Marche pursed her lips. "She was doing her 'duty' to her god. That's all."

I sighed out a breath. "Now I know why my mom is the way she is. That's what she was talking about when she was screaming at me about a curse in my blood... she was talking about Monica."

"Monica, the great powerful witch who almost destroyed a whole town," Marche said dryly. "Our dear old mom, who ended up dead in a mental asylum half a world away. We thought she'd turn out to be an exiled princess." She chuckled and shook her head. "You know, your mom Catherine always saw Moira as having performed a great sacrifice to stop the curse. She idolized her mother for clinging to the Church instead of succumbing to the temptation of witchcraft. I'm the heathen who embraced it." She shrugged. "I'm cool with that. I'm sad I lost my sister, but I like being who I am."

I was silent for a moment, taking it all in. "That whole

story is crazy... My great-grandma was an evil witch." I frowned. "What *did* happen to Monica's lover, anyway? Was there someone else casting spells on him? Why did he kill himself?"

"Oh. He was gay, as it turns out," she replied. "It must have been hell for him. No one realized – it was safer to stay in the closet back in those days. He'd lived with his 'best friend' for years, which, with the benefit of hindsight, was obviously his lover. When Monica's spell hit him, it really tore him apart. People remembered his 'best friend' storming away from Emerald Valley, cursing his name. Monica took away his free will and made him hers, and it destroyed him."

"Sheesh." I made a face. "That's a plot twist I didn't see coming."

"Apparently, Monica convinced herself that he just needed a little push to make his move on her. She thought he was just shy. Sacrificing that lamb started her on the path to total destruction."

I shook my head. My great-grandma wanted a boy to love her, so she messed with his free will. That was selfish. Maybe that was the thing; the reason why Prue's mom came back from the darkness – because she did it to try to save Prue. Monica only thought about herself.

"There's something else," Marche looked off into the distance. "The reason why both the smoke and leaves are telling me that you need to know this information. It's important, somehow, to this problem with the Blood Kings, and the swirling black hole of chaos that's forming in the middle of this city." She narrowed her eyes. "I don't know how the story of my mother fits in, but all the signs keep telling me it is connected. I'm hoping you can figure out why."

I shook my head. "I can't see a connection anywhere. There's an evil man at the center of the Blood King conspiracy, not an evil woman." I wrinkled my nose. "Maybe it's my mom. She *is* trying to take my own son off me."

"Maybe," Marche yawned hugely. "Although Catherine thinks she doesn't have access to any power at all. When her mother bound herself, she effectively bound the magic of her offspring, too. Catherine has no magic. You don't have any magic at all, and neither does Antonio."

Funny, how both of us ended up anyway, with me housing a vengeance demon, and him dating the son of a vampire.

"I could fix that if you want," she added. "I can unbind you. If you're interested."

"I think I've got all the power I need right now, but thanks."

Marche leaned her head against my shoulder. "I don't know how it's connected to this Blood King business, but I know that it is." She yawned. "My mother is dead – she's been dead for almost eighty years. Moira is dead too. I'm all that's left, and I'm not about to start building an army of evil supernatural men to overthrow all the women on the planet." Marche stubbed out the joint on the stoop and groaned, straightening up. "And that's the whole story. Now you know. You have the blood of a powerful madwoman running in your veins."

I shrugged. "It's kind of the least of my worries." Mavka was reclining in the corner of my mind, picking sinew out of her teeth.

"Okay. Breaktime's over." Marche got to her feet and stretched. "Let's go."

"What–" I shook my head. "Why? What are we doing?"

She peered down at me. "You've got work to do, don't you? You gotta go and get those fetishes. We gotta wake them girls up. I'll drive you, and we'll stop by the hospital on the way home so I can put their spirits back and re-tie their silver cords." She held up a doctor's briefcase and shook it. "I've got my kit ready and everything."

"Aunt Marche..." I shook my head. "It's going to be messy. I'm probably going to set Mavka loose in their chapter house..."

Wheeee! Mav crowed. *Let's go!*

Aunt Marche looked at me like I was an idiot. "I'm going to wait *outside,* Sandy. You kill the bad guys and grab the fetishes. I'll drive the getaway car."

"No, really." Aunt Marche was old, and I was worried about her. "You don't have to come."

"Can that demon of yours fly?"

"What? No!"

"Then you'll need someone to drive you. You need back up. Until the day you tell Sinclair what you can do and succumb to your destiny, you're stuck with me for the time being. Let's go." She held out her hand and waited.

I gazed up at my elderly great-aunt, a slightly hysterical giggle escaped my lips. "I guess you're my ride-or-die."

"Ride *and* die, if Mavka has anything to do with it!"

I let her help me up, then frowned. "Wait. Did you say Sinclair was my destiny?"

She grinned and slapped me on the butt. "One thing at a time, darlin'. Now let's go. We've got work to do!"

CHAPTER 24

Three days later, I was gently brushing bleach on a cute fresh pixie cut and trying not to cry.

My client wasn't doing any better than me. Her big brown eyes blinked back tears as she watched me work in the mirror. "I'm sorry," she whispered, wiping away a sneaky tear that managed to escape. "I just look…"

"You look beautiful, Belinda," I replied, smiling at her. "The cut really suits you."

"Well, it's not like I had a choice. It's all going to fall out soon. It's okay, though." She shook herself and took a deep breath. "My doctors said the prognosis is good. I just have to get through the treatments and I'll be fine…" The tears welled up in her eyes again, instantly overflowing and rushing over her cheeks. "I'm sorry," she said to me again. "I just can't believe he's gone."

"It's okay. *I'm* sorry."

"He's not a bad guy," Belinda sniffed. "He's not. He just got overwhelmed with my diagnosis, and with having to look after the kids and work and everything…" She shook her head. "I understand it. Cancer is scary. I guess he didn't like the idea of losing me, so he left me instead."

I bit my lip, not saying anything. I just nodded.

Her husband *was* a bad guy.

I remembered saying the same thing about Terry. He wasn't a bad guy, he was just a little absent-minded and not good with doing chores. He wasn't bad, he just knew what he wanted. He wasn't bad, he was just very in love with me, and he'd kill me if I ever left him.

I made so many excuses. Belinda was doing the same thing.

"He hates seeing me like this," she whispered again, staring at herself in the mirror. "It's causing him so much pain. He just couldn't bear it."

I pressed my lips together so I wouldn't shout at her, brushed the last dab of bleach on a tiny foil, and wrapped it up. She looked like a little silver porcupine, with foil spiking up all over her head. I hoped the hair would last a little while at least. "You're all done," I looked up at her and smiled. "You're going to look amazing." Picking up my color bowls, I walked over to the sink.

Prue stood there, glaring at Belinda with her arms crossed over her chest. "That fucker," she snarled. "He took three weeks of vacation leave from work to look after her and the kids when she got her diagnosis. He lasted *one week* before he bailed. Now she's forced to take care of the kids herself while she's sick as a dog." She bared her teeth. "I hope he gets what he deserves."

"He's already got it," I said. "He's lost a beautiful wife and family."

She pursed her lips. "I was thinking more like anal warts, or some sort of mysterious disease which causes him to hiccup all day, every day, for the rest of his life."

Just then, Chloe lurched past leading her client towards

the basins, zombie-like, her eyes blank. Prue and I watched her. "Ten bucks says she does it again."

"No bet," I said. "She's still making out with her new boyfriend in her head; she can't see a thing."

Chloe walked straight into the pole again. She backed up robotically, looking exactly like a non-playing video game character, and headed off in a different direction.

Prue sighed. "I'm happy she's happy, but damn, it's going to create a lot of problems down the track."

"Can't he just tell her he's a centaur?"

She shook her head. "Not without violating the Great Agreement. She has to find out on her own. And knowing Chloe, she never will. She'll marry him and pop out little half-horse babies, and not think anything strange about the fact that they have hooves instead of legs. She'll say something like 'oh, my great-great-granduncle Pieter had famously strong, hairy legs, too.' And she'll love her babies to death, never noticing anything weird, even while she's getting a farrier to reshoe them instead of the guy at Footlocker."

I couldn't imagine anyone – even Chloe – not noticing that she was dating a centaur. "But what about… what about when… when they…?"

"When they bone?" She shrugged. "Chloe won't notice anything weird. When she looks at him, she sees a tall, buff man. So when she touches him, her brain tells her that's what he *is*. I mean, when you hug me, you feel a body, don't you?" I nodded. "It's exactly the same. Your brain tells your body to feel me exactly the way I look, so you do."

"Oh." I nibbled on my lip for a second. That's some crazy magic."

"It's actually not – it's just how your brain works. It could be, though. Aunt Marche says there's untapped potential for witches who can create projections. I've been doing it since I was a toddler, so I apparently have a whole-ass talent for very powerful magic. She says I could learn to project whatever I want, and people will behave as if it's real. And it *will be* real." She wrinkled her nose. "My mom would love that."

I smiled at her gently. "You don't have to do anything you don't want to do," I told her. "Being a normal girl is cool."

"Ha. Neither of us is normal. Not even Chloe," she added, as we watched our vacant-eyed best friend slowly squirt twelve pumps of shampoo directly onto the floor, instead of into her outstretched hands.

Prue peered at me. "Don't you have another client? A newbie?" We walked towards the podium together to check the appointment book on the computer.

I looked at my watch. "Yeah, in a couple of minutes. A woman's perm, apparently. It's going to take up the rest of my afternoon."

The doorbell rang, and Detective Conrad Sinclair walked in.

As usual, my heart thumped out of my chest when I laid eyes on him. It was hard to believe he was only human; he seemed like a separate species, a celestial being of some sort, an angel and a demon at the same time. The magnificence of him was so explosive and otherworldly. Everyone in the room sensed the change in atmosphere; the anticipation and excitement he brought with him. Even Belinda stopped crying, sat up, and licked her lips.

Prue raised one eyebrow. "We're fully booked. Go away."

A hint of a smile hovered over his lips. "I have an appointment."

"Don't tell me you booked under a fake name again..."

"I had to. You canceled my login details."

"Prue!" I thumped her on the arm. "You *blocked* him?"

"This is a professional environment," she sniffed haughtily. "I don't need you mooning over him and screwing up all your colors."

Sinclair very deliberately turned his head to glance behind us. I turned and looked. We were treated to the sight of Chloe accidently waterboarding her client at the basin while she robotically gazed off into space.

"See?" Prue clicked her fingers. "I've got enough to deal with."

He tilted his head slightly; the dangerously flinty eyes narrowed. "Prue, we haven't talked about your mother's punishment yet…'

She pressed her lips together. "Sorry, Enforcer, sir. Carry on." She slapped my butt as she slipped past me. "He booked in for a perm, Sandy. *Do* the perm. I dare you." She hurried away to take the hose off Chloe before she accidently tortured her client to death.

Almost reluctantly, I turned to face Sinclair. "Do you really want a perm?"

"No. I just want to talk to you."

"You could have called, you know." I'd been waiting. It had been almost three days, and he hadn't called.

"I tried to call you–"

"No, you didn't."

"I did." He frowned. "You blocked my number."

I scoffed, offended. I wasn't a petty person. I wouldn't ever do something like that...

Suddenly, I remembered something. "Hang on." I wiggled my phone out of my pocket, and checked my contact list.

Damn it. He *was* blocked. "I didn't, actually. It wasn't me." I huffed out a long breath, realizing what had happened. "My son's cat's been messing with my phone."

"Your son's… cat?"

I nodded wearily. "They think they're hilarious. Him and Dexter messaged some fart noises to a few people in my contact list." Namely, my stepfather John, my old boss Jenny, and a few ladies from my mom's church. "He even managed to order pizza to be delivered to our apartment, twice. Extra anchovies. Turns out, my son's cat is an *actual* demon."

That's not all he did. Somehow, Dexter and Gor'gamuth managed to send a photo I had of Terry to his boss's wife. In an insane coincidence, the photo showed Terry with a couple of expensive power tools in the background – tools that had gone missing from his workplace a few months earlier. He was now suspended from work, pending an investigation. I had no idea about any of it until yesterday, when Terry had called me, screaming in rage.

Sinclair frowned. "Your son has a demon familiar?"

I eyed him back moodily. "What, you're going to kill him for it?"

"No, of course not. They're not all bad, you know. Sometimes they're quite helpful. They're mostly just mischievous troublemakers."

"Tell me about it," I muttered. "They're costing me a fortune in pizza delivery."

"He'll protect your son with his mortal life, you know," Sinclair said quietly. "Demons will do anything to stay in our realm. It's much more fun for them. If he's bonded to Dexter and given him his true name, he'll do anything to keep him safe so he can stay with him. Dexter's lucky."

I frowned. "Yeah, well. As long as they can keep their paws off my phone, I'll be lucky, too. Come on," I nodded him forward.

He looked startled. "What?"

"I thought you wanted a perm."

"Er..."

I let out a giggle. "I'm kidding. I'll give you a haircut."

He still hesitated.

"Something different," I said, remembering he didn't like

how I made him look too handsome. "Maybe lots shorter, less Rugged Prince Charming, more Hot Accountant, or something like that."

He nodded. "Okay."

He settled into my salon chair, and I got out my clippers, sans guard. He had gorgeous hair; the only thing I could imagine doing to him to make him less attractive was getting rid of it all. I started running the clippers up the back of his neck, shearing it to the skin. "So what's up?" I asked him. "How is your–" I stopped myself just in time. "How is your detective friend? Is her collarbone healing okay?"

"She's in a sling. She'll be fine." He caught my eyes in the mirror. "We've got a history, Sandy, but that's what it is. History."

I squared off his neckline, and nodded. The skin on his neck was softer than the rest of him; I ached to run my fingers over it. "It's none of my business," I told him.

"It's part of my history, so it is your business. I want it to be, anyway."

My heart thudded in my chest. I refused to meet his eyes. Instead, I snapped on a number-one guard and carefully ran the clippers over his head, creating a slight fade up to the occipital bone.

"You must have heard all the coma girls are awake," he said softly. "They're okay. Apart from a couple of them, who are still with Dr. Herd, recovering."

"I know," I whispered back.

"Luckily, the Vampire King managed to take out Mullins, as well as his partner, the vampire Squires. Mullins was the senior witch in charge of the spirit circles. He got the magic directly from Lord Seth, a gift, he said. He also called him The Wraith. I'm hoping that's another clue that will lead us to his true identity. He's a supe of some sort."

I nodded, not saying anything. He wasn't telling me

anything I didn't already know, but again, he couldn't find out that I *did* know.

He went on. "Mullins and Squires created a worm gate to trap the Vampire King – that's insane magic, the darkest magic. The King's fiancé managed to break out and kill everyone."

I pressed my lips together, pretending to concentrate on the haircut. I got my invitation to the royal wedding hand-delivered to the salon this morning. The Vampire King was so grateful to me and Mav for saving them, he'd promised not to breathe a word to the Enforcer. "Come on," I said to Sinclair. "I'll shampoo you."

He followed me over to the basins, and lay down in the chair. Suppressing the urge to straddle him, I started scrubbing his head. He relaxed immediately under my fingers, and gazed up at me with hooded eyes. "Why am I getting the feeling you already know all this?"

"Because I do," I told him. "I know things, remember?"

"Hmm." He blinked lazily up at me. "Is there anything you would like to share with me?"

"No."

"That was definitive."

I looked away. "Sinclair–"

"Call me Conrad. *Please*. Everyone calls me Sinclair, or the Enforcer. I want you to call me Conrad."

Giselle Russo had called him Conrad. Damn it. I never thought for a second I'd be a jealous person, but I wanted to scratch that bitch's eyes out. I channeled my energy into giving his head a good scrub, trying not to notice that he was almost growling in pleasure at my touch.

"There's more," he said roughly, when I started rinsing the shampoo. "We may have solved the problem of the spirit circles, but there's a new situation I need your help with."

"Related to Lord Seth?"

"Possibly. I've been–" He pressed his lips together for a second, then relaxed, and went on. "I've been told it's related, but my source is not sure how."

Ah, his mysterious Seer. I was hoping at some point he might tell me more about her. Again, I could hardly imagine him having normal family members. "So, what's going on?" I lathered a little conditioner on his head and started massaging.

He didn't say anything else. I waited patiently. After a long moment, he let out a low, manly grunt. "Damn it, Sandy, I can't think of anything else while you're doing that to me." Then, he shifted on the chair, his movement… *deliberate*.

My core burst into flames. I looked away frantically, and turned the hose on, icy cold, and blasted it at his head. For a wild moment I thought I might have to shove it down my pants. I took a long, slow breath out, trying to come back to reality. "Tell me about the new situation," I said, my voice shaky.

"You know Colin Shephard?"

"The senator? Yeah, I do." He was a representative from Virginia, my home state, but even if he hadn't been, I'd still know who he was.

Colin Shephard had an extremely high profile. Charismatic, charming and quite handsome, running on a platform of freedom and family values, Colin Shephard seemed to do the impossible – straddle the deep divide between liberal and conservative, beloved by both sides of politics. He was the first independent politician in U.S. history that had a shot at winning the presidency, and he'd just confirmed that he'd be running in the election in two years' time.

"Someone is trying to kill him," Sinclair muttered. "He's survived two assassination attempts already. Three of his staff members have been killed in the attacks."

"Whoa. That's... disturbing." I frowned. "Is it a political hit? A foreign agent, hoping to upset democracy?"

"No. Shephard is a normie, but he can definitely See now. It was a supe attack."

"How do you know?"

"The assassin is made out of stone."

"What? Like, a golem or something?"

"They're made of mud. This guy is made of stone. Marble, actually. I've checked the security footage of the attack and talked to everyone involved. The guy looks like a statue. Like Michelangelo's David came to life and tried to choke a senator to death." Sinclair scowled. "He looks human before the attacks, then when he strikes, he becomes marble."

"Oh. I've never heard of anything like that before." Not like I was an expert, or anything. Six months ago I didn't even know werewolves were real.

I turned off the hose and rubbed his head vigorously with a towel, and wandered back to my station, letting Sinclair follow me. I didn't think I could bear to see him adjusting himself again. He settled back in the chair and stared at me in the mirror. "I need your help, Sandy. I want to try and track him down before he strikes again. He'll be hiding in a crowd or milling around with Shephard's staff. I don't know who he is. Hopefully you'll be able to find out."

That meant working with him again. Getting close. Was it too dangerous? For my life, *and* my heart?

"Conrad..." I said, hesitating. I got out my shears, and trimmed the top of his hair a little, creating a texture in the short crop. "There's things... things about me..."

"You've got secrets. I get it," he said bluntly. "You can take your time." He fixed me with a hard stare. "I'll have to be patient."

"Really?"

He ground his jaw. "I can *try* to be patient. I've been told I have to work on a few... personality traits of mine."

"Like what?"

"The things I love... I tend to hold onto them too tight. I've been told I have to relax a little."

"You? Relax?' I grinned at him in the mirror. "Are you getting therapy or something?"

"Something like that."

I gave him a cheeky smile. "You're keeping secrets of your own. You're okay with me keeping some secrets?" My smile faded, waiting for his response.

"For a time. Sure."

Liar, Mavka murmured.

I turned my head away, thinking. "So you're okay with a few secrets, for now. That's good. I've had a crazy few months, Sin– *Conrad.* I'm only just getting used to this new life myself."

He nodded. "Okay."

I nodded back, and gave him a soft smile. "And you can try and not be so protective of me? You need to remember I can look after myself. I've got other... tricks up my sleeve." I kept my words deliberately vague, hoping he'd think I had defensive spells and charms from Aunt Marche. "I don't need babysitting. And I don't need you hurting yourself running to my rescue."

"I can try. It's not in my nature, but I'll try not to worry so much. I'll have to." He let out an explosive breath, and looked away. "I just can't get you out of my head, Sandy. God knows I've tried."

I froze. Like a deer in the headlights, I stared at him.

He turned back, catching my gaze in the mirror. "Listen. I'm not a normal guy, Sandy," he said gruffly. "I don't have a normal job. I've dedicated my life to taking down the baddest bad guys – the most *powerful* bad guys in the city. That makes me a target, and it makes everyone around me a target, too. If we're... together, you have to understand that."

I rolled my eyes slightly, trying to act cool even though my heart was beating out of my chest. Moving in front of him, I ran my hands through his now-short hair, checking the balance. "Is this the part where you tell me it's too dangerous to be close to you?"

Suddenly, he reached up and caught my wrist. "Yeah," he said bluntly, his eyes hard. "There's a whole mess of people out there that want me dead. If anyone wanted to fuck with me, they'd want to take things that are closest to me and hurt them. I go to a lot of trouble to keep those things secret and safe, Sandy." His eyes told me much more than his lips were saying. "And look at you," he added, rolling his eyes over my hairline, down my cheek, resting his gaze on my lips. "How can I keep *you* a secret? You're like a ray of sunshine in the darkness."

"Yeah..." I gently disengaged myself from him and moved slightly back. "I have a pretty tough core, though," I said, thinking of Mavka.

As soon as I thought of her, I realized she was gone again. Blinked out, gone to the place I go when she's ripping vampire's hearts out of their chest.

I shook my head, trying to focus, and ran my hands over Sinclair's head one more time, massaging a little wax through his short hair to give it some texture. His eyes followed me, never leaving my face. Finally, I wiped my hands, unbuttoned the cape, and brushed off the nape of his neck with my fluffy brush. "All done." I looked up and smiled. "What do you th–" My smile fell. "Oh."

His eyes finally moved from me, to look at himself in the mirror. He caught his reflection and scowled.

He looked more handsome than ever. Damn it, I'd done an excellent job. The very-short cut emphasized every single one of his model-like features; the square jaw, the high cheekbones, and his gorgeous full lips. Out of the corner of my eyes, I saw my client Belinda turn her head, catch sight of Sinclair, gasp dramatically, and clutch her chest.

"Sorry," I muttered to him. "Maybe I could bleach it, tone it pink, or something."

Sinclair sighed. "Don't worry. I'll grow it out." He stood up, towering over me, and caught my wrist again, and pulled me closer. "It's just something I'll need to get used to. But for now, there's something *else* I'm looking forward to getting used to…"

He leaned down, and gently brushed his lips against mine. The breath left my body completely, but before I could fall into the heavenly, sweet bliss of the kiss, a spray of water hit us both in the face.

"Sandy!" Chloe sounded shocked. She sprayed us both with her water spray bottle again. "Stop it! This is a professional workplace!"

THE END.

ALSO BY LAURETTA HIGNETT

Go back to the start with Imogen Gray series:

Immortal

Immortal Games

Immortal World

Immortal Life

Immortal Death

Then follow Sandy in the Foils and Fury series

Oops I Ate A Vengeance Demon

Dancing With The Vengeance Demon

Dating With The Vengeance Demon

Dying For My Vengeance Demon

Then go on with Prue's story with the Blood and Magic Series.

Bad Bones

Bare Bones

Broke Bones

Burned Bones

Bitter Bones

And then head to Chloe's series

Vicious Creatures

Fractured Gods

Ravenous Beasts

* * *

Fancy something different? Try this New Adult Paranormal Romance

Revelations Series

A cursed woman, destined to bring about the apocalypse.

The religious sect, determined to kill her.

The demon who wants to save her.

"It's Good Omens with a Twilight feel"

Book Cover by Mibl Art

First Edition 2022

❀ Created with Vellum

Printed in Great Britain
by Amazon

47733736R00142